EVERYBODY LOVES YOU

ALSO BY ETHAN MORDDEN

NONFICTION

Better Foot Forward: The Story of America's Musical
  Theatre
Opera in the Twentieth Century
That Jazz!: An Idiosyncratic Social History of the
  American Twenties
A Guide to Orchestral Music
The Splendid Art of Opera: A Concise History
The American Theatre
The Hollywood Musical
Movie Star: A Look at the Women Who Made Hollywood
Broadway Babies: The People Who Made the American
  Musical
Demented: The World of the Opera Diva
Opera Anecdotes
A Guide to Opera Recordings
The Hollywood Studios
The Fireside Companion to the Theatre

FICTION

I've A Feeling We're Not in Kansas Anymore
One Last Waltz
Buddies

FACETIAE

Smarts: The Cultural I.Q. Test
Pooh's Workout Book

EVERYBODY LOVES YOU

FURTHER ADVENTURES IN GAY MANHATTAN

ETHAN MORDDEN

ST. MARTIN'S PRESS
NEW YORK

Design by Glen M. Edelstein

Library of Congress Cataloging-in-Publication Data

Mordden, Ethan.
    Everybody loves you.

    I. Title.
PS3563.07717E94   1988   813'.54   88-11545
ISBN 0-312-02201-8

First Edition

10 9 8 7 6 5 4 3 2 1

To Robert Trent

CONTENTS

ACKNOWLEDGMENTS

The author wishes to acknowledge the enthusiasm, audacity, and sage counsel of his editor, Michael Denneny, though after six books this is becoming monotonous: or let us say a fond cliché.

EVERYBODY
LOVES YOU

The Complete Death of the Clown Dog

▰▰▰▰▰

THE RESTAURANT GOT A rave in the *Times*, and it was *hot*. If they didn't recognize your name, I was told, they wouldn't take your reservation. It was not that hot, it turned out, for they gave me no trouble. Still, it was horribly crowded, as if they had decided to run with the fame as long as it held out, and so had filled the room with tables, to serve the vested gentry at their lunches, then the chic cabaret watchers who would learn of the place from their friends because they never read, then the avid bridge-and-tunnel tourists, who would hear about it in *Cue*. Then the prices would go up, and the menu would lose its energy, and the waiters would mess up your drink order. And the place would falter and close.

I was taking an old friend to lunch to celebrate his promotion to managing editor of a prominent fashion magazine. He had been given little more than a few days in which to change the magazine's entire "book"—the major columns and features—and thus was invariably behind in everything that followed. Normally thoughtful and punctual, he became one of those nearly inaccessible heavy hitters who seldom return your phone messages or show up on time, the kind of Significant Other you are proud to know but can never see. At last I nabbed him for lunch, oddly timed to two o'clock, to fit into his schedule. Of course he was late, and as there is nothing else to do while awaiting the rest of your table but eavesdrop on your neighbors, I ordered a Kir and began to listen. To my right were three rowdy Communications people dishing a great load of apparently famous names; but I couldn't place those they cited. To my left were two men in their mid-thirties, whose quiet tone and conservatively sporty tweeds suggested the book trade.

They had reached the coffee stage. I supposed one was a writer and the other his editor, perhaps his agent, but I couldn't be sure because they weren't talking business. Many a telling silence passed between them. The one facing me—the authority figure, I guessed, whoever he was—sometimes smiled and sometimes nodded wisely. The one next to me, who was doing all the talking, had the heaviest regional accent I've ever heard, yet he spoke quickly, and filled his back country lingo with the articulate penetration of the literary man: as if he had picked up New York habits without losing his own.

What a backstory he must have, I thought—and suddenly, without preamble or explanation, he was spilling out his tale. I imagined that these two had met professionally and had just reached the moment—just now, here, at this lunch—when the business relationship turned into friendship. I imagined that the one speaking was a writer, and that he was sharing some profound and painful secret with the man who published his work. I imagined that he had come a long way to arrive at this lunch, at this career, at this friendship. I began to hope that my friend the heavy-hitting magazine editor would be unforgivably late, so I could hear the stranger's story.

This is the story he told:

In Hanley, West Virginia, close on to Wheeling, where I was when I was little, there was a pokey little circus run by Hopey Paris. Most places don't have their own circus on the premises, not even a little one like Hopey's with almost no animals and a busted trapeze and these admission tickets that must have been printed up before the Civil War that you couldn't even read what they said on them anymore. In Hanley we figured it was okay to have this circus, though most of us didn't much care about it one way or the other. Anyway, you never knew when Hopey was going to put his circus on, because he ran it by whim. Also he owned the dime store. I expect what he got out of the dime store he plowed back into keeping the circus going, since he didn't own anything else.

It was like this about having the circus. Some night in light weather, mostly at the tip end of summer when everyone would just sit around and wait for something cool to happen, Hopey would come up from his end of town and find a crowd on the steps of wherever it was they were . . . someone's porch, whoever had beer. He'd wait about three lulls, nodding and shaking along with the gist of things as they got said. Then he'd go, "Guess I'll have to have the circus tonight." And everyone would get everyone else and go on over because, look, what else is there to do? You go to the circus.

What a funny circus—but how much do you want for free? Hopey handed out the admission tickets in a little booth at the entrance and you would take your seat inside the tent, which stood in Hopey's backyard, hanging on by a thread to these old poles. It wasn't a big tent, of course, but, as it is written, size isn't substance. And then Hopey would come in with a whip and this hat he got somewhere to be a ringmaster in. You'd want to think he would look pathetic, wouldn't you? Hopey Paris trying to hold down a circus all by himself in Hanley? He didn't, though. He didn't look much like anything. But he did have a star attraction, the clown dog.

It's crazy about dogs, how some can do things and some can't. I knew a dog once that caught softballs in the air if you threw them underhand. Then he'd go racing off with the ball in his teeth and you'd have to trap him and pry the ball out with a stick. That was his trick, I guess, is how he looked at it. And my father had a dog named Bill who was quite a hero in his day. Bill ran away finally and never came back.

But the clown dog sure was prime. He had this costume, a yellow coat-sort-of-thing with polka dots that he wore fastened around his middle and a red cone hat with a little pom-pom at the top. Whether the circus was on or off, and in all weathers, never, never did you see the clown dog out of costume. And his trick was he could talk. That dog could really talk.

This was why we would always come back to see the same old one-man circus, with no animals or clowns except one animal-clown, like that was all you needed to call it a circus. The tent was hardly alive at all, the big-top tent itself. But you always had to go back because you wanted to see how the trick was done. Because no dog, not even a circus trick dog, can talk. But the thing about tricks is whether or not you can figure them out. That's the art of tricks, right there. And the clown dog, though he often roamed around his end of town like any dog, free in the sun, except he was dressed . . . the clown dog would never do his talking except in the circus. This was probably the deal he made with Hopey, who was, after all, his master. You'd suppose that they must have come to terms on something that important.

That's what's so funny. Because, speaking of dogs, my father never did come to terms with his dog Bill, though he would try, hard as stone, to make that dog his. He trained it and trained it. It must have run near on to two years of sessions in Sunshine's field, and Bill just didn't ever submit and be trained. My father was a ferocious trainer by the standards of any region, but he couldn't get Bill to obey even the most essential commands. And he never could teach him not to chase around the davenport, especially late at night, when Bill most felt like a run. "I will have that dog behave," my

◆ 5 ◆

father said, and I recall how he looked, like behavior was just around the corner. But Bill would not be suppressed. Sometimes he would come when you called, sometimes not. But when he did come, he had this funny look on him, as if he was coming over just to find out why you persisted in calling his name when it had already been established that he wasn't about to respond.

Bill was a mutt, not like the clown dog, who was a poodle, a very distinct breed. You can't miss a poodle, especially in a polka-dot coat and a cone hat with a pom-pom. But Bill was just another dog you might know, kind of slow for his race and disobedient but generally normal, except once when he was The Hero of '62. They called him that because he accidentally bit this management scud who was getting on everybody's nerves at the factory the summer before the strike.

McCosker, I think this guy's name was . . . one of those mouthy hirelings absolutely corrupted by a little power. He had been tacking up this notice by the front gate, some mouthy, powerful thing about something else you're not supposed to do, just busy as anything tacking away and being hated up by the people who were standing around watching. Suddenly Bill bounded over to where this guy McCosker was. I guess maybe Bill thought he saw something to eat near this McCosker's foot, but McCosker took it for some stunt and he made a sudden move and Bill got thrilled and bit him.

It was a tiny little bite on the ankle, kind of in passing, but McCosker screamed like he was being murdered and all the men cheered and patted Bill, and they all shook my father's hand, and mine, too. So Bill was The Hero of '62.

This is a funny thing. Because all Bill had done was what a dog will do every so often, whereas the clown dog was truly some kind of dog. Everybody said so. You just could not tell anyhow that he wasn't talking when Hopey Paris brought him on for his circus turn. Now, that was a trained dog if ever there was one. Yet nobody ever called the clown dog a hero. And the clown dog never ran away, either, which Bill did once. Once is all it takes.

I guess you have to figure that a dog that goes around in circus clothes isn't going to earn the respect of the community, besides him being a poodle, which is not one of your heroic breeds of dog. But I liked him, because he was the first thing I can remember in all my life. Hunkering back down in my mind as far as I can sail, the picture I reach is the clown dog talking in the circus, and the polka dots, and the hat. I wonder if he ever had a name, because he was always known as the clown dog that I ever heard, and I don't recall Hopey ever calling to him. Sometimes Hopey would act like that dog was this big secret, cocking an eyebrow and looking cagey if you asked after him, as if everyone in town hadn't seen the circus a hundred times.

I expect the clown dog must have liked me, because he used to follow me around some days that I know of with his coat and his dumb little hat. He looked so sad. I guess he sensed that he was supposed to be a secret, because he tended to hang back a little, like someone who has already been tagged out of a game and is waiting for the next thing to start. I don't recall that he even barked. And he never went along with us when we tried to get him to talk out of the circus.

Of course we had listened, with all the concentration of adolescents, to the exact words Hopey used in the act when the clown dog would speak, and we would try these words on the clown dog ourselves— imitating Hopey's voice, even, and standing the way he stood to be an imperial ringmaster. But we couldn't make it happen; never did the clown dog utter a word out of his context, the circus. It was the strangest thing. I was just thinking that I would have hated to be around Bill someday if someone tried to get him into a hat with pom-poms.

I was at college when Bill ran away, so I only know about it secondhand, from stories. I couldn't help thinking it was presumable in the end that Bill would take a walk one day and not come back. It was presumable. But still I was surprised to hear of it. It was Christmas, when I was a freshman, and the first sight I got of home when I got off the bus was my father cutting the grass with the Johnsons' lawn mower, and Bill nowhere to be seen. I knew something was wrong then, because Bill never missed a chance to play dogfight with the Johnsons' lawn mower, which always enraged my father. Bill would growl at it for starters, lying way off somewhere, and slowly creep towards it . . . you know, paw by paw. Then he'd run around it, fussing and barking, and at last he'd get in to rushing it like he was going in for the kill, only to back up snarling at the last second.

So when I saw the lawn mower and no Bill I

thought he must be sick, but my father said he had run off like as far back as October sometime. I listened carefully to this, though he didn't talk careful, not ever in all his life that I knew him. Whatever he was thinking when he spoke, that's what he'd say, as tough as you can take it. He didn't expect Bill back, he said, and he didn't miss him. He said it and I believe him. I can just see that now, what he said, and saying it, so plain it was like a picture somebody drew to prove something. I could see that way he didn't care right up front on him.

"No," he said lazily, because he is lazy. "I don't miss him. You run away from home and don't come back, nobody misses you at all. That's the rule."

I don't know of any rule saying you don't miss a runaway dog, even if he never comes back. If he's of a mind to run, there's usually a good reason. My father used to say, "There's always a reason for something, and sometimes two."

That was one of his wisdoms. He had wisdoms for most things that came up in life—lawyers, school, elections, working. He had his wisdoms for Bill, too, even when it was really clear that dog was born to go his own way in a nice wisdom of the animal kingdom.

I can see why that dog took off, anyway, because my father wasn't any too easy to get along with, especially when proclaiming one of his wisdoms. But despite what he said and how he looked saying it, I suppose he really did love that dog . . . or he *wanted* to love it, which would be the way people like my father express affection. It must have threatened to tear him up some when Bill deserted him.

That was a bad time, too, with the strike coming up sooner or later but sure as doom. I wasn't around for the strike. I was sixteen when I finished high school, and I could still have been young some more and not done much of anything with myself, but I had more ambition than to work in the factory or pump gas on Route 16. So I went to college on what you might call a soccer scholarship. My father always poked fun at me for playing soccer. "What kind of sport is that for a man, chasing a ball around with your feet? You look like a bunch of giant bugs," was his view of it. But soccer took me to college, on a full scholarship. It's true, I guess; soccer isn't much of a sport, and this wasn't much of a college. But one wisdom might be that college is college. Anyway, I went.

I came home for Christmas, because I was only two states away, one long bus ride. Besides, they closed the dorms on me and I had to go somewhere. That first night, Thursday, when I came home and saw the lawn mower and learned that Bill had run away, standing in the yard with my bag like a salesman, I decided to walk around town instead of just being home. Because I already knew about home, but I felt mysterious about Hanley, that it was a place filled with riddles that ought to be solved, even by someone who had lived his whole life of sixteen years so far in it.

I thought maybe I would take a look over to Hopey Paris's circus, in case that should be going on . . . or maybe I would talk Hopey into doing his show just for me, because it was extremely rare that the circus would happen in December. I had an idea that Hopey favored me over some others of my generation there in Hanley because I had always been keen to see the clown dog and figure out how he talked, and Hopey was pleased to be appreciated, even by kids.

He liked to think—I'm guessing at this—that his circus, starring the clown dog, which he celebrated as The Talking Dog of the World . . . his circus was what kept the town from feeling too complete. You might suppose that a town with a circus is more complete than most, but instead I sense that it is less complete, and therefore more open and more free. Because a circus is magic. And having its own private circus reminds the town of all the other magic things it doesn't have. It is like . . . it puts the town a little in touch with another town, a secret town that is the ghostly image of itself, a kind of myth in a mirror. Now, so long as the town is aware of its ideal twin, it will wonder about itself, and never think it knows everything there is to know, and not pretend that it is complete. Which I think is all to the good. So no wonder I liked to watch the clown dog's act. And that's why I went over to Hopey Paris's circus on my first night back from college—to watch the ghost dance by me again. Even after all those years, I still didn't understand how the clown dog did his trick.

This was the act. Hopey comes in with his whip and his hat and he stands in the ring. "And now we take great pride and the most highly principled pleasure"—this is exactly what he said every time—"in presenting for your delectation and enlightenment the one and only clown dog . . . The Talking Dog of the World!"

And out from behind a flap of the tent, in his coat and pom-pom hat, the clown dog would trot in. And he would sit on his hind legs looking expectantly at Hopey. That same old coat and hat. That poor little clown dog. Or I guess maybe he was well off, even if no one called him a hero.

In any case, Hopey would say, "Tell these folks here assembled who you *are*"—like that, with everything on the *are*. And . . . I swear to God, the clown dog would answer, as if he was going to growl first. But no, it was this funny talking—"Clown . . . dog." Like that, broken up into words. It was a high voice, tensely placed, like the sounds puppets make on television. And of course we were looking madly from the clown dog to Hopey and back to see the trick.

Then Hopey would say, "Who is the *clown dog*?" And the clown dog would answer, "Me." Something screwy would happen in his mouth, as if he was biting a fly or had bubble gum. And his head would tilt. But he talked, all right, and that was some trick. Just these two questions was all the talking, though. Because then Hopey would shout, "Leap, clown dog!" and that poodle just leaped right into Hopey's arms and licked his face. That was the whole act, and that was also the whole circus.

I miss that circus, for it is miles away from me now. But when I came home that Christmas, I didn't have it in mind as something you ever lose hold of, because I didn't realize about growing old. Now, that is a term for you, *growing old*. And it, too, has a trick: it contains the thought that things vanish. You don't grow old yourself as fast as old things grow old because even as you age you're still there but the other things are gone . . . what you might call completed. They function, and they pass, and you also pass along, and perhaps you come to the big city here, and you learn a new function, and think about who you are . . . and somewhere in there you remember the old things, and the other place, and suddenly you realize how much you miss them. And this tells you how you have your own completion to accomplish.

I didn't reckon on any of this at the time, passing through Hanley on my Christmas vacation. I was just out for a stroll. I should have stopped and seen everything the way a camera sees, marking it down so when I grew old everything that was there wouldn't have vanished even in completion. I just wanted a little peace.

The thing was, that if I was sixteen, the clown dog must have been well on to thirteen or fourteen. He just never acted old, so it was not something to realize. Fourteen is old for a dog, and that's as near as far as a dog can last without vanishing, even if he still acts spry and bouncy and leaps into your arms when you tell him. So I just went up to Hopey's door and knocked, thinking he'd be there like always and maybe he'd rustle up the circus just for me in honor of my coming back from college on my first holiday.

The house was lit inside but no one answered, so I went around to the back where the tent was. Except there was no tent there now. You could see the tracks in the dirt where it was, all the time before, and some of the bleacher seats were still there, a little wrecked, like someone was trying to take them apart and then suddenly changed his mind. And as I stood there wondering, I heard Hopey's back door open. I turned and saw him in the doorway, so I asked him where the circus had gone to.

"My little clown dog passed away," Hopey said, "so I cut down the tent and dissolved the circus."

It happened in October, he said, which would be only a few weeks after I left town for school. I didn't know what to tell him without making it seem like I was holding another funeral, and I was worried about words because I got distracted thinking about the clown dog's little hat and how sad he looked in it sometimes. You know how touchy it can be, lurking about a place and looking like a stranger. And what if I asked how did it happen and only made Hopey feel worse? I didn't ask. I must have stood there for a whole minute trying to get my mouth around a sentence.

"He liked you, you know," Hopey said suddenly. "Perhaps you suppose that I was busy in the store, but I knew who his friends were. He was a pickety chooser, but he had exquisite taste in people. Didn't you think so?"

"I think he was a shy little fellow," I said.

"Yes, that he was."

"I'm sorry, Hopey. I came over especially to see him again." Now that I'd found my tongue, I expected he would break down or get very quiet, but he was just so calm. The clown dog used to follow me around, I wanted to say. We tried to make him talk. But we never hurt him.

"Since he liked you," said Hopey, "do you want to plumb the mystery of how he talked?"

I had to smile now. "It was a trick, wasn't it?"

"It was a tip-top trick," Hopey replied, "because nobody knew how it was done. Bet I shouldn't spoil it for you after all this. Should I? Do you want to know?"

"I think I ought to plumb the mystery, if he liked me, after all."

"He didn't like everyone," said Hopey. "But I believe he was exceptionally popular in the town."

"I guess he had to be," I said. "No other circus dog that I heard tell of has ever been the headline attraction."

"Well, he certainly was that. And he led a rich life. He was The Talking Dog of the World."

Hopey asked me about college then, and I told him, and after a while there was this natural space to say good-bye, so I left. Hopey forgot to tell me the trick and I forgot to remind him that I should know it, but I didn't think it was fitting to go back there just then, and before I was halfway home I was glad I didn't find it out.

You'd think I would be unhappy to learn that the clown dog had died, but in a way that conversation with Hopey was the only nice thing that happened all Christmas. My father was in a terrible mood the whole time, spitting out wisdoms like he was on a quota system and falling behind. He kept talking about the strike that everyone knew was going to happen, and finally, a few days before I was due to go back to school, he asked me didn't I think my place was here with the people I'd known all my life instead of at some college?

It seemed to me that the place to be during a strike was as far from it as possible, and college would do as well as any. And that's what I told him. So he said if I felt that way about it, I might as well get going right now.

"Just like Bill," he said.

I was waiting for that. I didn't have anything prepared to say back to it, but I knew it was coming. I don't care. It was meant to hurt me, but it didn't, though I must admit it began to gnaw on me after a while . . . because I hoped it was true.

I really did. "Just like Bill," he said, but he meant more like: "Go vanish."

"Just like Bill"—because I was leaving him, too. Well, there's always a reason for something, and sometimes two. I never went back to Hanley, either; maybe Bill did, after I left, but I won't. I have heard those words often since in my mind, *Just like Bill*, in just the way he said it, looking so smug that he had doped it out at last, made the simple sum and added another wisdom to his collection. I could accept it if I had to, but the truth is I am no way like Bill, all told. I am not like anyone. Whenever someone asks who I am, I say, "Me," just like the clown dog did, because it cheers me to remember him, and to think back on how I could have heard the trick if I had wanted to, which is as close as anybody ought to get. That was a strange, but fine, animal.

The speaker stopped there; he had finished. After a moment, the man who had been listening to him quietly took out some plastic and laid it on the check, and as the waiter bustled over to them, my magazine friend burst upon me, loaded down with apologies. I had to hear them, of course, and soothe them, and assure him that I wasn't in the least put off, and by the time we had settled down the two men to my left had gone.

"The worst of it," said my friend, "is that our star writer has gone on an autobiographical binge—*this* after ten years of that wonderful 'Letter from Paris' column, and 'Down and Out at the Venice Film Festival,' and 'Backstage at the Oscars,' all that kind of thing *no one else living* does as well. Suddenly, he can't so much as turn on his word processor unless he's all set to write about his childhood, and his family, and all these *grisly events that shaped him*, for God's sake. I mean, please, thank you, but *who cares*, right? We all have families, who doesn't? But do *I* go around telling about it? Do *you*?"

"Shall we order?" I said.

"That's the marvelous thing about New York, isn't it? No one really *has* families, because we all leave them somewhere when we . . . yes, we've *got* to order because I'm utterly . . . how's the veal, though? Do they do it Swiss style?"

So we lunched and spoke of metropolitan things, such as what well-known actor was beating on, absolutely *beating on* his wife; that the apartment crunch is starting to ease up a bit, unless you want a terrace or a really *dependable* no-frost fridge; and where you can get ceramic refrigerator magnets bearing the logos of classic Hollywood movies.

We parted on the street like boulevardiers, urbanely waving, and quick to move along, and quite, quite sure of ourselves, and without any family to speak of.

◆ 17 ◆

The Handshake Deal

I DIDN'T COME TO NEW York to write; I came to get published. But what I ended up doing was play piano in bars, make party tapes, put out romance comic books for the firm that published *Superman* and *Wonder Woman*, and update *TV Guide*'s squibs on old shows in syndication. (When you read about what's doing on *I Love Lucy*, *Surfside Six*, or *The Saint*—even today—it's mine.) In the spring of 1974, I got my first respectable job, on the staff of *Opera News*, and in late summer of that year I talked my way into my first book contract. I called my parents, a few friends. They were shocked and thrilled. Then I thought I'd tell my brother Jim. He wouldn't be thrilled, but he wouldn't be shocked either.

In fact, he was silent, distracted, holding a shoe in his hand. I was about to ask him to try to remake contact with the planet earth when I heard a pathetic mewing from somewhere in his apartment.

"What's going on?" I asked.

"Mice," he said. "Mice are going on."

"Mice squeak. I hear—"

"Laid in a cat," he explained, "to catch some mice here."

"Laid in?"

"Borrowed it."

I decided not to pursue that one. Somewhere outside, probably, some poor slob was pacing the street calling out, "Felix! Felix!"

"Something wrong with it," he went on. "The mice come out to play and that fucker doesn't even notice."

"You don't seem very impressed with my news."

"Must be a cheese factory next door or something. Why should I be impressed? You always wanted to be a writer and you knew you were going to get there, so what the fuck? Tell me some news and maybe . . ."

A mouse zipped out of the kitchen and disappeared behind the sofa as Jim heaved the shoe at it.

"It's like an army of them," he went on.

"Where's the cat through all this? Hiding?"

"I locked it in the bathroom yesterday to hunger it up so maybe then it'll straighten out and eat mice."

"Jesus!"

"Fucking coward cat. I'm not giving it any Puss 'n Boots Number Four or so when it isn't pulling its weight here."

Someone hit the buzzer downstairs.

"That's my man Dave coming around," said Jim, buttoning him in. "Now that Johnny Boy's tomcatting out on him, you know."

Whose story is it, who tells it, and what is the

story about? Walking the three blocks to Jim's, I had thought it would be my story, about my ambition. It wasn't. But listen.

Dave and Johnny Boy. Okay, they're hard to do. Because it wasn't what they said to each other or whatever was in their eyes—easy to record—as it was the threatening clarity of their pauses. Their hesitations around each other. The way they would start to move toward each other, freeze, back off; and they would be smiling right then. It was all rather highly charged, needs the visuals. And there were those things you would hear about them, too—like "Johnny Boy's tomcatting out on him."

So just listen.

Dave came in and got the cat out of Jim's bathroom, first thing, and told Jim, "You got to aim your boy at a project." He was in the kitchen opening a can of cat food. He petted the cat as it ate. "Don't you need to train this baby?"

"The fucking cat and the fucking mice," Jim muttered.

"You wait, my friend, and I'll show you what it is."

"Mice in my fucking house, you know."

Dave was about thirty-five then, a rangy, ham-handed, jocular, greying blond southerner who went through life in a blue T-shirt on top of a white T-shirt. Johnny Boy, his inseparable companion, was a trim, muscly guy in his early twenties. Like Jim, they were ironworkers, freelancing on construction sites in and around New York. Dave drove a motorcycle and Johnny Boy had a mustache. Dave took it cool and easy and Johnny Boy ran to the moody. Dave was the chief and Johnny Boy, grinning, did as he was told. It was Dave who had named him Johnny Boy, and this story, I learned on the day of the mice, is theirs.

"Now watch," said Dave, after the cat had fed, taking it over to where the mice were disappearing. He set it on the floor, knelt above it, and petted it some more as it arched its back and purred. He whispered to it. When it tried to move, he held it fast.

"Listen," he said. "Listen to the mice, cat." The cat vaguely listened. "Its name," Dave told us, "is Waterloo. Waterloo the cat is listening to mice."

Soon enough, the cat grew still, focused on something. I saw its eyes widen, and I knew some mice who were in a lot of trouble.

"When you have something in mind for your little pal, you got to aim him at it, see?"

"Dave," said Jim admiringly, "you are a gentleman and a fuckmaster."

"Yep. Look at Waterloo. Look at this swift mouse-killer. Waterloo the cat is going for it."

Sitting on Jim's couch at the nightly bull sessions, Johnny Boy would fall asleep in Dave's arms and no one as much as glanced at them, except me. "He ran all over the site today," Dave would explain, hefting the boy into his lap, "and now he's all tuckered out." And when the party broke up, Dave would stroke Johnny Boy's hair and say to him, "Come along, lad."

They lived together.

Dave petted the cat, enjoying its concentration. He looked at Jim and Jim nodded.

"You got to aim him, Jimbo."

"I see that, my amazing Dave."

Dave turned to me, smiling. "Or what?"

"You aim him," I replied, "because that is a righteous thing." You had to talk wild to stay abreast of Jim's buddies. They were wild men. I liked a few of them a very great deal.

"Hey, Dave, guess what?" I said. "I just sold a book to the Viking Press."

"Don't they got enough books of their own?"

"No, to write one. I sold a *deal*."

"Oh, so that," he said, coming over. "Now, that's a headline." He shook my hand.

Dave and Johnny Boy had this game. Dave would break into popular song, using a familiar tune but making up silly words. Such as:

> I'll bake a tart
> In Capistrano.

He'd sing this sweetly right into Johnny Boy's ear, and Johnny Boy would patiently say, "It doesn't go like that, Dave."

"How does it rightly go, Johnny Boy?"

"'I left my *heart*,'" Johnny Boy would tell him, "'in San Francisco.'"

"No kidding."

"Yeah."

Or:

> They tried to sell us
> Egg Foo Yong.

Johnny Boy would say, "'They tried to tell us we're too young.'"

Dave would reply, "You're too young, puppy. I'm old enough."

"Old enough for what?"

"Old enough to take you," Dave would pensively drawl, and they'd back off and pace around each other as if they were going to fight. Then Dave would feint and grab Johnny Boy by the waist and swing him around right there on the street, Johnny Boy yelling like a kid on a roller coaster.

I told Jim, "I think those two are lovers."

"You got to be wrong there, sport. Johnny Boy's a cinch with the ladies. They line right up for Johnny Boy, you know."

"What about Dave? Does he have a steady girl?"

Jim thought. "I expect he's married somewhere down south if you got the right state. Probably more than once if I know Dave. So what, though? Dave is not a guy to lay out his credentials for you. Dave is not afraid of what someone knows about him."

"Don't you think they're radically affectionate for . . . for . . ."

"Two straight guys?"

". . . right."

I hadn't come out to Jim, so I wasn't sure what terminology we were to use in this context. But he was.

"Those two boys are very close, I'll say that," he said. "They are very close. They love each other. But not fucking love. Friendship love. I've seen other guys like that. Something clicks off inside them, see. And like this one has this crazy sense of humor . . . and that one can get everything organized, which the other can't. And they just go right for each other, so they have someone to talk to, you know. To talk about things together and set aside the cares of the day. They think about each other all the time, too. But that doesn't mean they have to fuck together."

"We come from the same part of the world in the same era," I said. "The same *house*, not to put too fine a point on it. Yet I sound like a metropolitan *flâneur* and you sound like Zane Grey. How did that happen?"

He laughed. I don't know the answer myself and anyway this is not our story. But I am telling it. So let me put my oar in here: I had seen plenty of gay couples very much like Dave and Johnny Boy, usually hanging out on Sunday afternoons outside the Ramrod, their eyes dim after a long post-dancing love scene; or strolling the sand at the Grove to greet a lesbian couple and sit down on their blanket, the two women smiling at each other in memory of their own first years together. The cool man and the keen kid, that bracing union of grace and energy that means money in the straight world and love among gays. I tell you, I have seen gay couples exactly like

Dave and Johnny Boy—except if you had plunked those two down in our setting, outside the Ramrod or on the beach at Fire Island, they would have stood out like a cancan ensemble in Middle-earth. Of course, this is a difference of culture, not of sexuality. All those tales of tensely available truckers and butchers that I hear (a little too often) from my midwestern friends similarly takes in what you might call enemies of the parish. Still, were Dave and Johnny Boy uninhibited cutups or was something going on there?

So what is the story about?

I mean, was something going on that I should know of for future reference? (Like now.)

Let me tell you.

After Dave aimed the cat and petted it and told it to listen for mice, any time someone came through Jim's door that cat would run up and lay a dead mouse at his feet.

"Don't you ever run out of these?" I asked, stepping around the mouse to hand Jim the sweater he had asked me to bring back from our folks'. "What is this, Walt Disney's *Cinderella*?"

"This is cat heaven," said Jim, throwing the sweater at the couch.

Dave, holding a quart of Dewar's, caught it in the air. "I'll drink to that," he said. After taking a swig the size of the wave that obliterated Atlantis, he told me, "Tell Waterloo the cat how your book is coming."

"Fine."

"Hear that, Waterloo?"

"Fucking mice bodies," said Jim, kicking the latest one out into the hall.

Johnny Boy was still out—as Jim put it—tomcatting on Dave. That means that one of the girls who lined up for him had lucked in and Johnny Boy was bunking with her and only saw Dave by day on the site.

"Here's a nice sweater," said Dave, playing with it. "I could use me one of these some time when it gets cold. Where do you get them?"

"Any store," I told him.

"It's a fucking old used sweater," said Jim.

"Nice color," said Dave. "What color of shade is this?"

"Charcoal grey," I said.

"That is a real uptown shade for a sweater on the site, yo Jimbo?"

Then Dave looked at me because I was staring at him.

"What's on your mind, my friend?" he asked me.

What was on my mind was what this story is about, but before I could answer we heard a man scream in the hall. Jim pulled the door open, and there was one of his neighbors, in a vested suit and carrying an attaché. He blushed.

"I . . . I thought I saw a mouse," he announced.

"Well, now, that mouse belongs to Waterloo the cat," said Dave, coming up to the door.

The man said, "Thank you"—as upper-middle New Yorkers will when they don't know what just happened—and moved on.

"See, Waterloo," Dave asked it, "the cat?"

Waterloo, now guarding the kitchen with grim eyes and ruthless tail, didn't turn.

"Everybody out," said Jim. "I got a date coming."

Dave and I ambled the three blocks to my building, and I took him up onto the roof to watch the sun go down, Dave blithely chugging his Scotch.

"What are you planning to do with yourself?" he asked me, and I told him; and "What part of the south are you from?" I asked him, and he told me. There was some more of that, back and forth, then silence. Dave kept passing me the bottle, and I would take a sip, and he would take a slug. We were looking down on the street and up at the darkening sky, out of conversation with nowhere to go. But some men are comfortable having nothing to say or hear, and Dave was one of those.

I remember thinking then that I was twenty-five, and had thus far done nothing worth mentioning. I was going to have to do something about that.

We drank and listened to the town. Even on the hottest days there's a wonderful wind up on my roof, fifteen floors above the street.

Dave stretched and leaned against the railing, handing me the bottle. Blue T-shirt over a white T-shirt. He nodded at me very solemnly. "Johnny Boy'll be back soon," he said. "I can always tell, somehow."

I was a bit startled, and stuttered, saying, "It must be refreshing to have the place to yourself, though."

He thought about it. "I don't think it is," he said. "Because when he's there I always know where my morning coffee's coming from. Johnny Boy goes around the corner for it. He gets up before me, and does his shower, and then out he goes. So when I'm just coming out of the bathroom, he's got all the stuff set up. Buttered roll, you know, or a Danish. He likes to surprise me. And he gets all fussed about the sugars. I like to look over and see him fussing with the sugars for my cup of coffee."

I was staring at him again but he was looking away, didn't see.

"I like to have him around," he said. "Guess I'm just used to his ways."

I nodded.

"He has to do this now and again. The ladies just love that young lad and he feels obliged to respond. I've no quarrel with that. Every lad should have his day off."

He passed me the bottle.

"His day off," I asked, "from what?"

"From being serious. Thinking about how it feels."

"How what feels?"

He shrugged. "Your brother should be telling you, not me."

"How it feels to be really close friends?"

He looked evenly at me. "Well, we've grown to depend on each other. Is that what you'd call really close friends?"

I tried to pass him the bottle, but he went on, ignoring it.

"We can swing into this balance sometimes. You know? Swing right into it. Then it's hard to swing out again. Very hard to do that, very close friends.

Now, maybe I don't like to see him go off with the ladies all the time, but he's got a right. He wants to show me what he can do. Show himself, too. He may well be there with some sugar right now. Right as we speak, here. And he's pleasuring her so nice, you know, just laying there, nothing doing but pleasure." He reached over and took the bottle from me. "And he's thinking, What if someone could pleasure me that way? If I was laying there. That's how it starts, you know. I believe so. Who do I know could pleasure me so? Who could I ask?" He hefted the bottle and took a long one.

I was staring at him again, speechless. And he nodded at me, and gestured in some odd way, and smiled, and shook his head. See, you had to be there; we need the visuals, the two T-shirts and the bottle of Dewar's and the endlessly kind wisdom in his eyes.

"So he asked you," I said.

Dave shook his head. "That's a tall order for a lad, asking like so. I had to figure it out and help him along. Mind, I was not needful to plow Johnny Boy for myself. I started in to pleasuring him because it was the best way to hold him, you know. And I was needful to hold him, that's true. Needful of his ways." He smiled. "Well," he said, and that gesture again: Think nothing of it? Let's discuss? None of the above? "Well . . . tell you the truth, I was not all so sure how I was to proceed. I waited till we were in bed one night, in that darkness, you know, with the traffic going by, and sirens, and the sign lights going on and off at the deli. And I got him to talking about things, and one thing that we talked on led to another thing. And finally I got to ask him to roll over for me, if he would be so kind, and he gave me no quarrel about it." Another swig of scotch. "He gave me no quarrel." He regarded me. "You know why?"

I shook my head.

"Because I believe my young lad Johnny Boy was brought here to be my buddy. My really close friend, like you're saying. And I was brought here to be his, you know." Another swig. "It sometimes happens. As long as you're very tender about it, everything is okeydokes."

I flashed just then on a wise old queen of my acquaintance who habitually hired street trash to perform his sex for him. Describing the comely clarity of one kid in particular, he said, "He's the sort of boy who was *put on earth* to wear a Mexican lace shirt and black Speedo shorts, and have them *ripped off him* by reckless *muscle* hunks!" I flashed on that, for some reason.

And I had been right about those two all along; I know everything. But that's not what the story's about, yet.

Dave shrugged. "What the hell," he said. "If that's what he wants. I just got to see him happy. And that's why he'll always come back. I got a hold on him." He extended the bottle. "Really close friends."

"What is it like when he comes back?" I asked, taking the scotch. "Is he embarrassed?"

"Hell, no! He comes in like a barn dance! Wants to tell me how it was."

"You don't mind that?"

"Mind?" He smiled. "He looks so happy talking about his ladies, now what kind of buddy would I be to mind?"

"Isn't there any. . . I mean, he walks out on you and then just—"

"He doesn't walk out on me, my friend the kid brother. He just takes a little side trip."

"Doesn't he do . . . I mean, just some punctuation . . ."

"Yeah, some punctuation here," Dave said, laughing.

". . . some token gesture, to say he's glad to see you?"

Dave was humming.

"To say he's back?"

"Well . . . he always shakes my hand." He nodded. "Does it real special, too. A long, solid shake like we just been through a war together. You know why? Because he knows, a way back of all this, that I liked what he was so I went after him. He knows. That'll occur from time to time, men going after lads like Johnny Boy. And he knows that the thing I went after him for isn't in the fucking. Do you know that? I'll tell you what it is."

This is what the story is about.

"It's in the feeling. The feeling that we have together." He passed me the bottle. "Like we're walking along the street about eveningtime there with a good dinner inside us, and we both know that when we get home we're going to talk things over and then I'm going to pleasure him, put a hold on my Johnny Boy. And nobody knows that but us. It's in the feeling, because we know it and they don't. See?"

"Yeah."

"That's why," he said. "Why one guy may just go after another. For the feeling."

"Is anyone after Jim?" I asked. "That you know of?"

"How much truth do you want, my young friend?"

"How much have you got?"

"Listen." He set the bottle down. "What it is. You got to be just a little afraid for someone to come after you. That's the kind of thing it is. And Jimbo ain't afraid of anything."

"That's his problem," I said.

He looked at me for quite some time.

"No, it ain't. It's just how he is. And I'm how I am. And you. Like that, down the line." He kicked a foot in between the railings, pulled himself up, and gazed up at the sky, dark now, and the city heavy below. We didn't speak for a while, and I heard the darkness moving around us.

"He'll be home soon," said Dave. "I know that much."

I thought of him aiming the cat for Jim, and talking to the man with the attaché in the hall.

"I know his ways."

I thought of the wise old queen gloating over the stagey savaging of his gutter Ganymede, and of Dave singing for Johnny Boy and talking with him to set aside the cares of the day, and asking him to roll over if he would be so kind.

"Shake his hand. Going to ask him how he feels."

I thought of my book contract, and the place of the visual in contemporary society. I thought of very close friendships, having a hold put on you. Then I thought of what I was planning to do with myself—but (as Immanuel Kant once said) every story is about love. It's in the feeling.

Dave finished off the bottle.

"Maybe tonight," he said.

"Johnny Boy," he said.

"To be home with me," he said.

"Coming home tonight now, don't you think?" he said.

"Dave, I wouldn't be at all surprised."

Do-It-Yourself S & M

W ELL, THE BOYS AND I ARE sitting around Dennis Savage's place, talking S & M. As with most New Yorkers, none of us is an expert but we all have firm opinions. One of the group points out that while S & M's rituals tend to the piquant, at least its platonic essence favors devastating hunks. Another (whom I have long suspected of harboring atrocious fantasies) observes that S & M has more sheer style than alternate love modes, recalling for proof a movie he saw in which a weight lifter made passionately tender love to a bound boy and, at climax, strangled him. A third is amused to note that S & M originated gay's unique gift to the world, fisting— the equivalent of Italy's opera and Finland's sauna.

Also on hand is a man I loathe, an activist who lives and breathes Movement. But which one? He isn't as much in favor of anything as he is against everything. Besides, he is one of the least charismatic people I've ever met, the Fearless Leader as schmengie; and shouldn't our heroes be men of style and vigor? Most social or political movements take their tone from the most admirable—at least the most striking—characters available. (Think of the champs and exemplars who instructed the spirit of '76—Washington, Jefferson, Adams, Franklin, Tom Paine.) Gay liberation is the only movement I can think of that often throws its worst people to the top.

Like this guy. In his veins flows dialectic, not blood; and when he talks love he means murder. Murder for you and love for him. After years of attacking that excrescence of gay life, Fire Island Pines, he finally decided to see it for himself. No sooner had he stepped off the ferry than he screamed that he had found Paradise and ran amok, chasing anything that moved. At the sight of his furiously hungry eyes, his K mart *pour le sport* attire, and his fish-white belly, the houseboys ran for their lives, locked themselves in their houses, and wouldn't reappear till the activist was back on the boat.

Of course, now that he's in the city, the activist has retrieved his cool, replete with abrasive, ecumenical putdowns and plans to rule the world. At Dennis Savage's, he outlined the utopian gay future, which included among other benefits "coupling by assignment," racial quotas for everything, and sumptuary laws beyond a Methodist minister's meanest dreams. Dennis Savage and I shared a profound look at this, but his other guests were blithely intrigued, for this was the mid-1970s, and we thought we had the world wired down. We took the activists about as seriously as we took Methodist ministers.

"Will we be able to put in for certain preferences?" the activist is asked.

"Yes," another agrees. "Like the ads: 'Applicant favors sizable S with full toy shop. Must be non-smoker and love screwball comedy.'"

"Smoking will be prohibited in any case," says the activist. "And screwball comedy is a sentimental fascism."

"Well, can I still have an S?"

Dennis Savage gets restive. This was not one of his better parties—short on connection but deep in lecture, a compound of closed systems, like a night of anonymous bathhouse encounters. Dennis Savage likes interlock, a density of communion and a streak of culture. Surveying this soiree of jerks, he becomes touchy, railing against everything like a sit-com mother-in-law. "S & M!" he scoffs. "It's a hoax. It's a mess of paradoxes."

He notes them, to murmurs of dissent, under the activist's beady eye: "S & M teaches us the ultimate hunk—doesn't it?—in those cartoons . . . Tom of Finland, Etienne, A. Jay. But let's look in the pages of *Drummer*, let's examine their real-life counterparts—skinny sillies scowling in a pantry! S & M assures us that its erotic transaction is the most intense in the gay world. Am I right? And what is it made of? Cheesy intimidation. Aggression. Name-calling. Is this love? Is this our revolution?"

The activist nods, smiling. It's sure news that the Movement won't tolerate S & M, comes the day. "And as for style," Dennis Savage continues, "it may be style to you, but all I see is dreary routine."

"You've never been there!" cried one of the group. "S & M is a frenzy! Why, people have killed each other in mid-session! You call that routine?"

"You must admit," said another, "that the S & M scene would make a wonderful movie."

"Actually," replied Dennis Savage, "I don't think it would make a competent Looney Tune."

Cries and whispers followed, then laughter, then the various exits, for it was getting on. The activist, however, showed no signs of leaving, and when he visited the bathroom—drink in hand, be it said—Dennis Savage held a war council.

"Help me get rid of him," he begged. "Throw a drink in his face or something."

"He's *your* guest, boyo."

"But he's after my bones!"

"So tell him to get lost."

He groaned. "You don't know these political types. They think it's homophobic to say no."

"Yeah. To *them*."

"I'll be your best friend," he pleaded, taut-ologically.

"Tell you what. I'll go down to my place and get my antique Hindu beheading sword. Out I go. You tell him I'm your jealous lover, and when I come back I'll charge him and he'll run out."

"What if he doesn't?" He grabbed my arm. "No, do it. It'll be fun, anyway."

I keep this curved sword, a present from my dad, hanging on my wall. It is carved in intaglio, long, dull, and mean. Sometimes I answer the door with it, held at the ready, and so I reentered Dennis Savage's apartment; but the activist had gone. Too bad. I was looking forward to playing the bravo.

"Boy, did he race out of here," Dennis Savage told me as I hunted down a last glass of wine. "I told him you're the most notorious S in the East Fifties."

"Did he believe you?" I asked, sipping and thrilled. "Maybe I should investigate the scene."

"I can see you getting into S & M. First, you'd assemble collateral reading matter, from Dante to William Burroughs. Then you'd make lists: The Ideology of S & M. The Iconography of S & M. The Ontology of S & M, above all, surely."

"Don't call me Shirley."

"Footnotes, anyone?"

I fondle the sword. "I believe I'll cut off your lips."

"Listen, there are only three questions to ask before getting into S & M, only three. One: How would I look in leather? Two: Am I willing to keep late hours—because, you know, S & M gives no matinees. Three: Am I the goon or the milquetoast?"

"I suspect you are a *trompe l'oeil* troll."

"That's all S & M is, really: costume, schedule, role. Is it compulsion? Liberation? Romance? No. What is it? Presentation."

"What isn't?" I ask.

"And you know why? Because there is no S & M. Everyone's an M. Everyone wants to be loved. *Possessed*. See? That is the dream of this presentation—'Take me away from all this. Take me out of myself! Rebear me into life!'"

"So there *is* an S in S & M, then—the bearer."

"Can you name?" he says, so wily. "Can you, now: a *genuine S* in the *world*?"

We have to rank out this cynic. Mind, race!

"Well?" he goes, so wry, so Ivy League.

I'm crazed. I can focus on nothing. I am back in seventh grade, when Mr. Van Santvoord swooped down on me crying, "Who kills Hamlet?" and I couldn't even recall who wrote it.

"Not a single name?" Dennis Savage taunts.

Yes, wait! "Mitch O'Connell."

"Mitch O'Connell is a sweetheart! He wouldn't squash a bug. And here I thought you would cite me some angry avatar . . ."

"S & M isn't about anger."

He waves this nonsense away. "Mitch is a lover, not a fighter. He dreams of April and tulips and scented encounters sealed with a puppy's kiss. Where do you get S & M in that?"

"S & M has love in it."

"Oh, sure. There's nothing as tender as a tit clamp. And cock weights are charity, loyalty. Yes! Yes!" he cries, like Fats Waller. "Push your beau down the stairs—it's true romance! Run him through the meat grinder—it's love, it's love!"

"In San Francisco, they would say that you sound like an old biddy who thinks there are fairies at the bottom of her garden."

"I happen to know that in your *whole life* you spent exactly ten days in San Francisco—most of them in record stores. So don't tell *me*!"

Well, it is true that no one would take Mitch O'Connell for an S at first acquaintance. He could perhaps play the role in some movie: dark, intense, taciturn. At times, he smoldered. But a collegiate spring in his ambitions typed him among the bourgeoisie, and the man was a flagrant romantic. He had It, but It wasn't easy to pin down, for he carried himself a bit off-kilter, as if he were trying to be blond, carefree, and gregarious. Still, he had *vast* shoulders and the boldest eyes ever seen, virtually navy blue. People kept looking at him; but he never looked back.

What did he want and what would he get? Well, you'll see.

But how did he find it? Through a natural mastery of S & M techniques.

And I don't mean as an M.

This will take us back to The Pines, summer of '73, when I rented a room for four weeks with, among others, Mitch O'Connell. The others came out only on weekends; I was temporarily permanent. Also in The Pines that month was my friend J. D. (for John David—he's a southerner, and you know those boys take their middle names everywhere they go). J. D. and I would sit on a bench in the harbor making fierce and facetious commentary as the boats pulled in. Friday afternoon was our gala, as the great and near-great collected, including our respective house-mates, who would greet us with city dish before trooping off to organize dinner, eat, nap, and dance. Those were the days, weren't they?

On this certain evening I wish to tell of, Mitch O'Connell arrived with an uncharacteristic aplomb. He was standing on the top deck of the ferry glow-ing, grinning, swaggering without having to move. He wore black running shorts and a gondolier's shirt and it seemed the whole boat was wondering who he was.

So were J. D. and I. "Is that Mitch O'Connell?" he asked. "He looks ten years younger or something!"

"He could be a movie star."

"He's dashing!"

"He's high as a kite on the—"

"He must be in love," J. D. whispered, and promptly clamped a fist in his mouth, amazed at the bitter beauty that stirs a sullen world. Bitter: for not all postulants are taken into the order.

"He is in love," I said, surprised that I hadn't realized it before. "He's in love with Bill Apgar."

"That little Californian boy?" J. D. drummed on his thighs in excitement. He loves a good story, as long as there's plenty of sex in it and a happy ending. "Lots of flash and no reality whatsoever," he once told me, describing the Perfect Party. But that's the way he likes everything. "Bill Apgar," he now observed, "is just right for Mitch O'Connell. He's *just right!*"

"Will you please stop hitting my arm?"

"Oh, think of them at beach parade tomorrow! Mitch's hulking, tempest-tossed dark ways next to the bright-eyed blondie boy! I *thoroughly approve* of this story!"

"If you hit me once more—"

"Look!"

At Mitch O'Connell, he meant, as Mitch disembarked. He gave us a frisky salute as he passed but did not stop to talk.

"Did you *see* that?" J. D. whispered, so loudly that some of the arriving passengers turned to stare at us. "Did you see how he *walked*? He was . . . *striding!*"

He was moving like the protagonist of the kind of

stories J. D. likes, like a man on a date with the love of his life. Now everything fell into place. Bill Apgar was also one of my housemates, and what I had taken for weekend blather and roughhouse I suddenly saw as the outline of a heavy flirtation. As Mitch vanished down the boardwalk, I told J. D. of their pensive stares across the breakfast table, of their moonlit walks, of how, when you came upon them talking in the living room, you felt as if you were barging in on the second act of a thriller. I told how Mitch called Bill "Billy" (no one else did), as if staking a claim on him; and how Bill reveled in the nickname. It *was* love. But something was missing— the happy ending, perhaps even the sex. Mitch's eyes glared at times; Bill's wavered. They had moved from the flirtation stage not into forthright romance but some densely ambivalent mystery.

Two boats later, Bill himself arrived. Though he was still in his early twenties, he had just sold a screenplay for an unholy fortune, and his weekdays were consumed with the doing of lunches and the taking of meetings. He stopped to chat with us, flushed and exhausted by success; I helpfully hummed "The Lady's in Love With You," but no one got it. Mitch was not mentioned.

"Do you think?" J. D. asked as Bill ambled off. "Are they really and truly . . ."

"Lovers?"

J. D. screamed.

"Oddly enough," I said, "I doubt they've as much as kissed."

"Is it *possible*?"

"Bill is afraid."

"Of what?"

Trying to verbalize an answer, I paused, and J. D. pummeled my arm again.

"Hey!"

"Of what?" J. D. repeated. "Of being fucked?"

"Maybe of being loved."

J. D. liked that at first; then it frightened him and he ran away. The story was getting too good: too much reality whatsoever.

Of course the setting itself, The Pines, only intensifies the passions of story, of any story. And The Pines, in the 1973 of no-fault sexuality, always tried to be as unreal, as fantastic, as possible. The heavy drug intake dulled the perspective, but the scenery, natural and human, beguiled and stimulated; and the recklessly appetitive prowling blew wide the vistas of Stonewall. How many thousands of men rode the ferry in those days believing, like Mitch O'Connell perhaps, that this would be the weekend that changed their lives?

It was nearly twilight. I lurked around the harbor some, pestered two housemates in the Pines Pantry till they asked me to go away, and finally passed on to the house, where I found Mitch and Billy wildly smooching on the couch like two frat brothers after a hell night.

Bill tried to leap up as I came in—he had had plenty of warning, given the noisy Pines decks—but Mitch held him fast. Stuck for a lead, I broke into a vocal of "The Lonely Goatherd" with creative dance steps. Bill struggled out of Mitch's grasp and put the dining table between them.

"I have nowhere to go," I told them. "My sidekick deserted me, my housemates threw me out of the grocery, and I'll lose my reputation if I'm found on the beach after sundown."

Mitch was moody, Bill all for company. He made me a Bloody Mary. He got out the cheese and crackers. He talked Hollywood and status games. He said they all play roles out there. Mitch said nothing. After a few minutes of this, I left: no place to go was better than that place just then. But Bill came running out after me.

"Please stay," he said.

"I'm not wanted."

"I want you. Anyway, this isn't the right moment for Mitch and me to be alone."

"Are you mad? Are you *wild*? You two had *Butterfield 8* working when I came in. What do you want, witnesses?"

He looked away. "No, yes, I . . . I just . . . did *you* ever . . ."

"Did I what?"

He took a deep breath. "It's overwhelming me. Why does it have to happen so fast?"

"He likes you. If you like him, say yes. If you don't, say no."

"Oh, it's that simple?"

"So far."

"You old grads of the Movement think the whole world boils down to whom you're going to sleep with tonight, don't you? Your whole revolution is nothing but sex. What about the other things in life?"

"They're all there. Our whole revolution is more comprehensive than you've been told. Whom have you been listening to? Some activist?"

He just looked at me.

"Activists don't make the revolution," I told him. "We do. *Chacun à son gout.*"

"Would you please come back in there and tell that to Mitch?"

"You're a nice kid. I wish you success in love, a great career, and a fast metabolism. But when it comes to kids, I prefer to seduce and abandon, not give courtship counseling. So huh?"

He thought, nodded, and started back inside.

I grabbed his arm. "I'm sorry. But don't call me old. And let me tell you something. No one can help you out in something like this. It's your story; you write it. Besides . . . generally it *is* simply a question of you like him or you don't. Yes or no."

Just then the rest of the house came rollicking down the boardwalk with the weekend provisions and we all repaired inside for a Fire Island cocktails, cooking, and dinner session, rich with subtext. After a while, Mitch stopped sulking and opened up some; by the third round of vodka he was giddy, making grimly robust jokes and sticking very, very close to Bill. I wondered how much of this was getting through to the others. They were not a particularly observant bunch, but let's face it, this was theatre. Still, much of gay life is theatre. Much of life, period.

Bill's performance seemed somewhat undirected. He was sort of unhappily amiable, possibly dreading the hour when the rest of us would go dancing and he would be left alone with Mitch for Act Three.

But two things happened. First, Bill got up during dessert, said he had to go visiting, and left. Second, Mitch went into his room without a word. And he was *mad*.

By then, everyone knew something about it. Everyone looked at everyone else and wondered. But The Life goes on, and what everyone mainly did was get into dancing uniform. It was plain that year: the basic white T-shirt and your second-best jeans. An early entrance into the dance hall was also favored that summer, at least by my housemates, serious dancers rather than event-attenders, who tend to arrive very late and thus Make an Entrance.

So off we went, clump after clump of us sneakering along the firm sand near the waterline in the midnight darkness, sure of ourselves, confident of our freedom. Why not? It looked easy then. Every so often, however, it felt hard to live up to the demands of that avidly bewitching style. It felt less like freedom, more like a mission. That night, I impulsively turned back on the verge of the Grove; The Life was too much with me. My housemates scarcely noticed, for I had been dragging behind them. Oh, perhaps for quite some time, in all—more than even I knew. Another tune I could most appropriately have broken into was "There's Gotta Be Something Better Than This."

I, too, dreaded having to play a scene with Mitch, and I paused outside our house, though all the lights were out. I virtually crept up our walk, scuttled into my room, and eased onto my bed, my head spinning from the predinner drinking. I lay there, pondering, organizing, making lists in my head.

Then it happened.

Footsteps on the deck. Lights on. Something's moving. Pause. More movement from somewhere deep in the house. Then:

"I'm glad you're here." Bill.

"And I'm glad you're here." Mitch.

"Are . . . are you sore at me?"

"No." Thoughtful. "No, Billy, I'm not sore at you."

"You sound . . . Aren't you cold without a shirt?"

Indefinable noises.

"Why are you putting a chair against the door?" Bill.

"So you can't get away."

Silence. I should say something, no? I could stir, or cough. I could sing the rest of "The Lonely Goatherd," perhaps launch into "An Ordinary Couple." But I never liked that one.

"Please don't be hard with me, Mitch. It's not what you think. I had to—"

"What do I think?"

"I wanted to go over it in my mind. See—"

"What do I think, Billy?"

"Can we talk about it? I didn't go visiting. I took a walk. Now I . . . I came back to tell you something. Don't be hard, now, okay?"

"Too late. You came back too late. I've been doing some thinking, too. Come here, Billy."

"Okay, except you . . . you look . . . hard . . ."

"There's a good reason for that."

"What . . . what are you going to do? Just tell me, okay?"

"I'm going to beat you up."

Nothing. Then Bill: "Any special reason why?"

"Did you hear me say 'come here' to you?"

I imagined J. D. asking, "What were they *wearing*?" and I ached to look, but I didn't dare move. Would you rush the stage to interfere with the actors' business?

"Mitch, you have every right to be sore, but if you just listen to— No, Mitch, wait!"

At a horse race you can leap and yell. Watching television you can make remarks. If the dam bursts you can run. I had to sit there motionless through these excruciating silences, eyeless in Babylon.

"Please listen to me!"

"You have this coming, so just take it nice and easy. You're such a cute little kid, aren't you? So beatable, now. So right." Scraping noises. Something heavy. Was Mitch moving the table? "Nothing you can do about it, Billy. Come here to me now."

"Mitch!"

"Billy . . ."

A chair went over.

"Oh, Mitch, please—

"Here we go now, Billy."

"Stop using my name! You . . . you said you wanted to be my friend!"

The table again.

"Just let me get my hands on you and I'll show you what a friend I can be."

That's what Bill's been afraid of all along, I

◆ 48 ◆

thought. But this was not the ideal time for a psychoanalytic reading of the case. Bill was sobbing. "Why are you hurting my feelings?" he wailed. Because you hurt his, I noted silently. "I wanted you to like me. Don't . . . not like this, Mitch, please!"

Oh? Some other way would be acceptable? He's tormenting you and you're loving it; so whom do I root for?

Bill spoke again, suddenly calm: "You don't have to move any more furniture. I'm going to come over to you and I'll . . . you can do what you want to me. I just wish you'd hear me out first. Then if you want to hurt me, you can. I can't stop you, anyway. You can wait a few minutes. Okay, Mitch? Okay?"

Silence. Was Bill "coming over"? Who in this scene is the bearer into life?

"You peeked, didn't you?" said Dennis Savage, when I told him the tale. "This is where you peeked."

Peeked? I was afraid to breathe. I was also consumed with admiration for this couple's instincts for S & M stylistics. No training, no arrangements, no practice. Just get in there and do it. Now Bill was whispering to Mitch. Damn! Key dish forever lost. Clearly, he *was* afraid of something, and Mitch demanded that he not be for the sake of romance—and if that isn't S & M, I don't know what is. In the gay utopia, when we couple by assignment, we'll be at the mercy of the activists. But for now we can always get locked in a room with Mitch O'Connell.

"I'll do anything you want."

Which of them said that? I was so rapt in thought

that I didn't hear this till it was an echo in the air, and I could no longer place the voice.

"*Now* you peeked," says Dennis Savage.

"No. I lay doggo, guilty, thrilled. *Who* will do anything? Only a gay. Wives won't swallow; husbands won't spank. But a gay who Won't loses love. What difference who actually said it? We all say it, or hope to. Bill was sobbing again; his sobs filled the house. Enough. Out I came, sweater in hand.

They were standing in the middle of the room, swaying in each other's arms, heart to heart. I doubt they were even aware that I passed them. I walked onto the black beach and fretted.

"That's your idea of S & M?" Dennis Savage asks. "Two cream puffs kissing?"

"On one hand," I tell him, "I'm concerned about your health. On the other hand, how do I know this antique Hindu beheading sword works till I chop-test it on your neck?"

"Now, that's S & M," he avers. "There it is: talk. Just talk."

"You think Mitch wouldn't have given Bill a beating if the kid didn't know how to handle him?"

We'll never know. Walking along the water's edge that night, I thought that everything I'd heard of S & M paled before the confrontation of Mitch and Bill. It was the *measured* nature of their text that got me, the calculation of anger and fear and need, the ritually repeated "Billy" and the maneuvering of roles, each an aggressor and a victim at once. But then that's one of the things that makes gay romance unique:

two bearers, in place of straight's bearer and receiver. Perhaps it was the incongruity of Mitch's attack that most impressed me, the dense love mixed
into the violence. Or maybe it was because I couldn't
see it; maybe S & M is never as good as it sounds.

Out on the sand that night, reviewing the event, I
decided that I knew nothing of S & M. But I know
hot dish when I have it. I ran off to J. D.'s house to
share it. His mates were advocates of the late entrance and were still engaged in working out a fastidious improvisation of costume. J. D. was all set to
go, in a cowboy's shirt, a fisherman's sweater, and a
painter's pants. "Who are you?" I would have said,
but before I had a chance to, he cried, "What were
they *wearing*?" Costume, schedule, role.

"Jeans," I told him. "Bill was in one of those
washed-out Lacostes he always wears. Mitch had—"

"And were they . . ."

"What?"

"For the first time? The last time?"

"This could be the start of something big."

Waiting for his housemates to assemble and de-
part, he was getting in a last-minute munch. The
two of us looked up to admire them as they came
out of their rooms, plumed and painted like Regency
rakes.

"I'm going to dance for my life tonight," said one
of them.

J. D. ate some peanut butter off a knife. "What if
Mitch had . . . done it?" he said.

"Done what?" asked another housemate, adjusting his cap in a mirror; he was going as an American
sailor.

"Beaten up his boyfriend," I said.

"Making up is hard to do," the sailor replied; the thought seemed to come easy to him.

"What happens to them now?" J. D. asked.

"Plenty of sex, I expect, and a happy ending."

Ecstatically floored, he was silent.

"All right," one of his housemates called out, "let's *get* there!"

"Let's *show* them!"

"We're going to *do this thing*!"

I couldn't go back to my house, so I decided I'd better go dancing after all. As we walked, J. D. was silent at first; then he hit me for more details of Mitch and . . . Billy.

"When you came out . . . who was. . . ?"

"Both."

He sucked in his breath. "And was it. . . ?"

"To die," I told him. "To *die*."

"But after you left . . . do you really think they. . . ?"

I shrugged. "It was the moment, wasn't it?"

"Don't you wish?" he murmured. Then he turned to the ocean and screamed at the top of his lungs, "Don't you *wish*?"

I speak fluent gay, but I swear sometimes I haven't the vaguest idea what we're saying to each other.

The Ghost of Champ McQuest

■▬◼▬◼▬◼

Faithful, indeed, is the spirit
that remembers
After such years of change
and suffering!

—Emily Brontë,
"Remembrance," 1846

DENNIS SAVAGE GROANED
when I told him I had invited Tom
Adverse for a midweek overnighter at our
Pines house.

"That dreary lump!"

"He'll repair the decking for us and blot up the
leaks in the roof. And I'll bet he can fix the upstairs
john so we don't have to jiggle it every—"

"He has the eyes . . ." Dennis Savage begins wea-
rily, his head all a-shake, *must* he explain, *why* will I
never see reason? "The eyes," he repeats, "of those

53

psychotic hustlers who keep tuning out and going blank on you because as long as they hold you at a distance you don't really seem human. So they don't have to feel conflicted when they pull out the knife to kill the faggot."

"Tom isn't dangerous around gays. He only gets into fights with straight men. And women, sometimes. I mean—"

"Where do you find them?"

"You introduced me to him. You said he gives a great massage."

That stops him. Ah, he remembers, nods. "A great massage, yes. Except for the jokes he tells over your shoulder. 'How many niggers does it take to start a Cadillac?'"

"He's got a racist, reactionary, and intolerant streak that is extremely unappealing, I admit. But what else would he be? He comes from a small town in North Carolina, goes right into the Marines after high school, survives Vietnam, supports himself by oddjobbing from hustling to housepainting, and spends his off hours failing to understand women and fending off their jealous boyfriends in bars. You must admit, it's a fascinating tale. He can't enjoy what he should have and he doesn't want anything else. He's all puzzled up."

"He's a vicious loon," says Dennis Savage.

"No. He's a big, sexy, kind man who's had a lot of bad breaks. *And* he's the only straight anyone ever met who had such a bad time in his world that he only feels comfortable in ours. If there were such a thing as homophilia, he'd get a medal for it. Don't you agree?"

"He's a lurid baboon," says Dennis Savage.

"Come on, he's a good guy."

"A *good guy*? He's so wacko, they're thinking of changing the word 'crazy' to his name!"

"They were getting up a list of the five most intolerant people in the history of the world. They had Hitler, Savonarola, Nero, Pope George Ringo I—and in fifth place, it was a toss-up between Caligula and you."

"He's a demented bore," says Dennis Savage.

More precisely, Tom Adverse was the Cherry Grove Carpenter, for those of you who con the folklore back into the early 1970s. Hammering and sawing away on roofs and decks in direly cut-off jeans, Tom Adverse was not only an amenity of the gay part of Fire Island but a regular stop on the new-comer's tour. Day-trippers to The Pines couldn't call their visit official till they had marched over the sands to scan the Cherry Grove Carpenter.

And scan they must, for Tom was truly a sight, dev-astating at first glance and mesmerizing on reconnais-sance. Still, he can't have been enjoying himself. He posed for mail-order porn, yet he was reportedly un-available. He did give massages, in those same car-penter's cutoffs, yet they were just that: massages. He had the winged shoulders, louche navel, and ruthless nipples of the absolute dreamboy, yet he had no atti-tude, no fire, no certainty of self. He palled around with quick, fierce gays, yet to most questions he gave dead eyes and said, tonelessly, "Uh-huh." There were a lot of things he didn't like to talk about. He preferred to play tambourine while the gay boys danced. The whole place drank him in; he didn't seem to notice.

Then he tried porn posing, strictly for the money: but look at his eyes in those pictures. They're sad. The only sad eyes I've ever seen in porn, a sorry hot.

So what did he love? Carpentry. Painting. Making and repairing. He felt alive in such work, placed, needed. Posing in the nude was giving too much away, at that to strangers who would plunder him of something he didn't know he had. Building and fixing was good work, doing oneself proud. And his rural right-wing style wasn't all racist jokes and Rambo politics. Once I was talking to him at the Pines ferry when a vastly noted New York fashion designer vastly noted Tom and approached with an offer. Normally this very wealthy and influential personage had only to ring out his name for men of all sizes to fall in with his schemes. Tom just looked at him.

"I know who you are," he said calmly. "You get young kids out here who don't know any better and you give them drugs to warp their heads around. Then you mess them up with sex stuff. So you can get away from me before I teach you one good lesson."

The fashion designer could indeed get away, and very immediately did.

Never till remember rest you will I.

—*allegedly recorded
during a "spiritual visitation,"
Denver, 1962.*

I suppose Dennis Savage was right to question Tom's suitability as a guest in our house, with his uh-huh and dead looks. But it was an odd house to begin with, known as Chinatown for no reason that anyone could name, and, this summer, veritably full of unsuitables—Lionel, for instance, one of my best friends but entirely too intelligent for anyone's good. Some people get 800 on their physics boards; Lionel got the Nobel Peace Prize. It was Lionel's resolute caprice to be attracted only to the dimmest, most impenetrable men. "I'm in love with that number," he would murmur in a bar. "He looks so *stoopid*." Lionel's number of the hour was Bert, so stoopid he spoke like a Valley Girl. When you first met him, you assumed he was doing a Valley Girl imitation. No, he simply spoke like a Valley Girl. I found it amusing, though it drove Dennis Savage crazy.

It was 1979. I had just turned thirty and was only now seriously considering the prospect of Growing Older, with all the loss and vitiation that it promises; today, of course, I look back on this time as my salad days. Dennis Savage's lover, Little Kiwi, had joined us but recently (alas, with his incalculably batty dog, Bauhaus), our supreme hunk-in-residence, Carlo, was still fancy-free and keen with dish on the giddy ways of the Circuit, and we all knew we hadn't yet learned everything there is to learn. We were young. We were healthy. We were having a grand time. The only person I knew of in our generation who had died was Jeff Willis, of my class at Friends Academy, killed in a car accident in his freshman year at Duke.

It is a quirk of the Island that while all houses in Cherry Grove run on the same rhythm—i.e., retirement torpor—each Pines house sets a unique pace. Some are as Arranged as Neapolitan marriages, others rather libertarian, some crowded with berserk guests, others strictly limited to the shareholders. Ours, set up by Dennis Savage, was classic Pines, slow to start in the morning, thinly lively by lunch, building to a heavily socialized dinner. However, there we diverged from the norm, which called for naps, drugging up, and the walk along the beach to dance at the Ice Palace. Lionel, Bert, and Carlo danced, but without artificial stimulation; and the rest of us usually hung around for games and assorted nonsense. Dennis Savage and I were playing out a craze for the old word game Jotto, and Little Kiwi was obsessed with mastering the Polaroid camera Dennis Savage had bought him, and with the construction of plastic models of dinosaurs, a group of which he had set up on the little table out on the deck, dubbed The Wonderful Museum of Terror Lizards. Never one to waste a passion, Little Kiwi would inveigle drop-ins and bystanders into posing with his models so he could photograph them.

Tom Adverse fit into our routine with his typical lifeless aplomb. "I could buff this," he would observe, running his hand pensively, caressingly, over the faded paint on the deck railing, or—looking over the kitchen end of the living room—"You ought to let me put in one of those spigots that come out with instant boiling water."

Cooking was another of his fields. Apparently he fended off gay hunger by busying himself with kitchen matters—it gave him a chance to turn his back, politely, on the roiling, wishful needs of men he could like but never love. Thus, hearing Dennis Savage, Lionel, and me arguing over whose turn it was to prepare dinner, Tom said, "Well, you know I could fix some four-happiness rice pastry for dessert."

Whereupon Little Kiwi snapped his picture.

"Do you like four-happiness rice pastry?" he asked Little Kiwi.

"Mostly I just know Rice Krinkles."

"Uh-huh," said Tom, not as much replying as punctuating the exchange.

Vietnam was another of Tom's topics, though the subject seldom came up in the house. Not that that mattered, since Tom never heard what anyone was saying in the first place. His every utterance was an outburst, a non sequitur, a frame without the picture. You would come upon him hammering away at something on the deck. You would offer a pleasantry or two about nothing in particular. And he would look up from his work and say, "On a scale of one to ten, I give *Apocalypse Now* a four."

Little Kiwi enjoyed Tom's line of speech for its sheer surprise. But after a while even he began eyeing Tom askance, because no matter how much you put in, nothing ever came out. I truly believe Tom was starved for friendship, grateful for any attention (as long as it didn't bear a sexual price tag), literally *relieved* to be asked among us. Yet he seemed unable to respond to people, almost preschizoid in his absentee companionship. So Tom fit in as he always did: by not fitting in. It's hard to complain about a man that terrific looking (though Dennis Savage found a way), and he did make himself useful around the house, tinkering and repairing. Besides, trying to cheer Tom up, to make him feel *connected*, was my good deed for the week.

Everyone helped, except Tom. The more welcoming you behaved, the weirder he got. Coming downstairs in the bright midmorning after his first night with us, he went right to the kitchen to make breakfast for the house.

"Carlo will love this," I said, noting the full complement of eggs, bacon, toast, three kinds of jam, and coffee that Tom was whipping up. He was even heating the milk. "One thing Carlo believes in is the full dinner pail."

"Uh-huh," says Tom. "I saw a ghost last night."

"A . . . ghost?"

"That's right."

And he goes right on with his work.

"A real ghost?" I pursued.

"I don't know how one of those things would be real or not," he replied, setting up the plates. "But it was a ghost."

He ladled out the food and brought two heaping plates outside. I took the milk and coffee.

"How do you say 'Come and get it' around here?" he asked me.

I shrugged. "Everyone just shows up, sooner or later."

He nodded. Hot food, cold food; nothing matters.

"So," I said, working on the imported roughcut Scotch lemon marmalade, a house gift from earlier in the season, so New York and hip and A-list, so sovereign of style and playful of taste. Tom, across the table, munched his toast naked. The toast was naked, too. "So, Tom, what about this ghost?"

"Yeah."

"I mean, was it . . . wearing a sheet?"

"What're these funny animals for?"

"That's Little Kiwi's Wonderful Museum of—"

"I could paint these deck things for you. Put some orange and navy blue on these chairs, so you'll stand out from the other places here. Hot boys looking up from the water during the beach parade after lunch, they'll want to be a part of this."

Note that Tom knew and was totally comfortable with the ways of the Circuit—the only straight I've known who was. All of the few nonhomophobic straights of my acquaintance would just as soon not hear about The Life in too much detail. Some faces go white at the very mention of the word "popper." You could describe the ins and outs of a Colt orgy to Tom, down to the last balling in and creaming out, and all he'd say is "Yeah."

Dennis Savage found that odd. "Doesn't this guy ever date?" he asked. "I can buy that he's happy around gay men, for whatever virtually unbelievable reason. But if he's really straight, shouldn't there be a woman in the picture somewhere?"

"There have been several. But there's always trouble, somehow. They break up pretty fast."

We had been cleaning out the pantry. He took me by the arm, led me to the couch, sat me down, and joined me.

"Tell," he said.

"No, because you're just looking for holes to poke into his story."

"Nay, I merely love to hear you make icons of various deadbeats and zanies just because you like their looks. First there's Carlo, your typical do-nothing Circuit joyrider, building a life entirely around the next meal, the next lay, and the next unemployment check. There are hundreds like him around here. I could buy a party of them for pin money. But no, after you get through recreating him, Carlo is our King Arthur, our Gandalf, our Little Boy Blue, isn't he? Our oracle! Our *guru*! And then we have . . . *Tom!*"

Who was standing at the doorway to the deck, now sporting the famous cutoff jeans, his face its usual blank. "I was going to fix lunch," he said. "Some chickens in the fridge. Could you stand to take them barbecue, or were you saving them for some other deal?"

"No, chicken is fine."

"Build a fire," he said, backing up, "out here on the—"

"Just don't step on my diplodocus," came Little Kiwi's voice, along with the click of the Polaroid. "Bauhaus, let's make some more candids."

Bauhaus barked.

"Oooh rillly," said Lionel's boyfriend Bert, coming up from the beach with Lionel. "Prehistoric *Cit-ty!*"

"Lionel, could you please stand there a second so I can take your picture? No, closer to the brontosaurus."

"Like *tot-tal* behemoth," Bert observed, coming inside.

"Bert almost killed a palaeosaur," Lionel announced.

"Nöe, I did-dn't," as they swept through the house.

Carlo came down and sat on the couch with us.

"Everything's happening at once," he said, grinning. "This place is full of loving, dancing gentlemen trying to figure what they're supposed to be doing with their own history."

"The first ten years of Stonewall," I crowed to Dennis Savage, "in a sentence!"

"I'll get you later," he said, rising.

"Crazy house," said Carlo.

"Look out for my iguanodon," Little Kiwi cried from outside.

"Saw something odd here last night," said Carlo. "Upstairs there. Wonder if you saw it ever."

"If I had to cite all the odd things I've seen in Pines houses over the years . . . You know, this is one of the Island's historic sites. It's had everything from visiting movie stars to a suicide."

"Yeah, well, now it's got a ghost, too. You know what I mean?"

"Uh-oh."

"Or what should I call it? Something creepy coming around at night. Unless the kid himself there is doing tricks with his camera."

"What exactly did you see?"

He thought about it. "Kind of hard to say it exactly. It's more of a feeling that something's there than a sight to see. There's some light to it, sort of, like a million tiny candles moving together. And you hear something, like very slow words. Like different people taking turns on a sentence. Couldn't quite make it out."

"You weren't afraid?"

"Happens too fast to be afraid. Got up to take a whizz and this thing comes down the hall, right past me. I just wondered if anyone else has checked in with you on this matter ever."

"Oddly enough . . . uh, this couldn't by any chance be some elaborate joke, could it? I mean, I love the million tiny candles and the sound effects are intriguing, but you realize of course that there are no such things as ghosts."

Carlo smiled. "I always think so. But I did see something last night in this house like I'm telling you about."

"Tom said something about a ghost, too. I just thought maybe you and he . . ." Carlo and I looked out through the sliding doors giving onto the deck, where Little Kiwi was holding forth on the size of the teeth in the stegosaurus, demonstrating on his model as Tom blankly stared, socially detained but emotionally touring, off on a tear among his private demons. "No," I said, "that's impossible. Tom is incapable of making anything up. What he is is what you get."

Carlo shook his head. "He's hiding plenty of stuff. Rough stuff inside there. He only shows you the smooth."

"Oh, certainly. I just mean that he can't create anything. There's no art in Tom Adverse."

"Forty years old," Carlo mused, "and he's still got a twenty-eight-inch waist. How does a guy that fine-looking get so wrecked inside?"

Tom suddenly wandered in—he's vague but he's abrupt—to ask where the charcoal was. Carlo had an appointment in another house, Lionel and Bert went back to the beach, Little Kiwi came inside to try "some shadow poses," and so the house reshuffled its hands, set up for the next play as surely as the stage of a repertory theatre. I could say that I was so busy with one thing and another (not to mention the Jotto championship, which Dennis Savage and I played as if for our lives) that I didn't bother with the ghost reports. I could say that. But then, how does one cope with ghost reports in the first place? What agency does one alert? What steps can one take on one's own?

Besides, there are no ghosts. There are only scientific explanations for alleged sightings. I reckoned the explanation would come along in due course, so I thought no more of the matter till late that night.

I had been putting together a party tape out of an antique miscellany—the overture to *The Boy Friend*, dated ballads by Bing Crosby, Julie Andrews, Diahann Carroll, and Danny Meehan, the Warner Brothers symphonies of Erich Korngold, a bit of *My Fair Lady* in Swedish, and so on, the whole tracked over with dialogue from old movies. I made such tapes for a living when I first came to New York, and though I had long retired from the field, I occasionally revved something up for an old friend, for the fun of it. When I began, this night, I was surrounded by company, because a thunderstorm had struck and dancing was out. Lionel was playing cribbage with Dennis Savage and (for narrative honesty demands a fair report) was wiping up the floor with him. Bert was getting his culture in, catching up on some old *Target* magazines someone had left behind. Little Kiwi was constructing a triceratops. Carlo was assisting Little Kiwi. Tom was sitting quietly in his usual daze.

Even a sixty-minute tape can take hours to complete, what with the split-second expertise needed to splice a conniption from Joan Crawford in her *Mildred Pierce* period into, if possible, Judy Garland's "Over the Rainbow," or to jump from Ella Fitzgerald's "No Strings" into Fred Astaire's in mid-chorus without cheating the beat. So, long before I was finished, the company had begun to scatter to their beds, and by the time I hit the finale—Bobby Short's "I'll See You Again"—only Carlo was left, idly rummaging through the *Target* books to see if he could find someone he hadn't had.

Time for a little talk.

"Carlo," I said, in the murmur of late-night Pines for the dishing of persons but inches away, "do you think Tom is straight?"

"He surely is. But he's nice, for a gringo."

"You don't find an interior contradiction in a Pines-loving, massage-giving, former porn-posing man who doesn't date women and doesn't know men?"

Carlo shrugged. "There's contradictions all over the place. Who's *not* a contradiction, when you look close enough?"

"You aren't. I'm not."

He grinned. "Ain't we got fun?"

"Did you ever run into Tom along the Circuit?"

"Sure. He's been around about as long as any of us."

"Well, did you ever try to set something up?"

He shook his head. "You look at a guy like that and you think, Hey, that's damn hot cake, now how about a slice? But wait a bit here. Never saw a man could talk to you for so long without knowing you're there. His quarter's twenty cents short, right? A smart guy would not want to take that on."

"He doesn't really seem dangerous, though, does he? I mean, he's strangely vacant, all right, but—"

"No, I catch that story. I truly do. See a tough guy like that who's kind of wounded and trying to be likable, and you think, I bet there's some real tender inside him, if only I could reach it. What a lover he'd make then, right? Is that the story? Some guys really go for that. So I'll tell you—don't go messing around looking for tender in Tom Adverse to strike that vein in there. Like what I told you before about the rough and smooth—you ain't going to hit gold. You'll bust a volcano."

In slow motion, whispering, he imitated an eruption; and went to bed.

Taping had energized me too much to consider sleeping. I took a walk along the beach, did some reading, and made myself a sandwich. I was halfway through it when Lionel came down. Besides dating idiots, he also mystifies his friends by wearing very questionable outfits. At the moment, he had on a white karate gi over an elaborate jockstrap of hempen webbing, the kind of thing you normally only encountered in the fashion layouts in *After Dark*. Lionel was also, at the moment, very shaken.

"What's wrong?" I asked.

He held out a hand: wait, let me collect my thoughts, choose my words. He kept pacing and looking upstairs.

"Lovers' tiff?" I asked.

"No, I . . . I don't know how to express this. You'll . . . will you promise to take me seriously?"

A thought struck me. "You saw a ghost, right?"

He stared at me.

"When Tom was the only one who saw it," I went on, "I dismissed it as Tom in a Mood. When Carlo joined in, I must admit, it was disquieting. But what the hell, what the hell. Now I *know* it's a joke! So call the pranksters downstairs and let's do a little giggling and pushing while—"

"Please don't humor me," he said. "This is not a joke and I'm not giggling. I saw something . . . phenomenological."

Now I stared at him.

"Surely not," I said.

He took another look upstairs, then sat on the couch. "I saw something," he insisted.

"Was it like a lot of little candles? Did it sound like—"

"It was silent. A sort of metaplasmic laser beam with shapes inside it . . . bumpy and . . . spinning . . ."

I know Lionel well enough to tell when he's joking around. He wasn't.

"You realize," I reminded him, "that ghosts do not exist. You realize that."

He nodded.

"I mean, there's no Santa Claus, no Shroud of Turin, and no ghosts. Right?"

He nodded.

"So—"

Bert came down the stairs so quickly he virtually leaped into Lionel's lap.

"Oooh," Bert gasped. "Like *tot-tal-ly* haunted!"

> *But, for the unquiet heart and brain*
> *A use in measured language lies;*
> *The sad mechanic exercise,*
> *Like dull narcotics numbing pain.*
>
> —*Alfred Tennyson,*
> In Memoriam, 1850

Lionel and Bert refused to go back upstairs that night, so I stayed with them, talking till all three of us fell asleep. The rest of the house was up early, and they found us strewn about the living room like dummies in the set of a war movie. So there was giggling and poking till Lionel spilled his story. Then Carlo chimed in with *his* sighting; and now the ghost became the house topic.

Dennis Savage, like me a fervent unbeliever, scoffed. But Little Kiwi immediately organized himself and Bauhaus into the Ghost Patrol and went around the house all day wearing a clove of garlic, a cross, and his Polaroid. He even made up business cards to hand out. "Remember our motto," he'd add:

> Ghost Patrol will come and so
> All the ghosts just have to go.

"You can start in my room," Lionel told him.

"Anyone who believes in this rubbish," Dennis

Savage announced from the kitchen, "gets no breakfast."

"Carlo," said Little Kiwi, "did you really see a ghost?"

"Well, I truly hell saw something."

The weather had cleared nicely, and from overhead came the noises of Tom Adverse, hammering and whistling as he patched the leaky roof.

"Rillly," observed Bert. "Why don't you get The Twisted Macho Man to like măybê for exam-mple scare it a–*way*?"

"Tom?" I said. "He's sort of a ghost himself."

"Oooh, *bark* me into the ca-*loset*."

"Don't worry," said Little Kiwi, adjusting his garlic. "The Ghost Patrol will exterminate this house. Remember our motto——"

"If you don't stop that," Dennis Savage began; but Little Kiwi put a finger on Dennis Savage's lips and made him blush.

"I play him," Little Kiwi told us, "like a stereo."

After breakfast, while Lionel considered completing the weekend in some quieter establishment and Dennis Savage accused him of giving way to bad dreams and California brain meltdown ("Oooh, gag me," said Bert), I went outside to check up on Tom.

"How're we doing?" I called up to Tom, happily ensconced on high amid the symbols of his calling, the affable eructations of the toolbox.

"Almost done here. I'm taking it easy awhile."

"How'd you get up there without a ladder?"

"Climbed up," he said, holding out a hand to me.

If he can, I can, I told myself, pushing off the front-deck railing to join him.

"It's great up here," he told me. "You can see clear to five counties." He laughed. Another thing about Tom is that while he has a sense of humor, it's invariably the wrong one. I think he tells those atrocious racist jokes not because he believes they're funny but because he wants to see how you'll react to his having made you listen to them. Denounce his morals and he'll go Uh-huh. But if you sell out a little and forgive him with a doubting smile as you shake your head, he'll put a hand on your shoulder or chest very lightly, one of those almost meaninglessly nuanced demonstrations straights make with each other.

I think they're all starved for fun.

"Just let me finish up here," Tom said, taking a swallow of the beer he chugs while he's working, "and you'll be dry for life."

"You know, the rest of the house has been seeing what you saw. The ghost. It's . . . uncanny. I've known people who believed in ghosts, but I never knew anyone who claimed to have seen one."

"Uh-huh."

"Tom?"

"Yeah?" Smearing the tar, casing out a shingle, lining it up.

"What do you think we should do about this? I mean, some of us apparently aren't comfortable sharing quarters with . . . Well, if it were mice we could trap them. But what do we do with a visitation?"

He nods. Nails in his mouth. Hammer. One side, other side, step by step. Start a thing. Finish it.

"Tom?"

He lays in the last shingle, dumps the can of nails into the toolbox, toys with the hammer.

"I know who it is," he tells me. Why not? He doesn't care what I think. "Visiting at night here? I used to know him."

"Hey!" Little Kiwi called up to us from the poison ivy and tundra that holds the Island together between foundations. "Have you seen any ghouls around here? Bauhaus and I are the Ghost Patrol."

"Hey, Little," Tom called down. The notion of a fully grown (if boyish) man named Little Kiwi was more than he could accept. At first, Tom called Little Kiwi nothing, then compromised on the first half of his name, solo. No one, including Little Kiwi, seemed to notice. "Hey, come on up here with us."

"There's no stairs."

"Chunk up on the fence there and we'll pull you along."

"Hey, this is great," Little Kiwi ventured after Tom had helped him up. "The Ghost Patrol can really do a lookout up here."

"You can see clear to five counties," said Tom.

Little Kiwi laughed.

"Who wants a slug?" Tom asked. His term for beer.

So we all sat on the roof and slugged beer.

"Tom," said Little Kiwi, "did you see the ghost?"

"Yeah."

"Can I take your picture?"

"No, I don't want my picture taken anymore."

"Why not?"

"I guess I took too many when I was young. I'm all pictured up by now."

"I want to get a photo of the ghost. What does it look like?"

Tom went into his secret hell, but he stayed with the theme. "He's a very sad guy. Very nice guy and very sad. Good-looking. It was hard to know what to do with him because his feelings always got hurt very easily."

"Whose feelings?" Little Kiwi asked.

Yes, whose? Tom could have been describing himself.

"His name was Champ McQuest, and this was something like 1972. Maybe 1973. Champ McQuest."

Little Kiwi, not following the computation, looked at me.

"He's recalling an old friend," I said.

"He was so sad," said Tom, "that no one could cheer him up. I gave him a massage for free once, to make him happy." Tom shook his head. "Not even that."

"Then what happened?" asked Little Kiwi.

"He died out on drugs. That stuff's so mean. He just got out of control with it."

"That happened a lot then," I put in.

Tom nodded. "Everything was an experiment. Because you didn't know what the end was. But it was the nicest guys who got wrecked the worst. You remember that, Little. The *tough* guys are still standing when the dust clears."

"I'm afraid to be tough."

"Champ had a lot of friends. Everybody loved

◆ 73 ◆

him. But no one could figure out what was hurting him. Now he's trying to tell us something. A message from the past."

"What?" I said. "You think that's—"

"I know it." He looked at us, one after the other. "I knew him close and I know he's what's been coming around at nights here."

"Why would he tell *us* anything?" I reasoned. "He's trying to get to you, isn't he? Maybe there's something the two of you didn't finish . . . Jesus, look at me talking as if there really were a—"

"What are you three hayseeds doing up there?" Dennis Savage called. "Half the house is in a state of panic, I don't know where our next dinner is coming from, and you're on the roof guzzling beer. And Little Kiwi, I told you to lose that garbage around your neck."

"Come up and make me," said Little Kiwi, aiming and snapping his camera.

"Little's getting tough," said Tom.

"I'll make you but plenty when you come down! And stop taking those pictures!"

"In one minute," said Little Kiwi, "this candid photograph will be developed, and then I'll send it to the Curiosity Section of the *New York Times*."

"The world's nuts," said Dennis Savage, stomping off. "But come dinnertime, let no one complain to me because there's nothing to eat."

"There have to be ghosts," Little Kiwi mused, "or there couldn't be Ghost Patrol."

"What is Champ McQuest trying to say to you, Tom?" I asked.

Tom was quiet for a bit. Then: "He was a very sad guy."

> *They're out there whether you like it or not.*
>
> —*A crank on a local television news show, Philadelphia, 1977*

Wise old queens know everything, and it was to a wise old queen that I took The Problem late that afternoon. Not that I fancied asking him how one exorcises a ghost. But this man had been all over the scene for a good thirty years; he was *old* gay, older than clones and discos and politics. He was not a Circuit rider, but a considerable fortune put him at the very helm of the New York section of Stonewall while protecting his crony ties with the Big Boys at City Hall. He gave some of the greatest parties ever given, yet—and this is considered questionable—he was never to be glimpsed in the center of his dos, prancing and quipping, but far to the edge, talking to a friend or silent and watching. Some men know everyone; this man would have thought them parvenus. This man knew everyone he felt like knowing. There was a good chance that he had known Champ McQuest.

He is not a showy man. He prances and quips in private, for his personal pleasure. His Pines house is far to the east, on the ocean along the most chic strip of the choice quartier: but this is no palazzo. He doesn't even have a pool—he uses the Atlantic Ocean. He lives simply, easily, securely. When he throws a party he goes for it; when he lives he just lives.

He was one of my first clients in my party-tape era, eventually my best one, because his tape commissions turned into a sly challenge match. Not realizing how varied, extensive, and bizarre my record collection is, he kept asking for more and yet more recondite compounds. "Intimate, Brahmsian, a lot 'cello," he'd say, or "Honky-tonk, Sophie Tucker and ragtime—make it all sound like a battered upright piano with a broken middle C." I never failed him, and finally he asked me not only to tape a soiree but attend it, perhaps hoping that I'd at least insult the dress code or fake the politesse. I did neither, and we became friends. I relate all this to underline how necessary it is to understand your associates, for only then can you be sure what you can ask of them, and what they can give you.

Of course he had known Champ McQuest.

"One of many such," he said. "Those chillingly handsome young men who fell into the city in droves in those first years after the Riot. The gates were pulled down," he recalled, with a somewhat regretful smile. "The citadel was opened up. Champ was not the handsomest or the youngest, but he may well have been the nicest."

We were sitting on his back deck, looking at the ocean. This far east, there were few sunbathers; even the beach parade, a routine of Pines afternoons, tended to give out and turn back several houses to the west of us. Two boys were wrestling in the sand. A jogger robustly pumped along the water's edge. A straight couple laden with grocery bags trudged toward Water Island.

"Young men, young men, young men," he sighed. "Some of them place themselves well, others put on stomachs and tend bar to East Siders slumming in Chelsea, and a few fall into very wrong hands. Handsome young men. I've wondered what life might have been like if I'd been born when they were. Born, I mean, into this demotic everything-is-possible Stonewall thing, where you go to a gym and grow a mustache for love instead of paying for it. I never mind paying. That's what money is for. But if I had been *younger* . . ." He slurred out the word with a trace of wonder, as if the concept could scarcely be imagined, much less debated. "If I had been young when everyone else was young . . . and if I had not been rich and powerful." He hugged himself, shrugging playfully. "Well. Would *I* have gone to the weight rooms and worn jeans and frequented orgies just on the basis of who I was or pretended to be? Would I have delicious companionship *just because I showed up*? I love to ask. But I don't quite see it. All that effort, all that . . . *handsome* running around. It's so much easier to buy love than hunt for it. And then . . . even if you find it . . . don't you have to *deserve* it? You have to be as worthy as your partner, don't you? You have to be a *handsome young man*! Much, much more fun to buy your love, wouldn't you?"

"But can you buy love?" I asked. "Or just sex?"

"Writers are so naïve. You can buy anything, in fact. You can buy murder, don't doubt me. Don't. Don't."

The two boys on the beach, spent by their wrestling, lay side by side in the sun. One put his hand on the other's head.

"Anyway," he went on, "you can't necessarily have your love for free, either, so where are you then? Champ, now, dear Champ was certainly one of the elect. Yet he was always falling for men who didn't respond. *He* had no love. And my. *My*, how it rent him. The *passion* of a boy in love with a boy! The incredible *dis*regard for the *stand*ard *caut*ions!"

"Why did he die?"

"He was too sweet to live. He was too sensitive to survive. He fell prey to overwhelming despairs. Choose one. Freshen your drink?"

The two boys on the beach ran into the ocean and started wrestling again.

"You mustn't get into a state about Champ McQuest," the wise old queen warned me. "There were so many such. So many handsome young men who never even made it to bartender. And Champ was *born* to doom. Who knew *anyone at all* as glum as he? Did you? Tom Jones in the Dostoyevski edition, that was Champ McQuest."

"What did he die of, though?"

"Oh, he was one of the overdoses, technically. There was quite a lot of that at the time. Many of them simply lay there and gave out the soul, but some actually *did themselves in.* One went out a window shouting the name of the model agency that had dropped him for galloping debauchery. Alas, he had defied the cautions."

"And Champ?"

"Hm . . . can one recall a specific event, some *triggering* thing? He had such a greed for agonies, poor boy. It happened in your house, didn't it?"

I was speechless.

"Aren't you in the house they call Chinatown? Way over on The Other Side by the cruising park? It used to have a myriad of Oriental gewgaws hanging from the eaves over the deck. Wind chimes and fairy bells and a whole orchestra of gongs. If the breeze was right you could hear 'Limehouse Blues.' But you stalwart sprouts of Stonewall have taken all that down, haven't you? All the . . . decoration. You want to be your own decorations."

"Champ McQuest died in our house? Jesus, I knew there had been a suicide, but I—"

"Oh, I shouldn't call that a suicide. I shouldn't. Such a *deliberate* word, don't you? There comes a time in certain lives when one is too miserable to live, so one simply dies. *How* one dies is of rather small moment. Champ was very mixed up, and very unhappy, and very drugged. So it all came together on him one night, and the next day he was no longer with us. You know, I think . . . I just *think* I have something you should see. Sip your wine and gaze upon the sempiternal sea while I make sure it's out here."

He went into the house. While he was gone, the two boys came out of the ocean arm in arm, grabbed their towels, and dried each other off. They stood for a while, looking at each other.

"Well, we're in luck," said the wise old queen, returning with a small black rectangular box. "I must say, I *thought* I'd taken it out here."

I would have said something, but my attention was held by the two boys from the beach, who were coming up the walkway onto the wise old queen's deck.

"Russ and Billy," said the wise old queen.

They called to him, waved at me, and went into the house.

◆ 79 ◆

"Believe it or not, I don't do anything with them. I just like to watch them together. Why? Who can tell us why? Maybe even money is not enough. Maybe the reason some homos stay straight is out of *fear* of the *dream*. They fear to be . . . all homoed up into starving wraiths who get nothing. Take your wine along, I've this to show you now."

The box held videotape.

"Russ and Billy will be napping, luckily. I wouldn't want them to see this. It's strong material. What we used to call 'private films.' Of course, everything's transferred to video now. What pleasing novelty to see dear old friends back among us from the past. But don't expect state-of-the-art . . ."

Waves of static gave way to what looked like a piece of cardboard bearing the ballpointed legend, "Sailor Dick and Pants-Down Johnny."

"A certain half-baked Seventh Avenue *tycoon* who must remain nameless or I might vomit used to hire boys to make these . . . what to call them, my dear? Noose operas? Where it looks as if one boy is getting hung by another?"

"Hanged," I told him. "Not hung."

"Is there a difference?"

"Porn stars are hung. People are hanged."

"Ah, there's Champ. How tired he looks. I wouldn't appear in a piece this tawdry to save my life. Of course, they're totally fake and harmless, and the money was terribly good. Still . . ."

Champ was pretty much what I had expected, a solemnly nice-looking chap who seemed very uncomfortable to be where he was, in a spotlit corner of a dark room, sitting in a chair. The raspy voice of an unseen man directed him in a stripping scene, item by item. "Leave your socks on," the voice ordered. "Now let's see a little action."

"That's our friend from Seventh Avenue," said the wise old queen. "He liked to *superintend* his shows through a microphone, right into the sound track. Everyone else was making silents. Not he. Lavish productions, spare no expense."

"Don't rush it, baby," the voice grated out. "Take your time and you'll get your dough."

"Rather Brechtian, wouldn't you?" said the wise old queen. "All these directorial impositions *during* the show?"

Champ stopped masturbating and said something toward the camera. He seemed hostile, but he wasn't miked, and I missed it.

"Silly name, isn't it, Champ McQuest? It was originally something extraordinarily simple. David Jones? Donald Jones? There was so much of that then. So many David Joneses coming to the city to turn into Pants-Down Johnny."

"Or Sailor Dick."

"No, the sailor is an unusual item. He looks like a pro to me."

That he was, as I soon saw: sturdy, self-possessed, edgily efficient, and incongruously mustached in his navy whites. He hulked into view through a doorway and stood there, a pose in the shadows. The brutal voice told Champ to undress the sailor, step by step as before, and go down on him. They obeyed the command in the awkward simulation of hot that bedeviled early porn; and the technical setup was so poor that most of the action spilled out of the light into darkness. It was hard to see, much less believe.

"Paramount is eating its heart out," said the wise old queen.

"Fix the lights," the voice muttered to someone, and the beam slowly and effortfully reached out to the two actors. As the light hit him, the sailor gazed up, straight into the camera, and it struck me that he looked just like . . .

"Sweet Jesus!"

"A friend of yours?"

"It's Tom Adverse."

"Ah."

"You must know him—the Cherry Grove Carpenter."

"I've never been to the Grove," said the wise old queen, airily. "Is it nice?"

"Okay," said the voice. "Take him over now. Real slow. Slower. Keep him calm."

The camera swung over to another spotlight, this one trained on a length of rope dangling from the ceiling and noosed at the end. Tom brought Champ over to it, and the two of them waited, apparently for instructions. But we heard nothing.

"A penny for his thoughts, wouldn't you?" said the wise old queen.

"Okay." The voice had returned. "Now loosen up his neck muscles so he'll respond to the rope when he drops. Easy does it. Got to soothe him up for this."

Whoever he was, the man running this show suddenly symbolized everything I loathed in that early era of Stonewall, all the selfish money and back-alley egomania that still helps keep our world disjointed, all a-spin upon itself. "God, what a voice," I said.

"Yes, he should have sung opera."

"Loosen him up, come on. Think about how nice it'll be to do him now. He's almost ready. Turn him around to show us. Yeah. Stand over to the right a little so . . . yeah, so we can see what you got. Beautiful, baby. Nobody does it like you." A beat, then: "Look at them, huh?"

Champ said something to the voice, again off-mike. He spoke to Tom, too, and Tom looked inquiringly at the voice. It told them, "No play, no pay, baby. That's what it is."

Champ and Tom had a few more words, but the voice cut in with, "Noose that boy up and hang him," and Tom threw his left arm around Champ's middle and reached for the rope with his right.

"Jesus."

"They're standing on the floor, you know," said the wise old queen. "Nothing can happen."

"I know, but . . . I think Champ has a crush on Tom."

"*Had* a crush."

To myself I said, Don't be too sure.

Champ was fighting like a tiger, but Tom easily overmatched him. Within a moment he had looped the rope over his head and zipped it up. In the shadows let me come and sing to you.

"Lovely," said the voice.

"It's so beautiful when they struggle," came a second voice.

"Poor Champ," said the wise old queen.

Tom was holding Champ from behind, holding him tight and talking into his ear. Champ was shaking, but after a bit he suddenly grew quiet. I could hear the voices breathing. What was Tom telling Champ—"Work with me till we finish this gig and we'll get our money and split"? Would they go out to celebrate? Was this as far as Tom ever went, stylized snuff duets?

Champ broke free of Tom's grip, but Tom reached for him and Champ turned and impulsively threw his arms around him.

Surprised, Tom thrust Champ away with an odd look on his face. Champ tugged at the rope. Tom stopped him and with a single movement pulled the noose open and slipped it off.

Champ turned away from Tom.

Tom looked at the camera.

"Tasty boys," said the voice, and the screen immediately went dead.

"Isn't it savory," said the wise old queen, "that Russ and Billy will never know about such things?"

> *One must not forgive. One must understand.*
>
> —*Cosima Liszt von Bülow, 1870*

When I got back to the house, it was nearly dark. Dennis Savage and Lionel were in the kitchen, arguing over whether or not to put garlic in the salad. Bert was napping on the couch.

Little Kiwi, on the stairway, beckoned me upstairs in elaborate pantomime. He and Carlo joined me in my room.

Door closed, Little Kiwi said, "We have a plan. We're going to lay for the ghost tonight. Carlo is part of the Ghost Patrol, and you can be, too."

"Look . . ."

"We're going to lay for the ghost."

Carlo grinned at my questioning glance. "He learned a new expression."

"Carlo taught me. Don't you want to help us trap the ghost? We're all going to stay up, and when it comes out, I'm going to take its picture. Ghosts die when you photograph them, you know."

"Why don't we just wait out the weekend," I suggested, "and let it vanish the way it came?"

"We're going to lay for it."

I looked in on Tom. He was lying faceup on his bed staring at the ceiling.

"You okay, Tom?"

"Uh-huh."

"Want to talk?"

"Thought I'd get some sack time in. I'm kind of beat."

"Okay."

As I turned to go, he said, "You could tell those guys they shouldn't fool around with it. It's more serious than that."

I waited.

"I haven't been out here in a long time," he said. "I didn't want to come particularly."

Tom, I saw you and Champ McQuest in a private film.

"It's just that nothing's going on in New York now. No work for me. Thought I'd take a vacation here. It doesn't seem the same, though. I feel cold."

He pulled the spare blanket over himself.

"Everyone's been nice to me. I really appreciate it."

What happened after the film was over? What did you say to each other? Everybody loved him but you, right? Or did you love him gringo-style, without touching? Come ye out, Pants-Down Johnnies, in Tom Adverse's Club Stonewall, where you can have anything you want. Except Tom Adverse.

"A while along, it's almost like you don't have as many friends as you once did."

"Hey!" said Little Kiwi, leading in Carlo and Bauhaus. "This is the night, so everyone should get ready."

"You be nice and tough, Little."

Of course, you can't be both nice *and* tough, but, typically oblivious, Little Kiwi sat on the bed, patting Tom's chest and heartening him for the work ahead.

"Uh-huh," said Tom.

Carlo glanced at me, everything in his eyes: poor busted guy.

"I suppose you heard we're going to lay for the ghost. Behind a barricade!"

Tom put his hand on Little Kiwi's shoulder. "It's more serious than that."

> *One cannot understand. One must simply forgive.*
>
> —*The Cocktail Dandy, 1988*

It was another of those nights, boys and girls—no rain, now, but everyone sticking close to home as I fiddled with my tapes and the others sported about. We sat in on a television movie, held a game of Risk (everyone played except Tom), and still no one headed upstairs.

Apparently we were staying up to see the ghost.

It got so late that Dennis Savage and I had to rustle up an antipasto plate to keep everyone fit and happy. "Like, *tot-tal* salämi," said Bert, tucking in. Then we heard Bauhaus whining upstairs and Little Kiwi gave Carlo an Extremely Meaningful Glance and slithered away.

"I should know better than to ask this," said Dennis Savage, "but what's Bauhaus doing in the bedroom?"

"The kid himself leashed him up there," Carlo explained, "as part of his Ghost Patrol."

"Oh, for heaven's sake!"

Tom went outside, I assumed for a cigarette. House rules banned smoking indoors.

"I think this joke is getting out of control," said Dennis Savage.

"It's no joke," Lionel told him.

"Like, it was rillly a *hor-ror* show!" Bert agreed.

"It was marsh gas," said Dennis Savage.

"In a second-floor hallway?" Lionel challenged.

Beeping like the old RKO radio tower, Little Kiwi, upstairs, yelped out, "Ghost Patrol calling Carlo Smith. Come in, Carlo Smith."

Carlo grinned. "Got to go," he said, getting up. "Duty's calling."

Yes, I'd guessed right. Tom was standing on the deck looking at the ocean, the white gnat of a lit cigarette the only motion in the picture. A pose in the shadows.

"This jive about ghosts," Dennis Savage warned us, "is offensive to Stonewall pride. Are we not men?"

"Sometimes it can be very difficult to believe in anything," I said. "Some people can scarcely deal with the most ordinary things in life, no? Until we are all direct and articulate with each other . . . until we can face each other fairly, how can we possibly approach the metaphysical?"

Dennis Savage stared at me. Lionel mimed the tugging of a sage's grey beard. Bert said, "Oooh, *school*."

"I mean," I went on, "how can we even discuss the existence of supernatural phenomena when some of us can't even believe in . . . Where'd Tom go?"

The porch was empty.

"Believe in what?" Lionel asked.

A crash overhead.

"Little Kiwi," Dennis Savage called out. "Would you come down here, please?"

◆ 88 ◆

"In a minute!"

"*Love.*"

"What's going on up there?" Dennis Savage cried.

"Ghost Patrol! Remember our motto—"

"It's the most commonplace thing, all about us. It's the very essence of our revolution. Yet some of us can't . . . see it."

"The two of you goons get down here pronto and stop wrecking the house!"

Upstairs, Little Kiwi complained to Carlo, "He never lets me have any fun," and there was another crash, followed by a thud.

"I'm going up there," said Dennis Savage, rising.

"You'll be sorry," Lionel told him.

The lights went out upstairs. Dennis Savage paused. In the silence, we heard Little Kiwi giggling.

"I'm telling you," Lionel insisted, "there's something in this house."

"Oh, please," said Dennis Savage, and up he went.

I excused myself and went outside, following the cigarette light to Tom, brooding down near the water. He nodded at me, but said nothing. After a while, I asked him, "What makes you think it's Champ McQuest?"

Nothing.

"Talk to me, Tom."

"It was fine of you to ask me out here, I know that. I want to be nice when people do a friendly thing. But I think I better go back to the big city tomorrow, get me off your hands."

"Come on to the house. You'll feel better inside the party."

"If you get the chance to be nice to someone, you should take it. That's a lesson I learned."

"Didn't you say one has to be tough?"

"There are people to be tough with and some to be nice with. That's the lesson that I mean."

"Come on back, Tom."

"Yeah. Okay."

He threw the cigarette into the water.

"God fucking damn it to hell," he said as we walked back. "Jesus shitfaced baboon sucking *damn* it all fuck!"

Nothing specific. A mood piece.

Then Tom halted. "I don't want to go back there," he told me. "You know somewhere else I can stay?"

"What's the matter?"

He turned back to the ocean. "I've been making so many mistakes that I just can't rectify. No *way*. You know that feeling?"

"Who doesn't?"

He was turning from the ocean to the house and back, a man without a place. Suddenly he stopped moving. "Why'd the house go dark?" he asked.

I looked back. All the lights were out.

"I think they're trying to lure the ghost out."

"Man, they shouldn't be doing that."

"Listen, Tom, what exactly did you see when . . . what did the ghost look like?"

He thought about it. From the look of him, I expected no more than an uh-huh, but then he told me, "It looks like a movie."

Just at that moment the house lit up to shouts, screams, and the barking of Bauhaus, and Tom and I ran up onto the deck and inside. Everyone was on the second floor, amid a barricade of chairs. Little Kiwi was studying one of his Polaroid three-by-threes. Carlo was flat on his back on the rug. Dennis Savage, his face as white as Mr. Softee, staggered over and grabbed me by the arms.

"I *saw* it!" he cried. "I saw a *ghost!*"

"It came through so fiercely it knocked Carlo over," Lionel reported.

"Like, shove me down the sli-yed!"

"Oh, no!" Little Kiwi wailed. "There's no picture in my photograph!"

He held up his Polaroid print: empty black.

"Maybe the flashcube didn't—"

"Ghosts probably don't—"

"Everyöne was like môving so—"

"Where is it now?" I asked.

"It went out the window," said Lionel. "Just . . . zoom."

Tom was not, as I had assumed, behind me. "Tom?" I called.

The reply was a fabulous series of crashes from the porch.

"My dinosaurs!" Little Kiwi shouted.

I raced downstairs and outside. The whole porch was a wreck. Tom was on his knees, in a stupor, slowly picking up the pieces of Little Kiwi's model collection.

"Tom?"

He shook his head.

"Are you okay?"

He laid some plastic parts on the deck table and looked at me.

"It's all right," said Tom. "He said it's all right."

I felt the others piling out behind me.

"Tom," said Little Kiwi, "you didn't knock down my dinosaurs, did you?"

"He said it wasn't me. He won't be back again. He wanted to make sure I . . . he talked to me . . ."

Tom knelt again and picked up the iguanodon.

"It's all right now. He talked to me."

Carlo righted a fallen deck chair; next door, two men had come out on their balcony to investigate.

"He talked to me."

Tom began to weep: this big, beautiful, kind man with a broken middle C.

"He said . . . he said . . ."

"What, Tom?"

"He said, 'Remember me.'"

It was not a message from the past, then, but for the future.

Tom held out his arms, showing us the wrecked patio. "I'm sorry," he said, the tears running down his cheeks. "I did this to you."

"You didn't do this," said Carlo, coming up to Tom. He put his arms around him, and this time Tom accepted the embrace.

("Does this mean there really are ghosts?" Dennis Savage murmured in my ear.

"*I* didn't see one," I whispered.)

"It's all right," said Tom, very gently breaking away from Carlo. "Okay?"

He put the iguanodon on the table.

"Okay, now? Is it okay?"

Yes, Tom. It is okay.

The Boffer

I CHERISHED MY TOYS. I shielded them, hoarded them. I kept my toys neat and slick and whole and true, and by the time I finished college and came to New York, my toys were still alive and perfect, in closets in my parents' house or on shelves in their garage. My toys. And when I took my present apartment at Fifty-third and Third, I brought some of them along—the Meccano construction set my dad lugged home from France in 1955; Plasticville: The City in a Box; my Sneaky Pete Complete Home Magician Outfit; and about a ton of Lego.

The Lego I eventually passed on to my little cousin Scott, and it gave him such a kick that I added Plasticville. The day I came over with it, I showed him how to set it up, snapping the building walls into right angles, aligning the fences, dotting the crisp lanes with mailboxes, benches, and lampposts. A serene American village then lay before us, with a church, a K mart, a barn, a school, and

93

houses. An informal civics class. See? They get the kids when they're too young to know any better; they recruit them, make them straight for life in a village with a church and a K mart.

At least it didn't work with me. The Meccano set still rests under my bed on Fifty-third Street, but the Sneaky Pete Complete Home Magician Outfit I had to give to Little Kiwi, to distract him from his obsession with *A Chorus Line*.

Dennis Savage blamed me for this, of course. I had taken Little Kiwi to the theatre for his birthday one Wednesday afternoon, and he was so entranced with the show that he went out the next day and came back with a *Chorus Line* cast album, coffee mug, and T-shirt. The record he played day and night, the mug he not only used for everything from water to ice cream but carried around with him like a shaman's fetish, and the T-shirt he wore incessantly till Dennis Savage wrested it off him and scrubbed it in the sink. (At that, Little Kiwi couldn't wait till it had dried and put it on half wet.) This is not even to mention the *Chorus Line* ·scenes and numbers he insistently favored us with. At the nine thousandth haunting repetition of "Kiss today goodbye," Dennis Savage groaned and told me, "You started this. Do something."

I started this because I sometimes think it the truest act of friendship to introduce someone to something instructive or delightful that might—who knows?—change his life. Still, I did something. I gave Little Kiwi my Sneaky Pete Complete Home Magician Outfit: and *A Chorus Line* dissolved before our eyes. In a trice—in a bath towel, actually, which he wore as a cape—Little Kiwi reinvented himself as La Dolce Pita the Magnificent, complete with his assistant, Ferdinand (the inevitable Bauhaus, Little Kiwi's dowdy dog, half German shepherd, half weasel, and half kraken; and I know that's three halves, but you don't know Bauhaus). Visiting Dennis Savage became recreationally hazardous. Without even waiting for a lull in the conversation, La Dolce Pita the Magnificent would run through the Sneaky Pete program, beefed up by card tricks with a deck he found in a joke shop, all this to the tune of Johann Strauss's "Roses From the South" on the stereo. Those who have taken these journeys with me in the past will not need to be told that La Dolce Pita was somewhat less than magnificent in his command of the magician's arts.

"The Disappearing Coin!" Little Kiwi announced one evening, flourishing the oval yellow tray with the secret compartment. I was a whiz at this in my youth: one deposits a coin in the tray, covers it, deftly pulls a lever that whisks the coin slot to the side and a second slot, empty, in its place, and presto! the coin has seemed to vanish. Reverse the action, and the coin reappears.

"If some gentleman in the audience would provide a sovereign," La Dolce Pita requested, with an opulent wave of his hand. "Never you mind," he went on, in the administrative croon of the hopelessly tenth-rate performer, "for though the coin will truly disappear, La Dolce Pita the Magnificent will restore it with a murmur of the magic code."

There was a lot doing at Dennis Savage's that late autumn day, for he had received another round-robin letter from his Hamilton alumni group. The men whom Dennis Savage had been close to in his college days had doggedly stayed in touch all these years, though all but he had married and most were raising kids and many had moved to distant quarters of the map. The wives took turns garnering everyone's news by phone and then sent out a kind of homemade newspaper to all the gang every six months or so, with news stories, burlesque gossip columns, photos, and even editorials on the state of the nation from a post-yuppie platform.

I found all this rather touching, even if it tested one's patience to have to attend to Dennis Savage's moony nostalgia for the days when he was embosomed in the tersely supportive confraternity of the collegiate male. He would cite names that had no meaning to me beyond the haze of data generally attached to the whole four years—the road trips with Henry Christian, Budge Lewis, and Pete Hedstrom; the two-man volleyball with Jojo Baker; the bull sessions with Cal Colson and Warren Acker—and mainly, the sheer ground-zero miracle of knowing, trading confidences with, and having a violently secret crush on Chad Jeffers, Dennis Savage's best friend. Now, this name stood out. This name had meaning. One had only to breathe these three blessed syllables to provoke from Dennis Savage a litany of such plangent, mesmerized eyewash that he'd come off like a Cherry Grove queen returning from a day in The Pines to throw himself across his bed with a terminal case of Houseboy Attitude Breakdown.

Ah, these scars of our college days, the mark they

leave on the gay soul! The beauty! The purity! One never quite recovers. For of course the world after college is unbeautiful, impure. I myself regarded college as an idiotic detour on my way to here, but I could share Dennis Savage's enthusiasm. It was always a big event when one of these alumni newsletters arrived, and Dennis Savage and I were far more involved in digesting the latest one than in taking in La Dolce Pita's performance.

"Just a simple coin, such as may be found in any fine gentleman's pocket."

"It says here," I noted, "that Warren and Janey Acker just had their sixth child."

"Three boys and three girls," Dennis Savage rejoined. "One gender after the other."

"So neat, so sure, so Hamilton."

"Any coin will do, but a quarter works best."

"Did you see about Pete Hedstrom living in San Francisco? Is that a message, do you suppose?"

"Never," said Dennis Savage. "That's his hometown."

"Everything is magic, if you only know. The coin is there, the coin is gone, the coin is there."

"Is Budge Lewis's real name Budge? Or is it short for one of those fancy WASP surname-first names like—"

"Roses From the South" suddenly cut off and we looked across the room to find Little Kiwi at the stereo, holding up the playing arm and glaring at us.

"Look, can I please have a quarter?" he cried.

Bauhaus growled.

Digging into his pocket, Dennis Savage muttered,

"What do I get for a quarter?" and Little Kiwi went on with his act as Dennis Savage handed me a letter.

"Wait till you see this," he said.

"You view the coin. I cover it. Now the magic code word . . . *Robitussin*." As I read the letter, Little Kiwi fiddled with the lever. "And presto!"

"Bravo!" said Dennis Savage, and I clapped mechanically, the two of us too intent on the letter, handwritten by Mary Beth (Mrs. Henry) Christian, to look up.

"Oh, *no!*" Little Kiwi wailed. "It still doesn't work." The coin had not disappeared. Better yet, Little Kiwi promptly dropped the tray, and about two dollars' worth of nickels and dimes fell out. "So *that's* where they went!" he said. "They don't make these tricks right."

"Jesus Christ," I said, "an alumni reunion!"

Dennis Savage nodded. "The Colsons just moved to New York. It's a housewarming party, obviously, but apparently everyone's going to be there."

"Everyone?"

"That's what Mary Beth says."

"Including Chad Jeffers?"

"Now La Dolce Pita the Magnificent, assisted by Ferdinand, will present the notorious card stunt known to an elite few as The Bashful Deuce. Notice the colorful way I shuffle the deck to assure complete honesty."

The cards flew all over the room.

There was silence for a bit, then I said, "*Including* Chad Jeffers?" and Little Kiwi said, "Oh, gee," and Dennis Savage said, "You know, I haven't seen him in over fifteen years."

"Seen who?" asked Little Kiwi, picking up the cards.

"Maybe it's a cute idea to have an eighteenth anniversary reunion party instead of a twentieth," Dennis Savage went on. "Maybe they should have done something like this long before. Maybe every so often I think of the way things were back then and all. And I miss that life. No maybe about it. I traded it all for the Eagle and the Saint and the Pines and the meat rack and the Everard and the backroom bars and a few other things I haven't dared mention to you—"

"If you mean that orgy in Burke Fuller's loft when a Colt model took a bath in motor oil and you licked him dry, Lionel told me all about it."

"—and I've never been sorry," he continued, closing his eyes briefly in a kind of visual scream but holding to his rhythm. "I've never been sorry for that trade. They were straight and I wasn't, and the wisest thing I ever did was to admit that and get on with my real life instead of trying to live like them."

"So?"

"So why should I go to their party? The lone bachelor amid the marrieds and the dates. I'd feel like a fool. I'd look like a . . ."

"A queer?" I asked.

Little Kiwi was looking at us from the floor, attending, taking in this new thing.

"Don't you want to see them again?" I said.

"Oh, yes. You don't know how much. I suppose in a way I've been hoping that something like this would come up. But now that it has, I'm afraid of it. Aren't I?" He shifted position on the couch. In the avid stillness of the listening room this seemed almost violent, and Bauhaus growled. "That's how it feels, anyway. Like fear."

"Fear of what?"

"I have no idea. But it's there." He shrugged. "It would be great to go, though, wouldn't it? And yes, I imagine Chad Jeffers will be there. Boston's not that far away, and he was always a real gung ho about alumni stuff. If he goes to every homecoming, he'll certainly come to this. Clapping the guys on the back. Dredging up the old sagas. All that. Oh, he'll be there. He's so good at this kind of thing."

There was that look again, and that mooing tone, and Dennis Savage was going into his nostalgia trance.

"And then someone will tell one of those dumb old jokes again, and Chad will smile and his eyes will crinkle up."

"What is crinkle?" asked Little Kiwi.

"Oh . . . it's this odd face he gets sometimes when he's really happy. It was the most devastating thing, and I'll bet you he isn't aware of it even now. It happens when he smiles. His eyes narrow and the edges get squishy, as if they had been made by a cookie cutter. It's very boyish, and he's such a . . . a manly guy that the combination of . . . well, you just . . ."

"Quietly dream of him for eighteen years?" I said.

He slowly shook his head. "These crushes we get on our straight friends have to be laid aside when we come into Stonewall. It's like having tantrums when you're eight or pimples when you're fifteen. You outgrow it."

Like my toys.

"This all sounds very sensible," I said. "If you ask me, you have a very adult take on this and there's no reason why you shouldn't go to the party."

"Little Kiwi," said Dennis Savage, "what are you doing?"

Little Kiwi was staring at us, grinning and squinting at the same time. It made him look like a jack-o'-lantern.

"I'm trying to crinkle like Chad Jeffers."

"It's not something you can put on," I told him. "Your features have to do it naturally."

"In the world of magic," he told me, "everything is possible. There is always a trick you can do."

"Actually, he had a lot of boyish qualities," Dennis Savage went on. "He'd look like a Cub Scout if you taught him something. He used to come to my room to listen to *Tosca*, and he'd get so serious and happy about it, you know, when I'd explain what was happening on stage. He really liked that. He liked to learn. I think that was the bond between us, in fact."

"That boring old Leinsdorf recording of *Tosca* was your bond? Maybe if you'd played Callas for him you could have gotten him into bed."

"I didn't want to get him into bed. One didn't think of those things then. This was an enchanted time, the vale of innocence. We weren't trying to plunder each other, don't you see that? We were all in love, but it wasn't erotic love. It was some sort of ideal love, very trusting and delicate."

I glanced at Little Kiwi and he said, "Get her."

"Oh, for heaven's sake," said Dennis Savage.

"Can't you imagine anything but cruising and dancing? Is that all there is?"

"I'm just trying to imagine you teaching somebody."

"I *am* a teacher, as you well know, you festive pigpen! What do you think I do all day while you're out boulevarding around the town?"

"Oh, yes."

"Don't 'Oh, yes' me, you tank-town swell!"

"So are you going to this reunion shindig or not?"

"You just *bet* I'm going!"

"Can we come, too?" asked Little Kiwi.

Startled in the midst of his offended reverie, Dennis Savage surveyed us: me in jeans and a spaghetti-stained T-shirt, Little Kiwi in his bath-towel cape; and let us not omit quaint Bauhaus, just then dancing around the room on his behind to ease an itch.

"Well," said Dennis Savage, "that . . . would be complicated."

"A Stonewall loyalist would take his buddies," I observed.

"And I want to see the eyes of Chad Jeffers," Little Kiwi put in, "when they crinkle. I might be able to use that in my magic act."

"Yes, well . . . we have to consider whether we would all be comfortable in the admittedly narrow environment of a—"

"You're ashamed of us," I said.

"It's very difficult to be a stranger at a party like this. It's hard to break in."

"Not if you're connected," I told him. "Introduce us around, set us up right, and presto—"

"The magic is made!" said Little Kiwi. "Everything is magic."

"Everything is friendship," I corrected.

"Everything is straights," Dennis Savage reminded me, "at a party like this one. Do you really want to try to reenter that world, you, even for a night? Really?"

"I do," said Little Kiwi. "I'll knock them over with my tricks."

Dennis Savage winced, but he pressed on, certain that reason would discourage us. "It's a closed society," he explained. "I see it as a memory open only to those who were there originally. With all those code words and legends and nicknames, you know."

"Nicknames, huh? What's yours?"

"The Boffer."

Jolted, I said nothing. Little Kiwi asked, "What does that mean?"

"You can't go to this party," Dennis Savage almost pleaded. "I'm afraid to go myself. I just don't think I can handle—"

"The Boffer," I said. "Well, now, The Boffer."

"Just to be there again is trouble enough, surely, but—"

"It's an honorable name," I said.

"What does it mean," Little Kiwi asked, "if you're The Boffer?"

"It means he goes on road trips," I said, "and he calls the Mount Holyoke girls 'Hokes' and gives pointers to the freshmen. It means he teaches Chad Jeffers how to boff a sweet young thing, and how to know about boffing, and how to be a boffer. It's sacred brotherhood stuff. It's the boffing science on the theme of the virgin Hoke. It's fucking."

Little Kiwi's mouth was open, and Dennis Savage said to me, "And you still want to go to this party?"

"More than ever. And I know why you don't want us there—may I? You're afraid Chad Jeffers will figure out that you're . . . light in your loafers . . . is that the expression he'd—"

"Blackmail," Dennis Savage said, his tone pure outraged innocence but his eyes cloudy with ambivalence. "This is blackmail."

"Everyone will be there with his wife, right? His true partner. Does it not behoove a Stonewaller to bring *his* partners? His lover and best friend? That's what we have for families and that's what you should bring."

"You should bring your magician," Little Kiwi put in, "to regale the guests with the Chamber of Disguise where I put objects into this little house and they vanish."

"I remember that one," I said. "There's a mirror inside that conceals the back half of the chamber. You put objects in *behind* it and they seem to disappear."

"You shouldn't tell about the tricks," said Little Kiwi. "As one magician to another."

"Oh, hell," said Dennis Savage.

"If you *talk* about the secrets too much," Little Kiwi observed, "they lose their secret qualities."

"Hell, of *course* you can come."

"You can know too much about magic, you know."

"I doubt I could get through it without you. You *have* to come. I was just playing around."

I question that.

"I just don't think you'll enjoy it, that's all. It's such a . . . a reversion into old business."

"Oh, I'll enjoy it, my dear old Boffer," I told him. "Old business is true business. Hidden objects must be retrieved from the Chamber of Disguise."

"And I, La Dolce Pita the Magnificent, must demonstrate the truth of magic, assisted by Ferdinand."

"The dog," said Dennis Savage, with penetrating finality, "stays home."

And Bauhaus growled.

This was not a simple matter of getting dressed, grabbing a cab, and showing up. Phone calls and letters passed among the Hamilton folk, as the party took shape and Mr. and Mrs. Cal Colson confirmed the date and old grads from Portland to Atlanta made their travel plans. Here was a Heavy Party. To top it off, Dennis Savage and I took Little Kiwi to Lord and Taylor for a new sports jacket on the afternoon of the do. Little Kiwi crinkled at the salesman while trying it on, and the salesman pretended not to notice; but he and two colleagues were buzzing like bees in a petunia patch as we left.

"What do you think they were thinking about us?" asked Dennis Savage after we got out of the store. "Those salesmen."

"They thought we were some sort of gay ménage," I answered. "What do you think people take us for, palling around like this?"

He said nothing.

"What do you think people will take us for," I

gently added, "at the Hamilton party? A law firm? An archaeological dig?"

"They'll know what we are," he said, firming up his jawline. "They will know and they should know."

"And what will they say? After we leave, of course, like those salesmen."

"After we leave? Who cares what happens after we leave?"

At home, we separated in the elevator, but I went up to his place for dinner. He seemed remarkably calm, considering how close he was to bumping up against his dearest legends. How many of us, boys and girls, get to greet our own history? Now, it is true that half the party—the wives—would be strangers. But the other half—the Hamilton alumni—would be men who had known Dennis Savage intimately when he was dwelling behind the mirror, when he couldn't be seen. Now they would see him. He must have had highly mixed feelings about all this, but he wasn't showing us a thing: just a man in an apartment, a decent hand at dinner, a sharp dresser, a good friend, wise enough to know that no one, whatever his genetic advantages and luck, gets all that he wants out of life, and that we all pay a price for that which we do get. He knows this and I know this, and we can live with it. And that might very well explain why we get on so well.

"Why do I just have jackets?" Little Kiwi complained, coming into the living room ready to go. "Why can't I ever have a suit?"

"You look so nice like this," said Dennis Savage, straightening Little Kiwi's tie. "What do you need a suit for?"

"For when I go on the stage, as La Dolce Pita the Magnificent."

Bauhaus barked.

"Plus Ferdinand."

"That's a little rich for the contemporary marquee," I observed. "Why don't you take a trimmer stage name? Something like . . . The Boffer?"

Dennis Savage knifed me with a look.

"I guess we'll be hearing a lot of that tonight, won't we?" I continued. "There we are, making our entrance—and all those wild and crazy Hamiltonians will rush up and cry, 'Say, it's The Boffer!' and 'Hey, Boffer!' and 'How're they hanging, Boffer?'"

Little Kiwi giggled. "The Boffer," he said.

"Then comes the moment of moments. All is still. The crowd piously parts. And across the crowded room on this enchanted evening, you will see a . . . no, not a stranger, but a comrade, a vision, a ghost of your sweet youth of bracingly platonic rhapsody: Chad Jeffers, younger than springtime. He wafts toward you . . ."

"Crinkling," said Little Kiwi.

"Crinkling all the way, yes. Then he leans over and murmurs into your ear, 'Hey, there, my . . . *Boffer*.'"

Dennis Savage smiled. He would not be needled this night. "He never called me The Boffer. He called me something else."

"What?"

He shrugged.

"Shall I guess? Groucho, perhaps? So fitting."

"Daddy-o?" asked Little Kiwi.

"Attila the Nun? It's chic and it's true."

"Everybody hush," said Dennis Savage, "and let's go."

"I guess we'll hear it soon enough, anyway," I said.

"Doubtful," he said, getting his coat. "It was a private nickname. He only used it when we were alone."

"Listening to Erich Leinsdorf murder *Tosca*."

Riding down in the elevator, Little Kiwi said, "When I go on the stage, I'm going to wear a three-piece suit."

"Why do you always have some bizarre project going on?" Dennis Savage asked. "Don't you like your life?"

"How would *you* like to be your houseboy?"

"It's a responsible position," Dennis Savage reasoned, his voice quiet, his mind elsewhere. "The free time . . ."

"It's woman's work! I should have a real job."

Finally hearing Little Kiwi, and realizing what upheaval this complaint portended, Dennis Savage looked alarmed and turned to me—but this is a story for later. I put on my innocent face and whistled a happy tune as the elevator door opened, and we headed out for the party.

First of all, the Colsons had a terrific apartment, one of those room-after-room things on West Ninety-second Street; and the rooms were *big*. I know three people whose combined apartments would fit inside the Colsons' powder room. No doormen, true. But the expanse of sheer place that confronted us as we entered the apartment was as daunting as welcoming, at least to those of us who dwell in the dollhouse accommodations of the post-war high rise.

We scarcely had time to take this in before The Receiving Line was giving greeting. The Line was all women, and we weren't inside for more than three seconds before Little Kiwi had his trick deck out and was asking the girls to pick a card.

("I frisked him before we left, I swear," Dennis Savage whispered to me.

"He probably had it planted in his overcoat.")

"I'm Mary Beth Christian," an attractive, slim yet motherly woman was telling Little Kiwi.

"Linda Baker," said another, more amply curved, somewhat severe of mien, just as attractive.

"Terry Finn," said a third, a delightful post-tomboy deb with a halo of blond curls.

Little Kiwi was shaking hands with them. "I'm Virgil Brown," he said. "But basically I'm known as The Little Boffer."

Their smiles froze, but they took it in stride, as bourgeois maidens are taught to do, especially when Receiving. Then Dennis Savage and I grabbed their attention and thus we moved into the party, Little Kiwi trying one last "Pick a card" as I hustled him forward.

"Just keep moving, Little Boffer," I told him.

We were in the center of a very fully done room—icy glass tables to the left of us, truculent couches to the right of us, and all about us vases of a very precise shade of antique green. This always means trouble. Naturally we had arrived somewhat late, as if prancing into a dance hall last and most awaited, *grandioso, chic deluxe,* and the rooms were spilling with Hamiltonians, strollers and couples and groups and whole coteries. And, pretty much as I had pictured it, a gang of males rushed upon Dennis Savage crying out, "It's The Boffer!"

He shuddered with a glad, stinging thrill as they surrounded him, shaking and clasping and pushing him in that way they have, that old-boy style. He nodded and reached for them, as if he were going home again even as he knew one cannot. They were crashing all over the place at the dead center of the party, he and his old boys, and their wives were coming up, drawn by the hoopla. Dennis Savage was encircled, and terrified, and content.

Or did I read it wrong? He was swimming smoothly in this sea of bright shadows—and I was watching carefully to see how much they liked him: they were wild. Little Kiwi was taking it in quizzically. This was a side of Dennis Savage he had never seen, opened to his gaze not by action but by reflection, in the excitement of the men roaring and pawing at him, in their attempt to share with him a relapse into the boisterous, bracing freedom of their youth.

Dennis Savage was calming them, and laughing, and nodding; they were strident, insistent. Then someone came up to him out of nowhere and said, "Hey," so softly that I had to read his lips. But Dennis Savage heard him, and turned, and there was Chad Jeffers.

Yes, he was terribly handsome, and shockingly young looking, one of those do-or-die, take-no-prisoners preppies who somehow never lose that sense of having been rejected for the role of Prince because they are too nice, too real.

"There he is," I told Little Kiwi.

Rather, I told the place where Little Kiwi had been. He had slipped away. Trying to keep an eye on Dennis Savage, I surveyed the room—ah, there he is, shuffling cards and effervescing at Linda Baker, who severely took a card, gave it back to him, and when he had reshuffled the deck and produced a card, severely shook her head. Wrong card. Well, all that's harmless enough. Dennis Savage was shaking Chad Jeffers's hand in a grip of death, and that can be harmful: because the grip must yield after the time passes and the boys separate to find themselves as men. You can keep your toys under your bed, perhaps, but you can't shake hands again, not with your enemy.

You may wonder at my choice of word. Well, you'll see what I mean presently.

You can imagine that I watched Dennis Savage's reunion with Chad Jeffers as a camera turns. I wanted to measure this data securely. But there was little to see. They were at ease with each other, focused on their conversation but, very clearly, free of those overtones of injured affections that long-lost friends sometimes give off when they speak. I imagined them tracking down old capers and catching up on recent curriculum vitae. I tried murmuring unlikely dialogue to the rhythm of their talk: "'Remember the night we gave Doofus McWasp an apple-pie bed?' 'Hey, and the time we road-tripped those two

Smithies all the way to Canada and *really* ran out of gas? What a high!'"

Little Kiwi joined them. I continued to improvise as Dennis Savage introduced him: "'This is my hot little fuck buddy, bet you wished you had one, right, Chad?'"

As Chad shook hands with Little Kiwi: "'Can I borrow him, Boffer? It's perfectly safe, in the Hamilton way. I use three condoms, one on top another, each made of sheep entrails and individually packed in your choice of spermicidal creams, jams, jellies, pastes, and . . .'"

A dark-haired woman had pulled up next to me to listen. She was smiling. "You're not from Hamilton, are you?" she said, as a merry wife of Windsor might tell Khomeini, "You're not an old Etonian."

"Hi, there," I replied, feeling a blush make a jerk of me.

"Nor I," she said. "Susan Drinker, outsider."

"Bud Mordden, best friend," I replied as we shook hands.

"I married into this pep rally. What's your excuse? Something unseemly, I hope."

"Some people think so."

"That's my husband," she told me, pointing at a former stalwart lad now settling into the flabby grandee phase of the respectably accoutered straight. Family, career, and a house in one of the more ruthless suburbs of Boston. "Jensen Drinker," Susan went on, "president for life of the singing group known to glory as the Six Hamiltones." Jensen was speaking in a very confidential way to a small bevy of alumni. He was holding a pitch pipe and what looked like a college yearbook, and they had all changed into blue blazers. "I believe they are popularly known as the *Sex* Hamiltones. We can only guess why."

Did she just wink at me?

"Let's really get down," she sighed, sinking into a couch, indicating the place next to her with a toss of her head. "One thing you have to say for the University of Pennsylvania. *Their* alumni don't drag innocent wives away from their children, especially on the littlest one's birthday. Oh, she sounded very brave about it on the phone this afternoon, but she'll be weeping at dinner and her two brothers will bully her and make it worse."

"Did you go to Penn?"

"Class of '75."

"Egad," I said. "Class of '69." I held out my hand again, and as she took it, she said, "Buster, you just made the team. What do you say we kibosh the Hamiltones's act with a fast chorus of . . . What *is* the Penn song?"

" 'Drink a Highball at Nightfall.' "

"Sounds really barfy. Teach it to me."

Three lines into it, the two of us giggling like freshmen cutting an orientation tour, Little Kiwi came up with his magical deck of cards and launched one of his tricks at Susan Drinker.

"Now *this*," she averred, "is really cute. This makes the party. Did he go to Penn, too?"

"I went to the Lake-of-the-Woods region on a fishing trip," said Little Kiwi, carefully shuffling his cards. "But I didn't like the food. I told my pop I wasn't going to fit in, but he made me go, anyway." Somewhat tentatively, he pulled out a card to show Susan Drinker. "Was this your original card?"

"Yes," she said, sporting that smile again. It said, People are interesting because sooner or later everyone's bizarre.

"I *knew* I could do it!" Little Kiwi exulted. Then he looked at the card. "No, that wasn't it."

Susan shrugged, still smiling.

"Why can't I do it right?"

"He's sort of a Peter Pan figure," she told me. "He should fit right in at this party, because this is a night for all the little boys who never grew up. Why *are* you all here?"

"We're friends of that fellow there," I said, pointing out Dennis Savage. "The one talking to—"

"Golden Boy. I can't remember the names of all these historical personages, but I know what each of them represents. To Jensen, anyway." She laughed. "What do they look like to you?"

I grunted.

"Ask Peter Pan to sit with us and we'll sing him a chorus of the good old Penn song." We made room, and Little Kiwi sat between us. "My ten-year-old is going to look like him in about ten years, and he's going to break hearts like a highwayman. And he plays beautiful piano. Men never realize what that does to a woman."

"Why don't you tell *me* that?" Little Kiwi asked her. "I can talk, too, you know."

She quietly sang to him:

> Drink a highball at nightfall,
> Be good fellows while you may;
> For tomorrow may bring sorrow . . .

"That's silly, isn't it?" she said. "This notion that everything after college is a letdown. It's just silly. I didn't like college. All that homework. The catty sororities and the frat boys using you to prove themselves. I couldn't wait to be married. I live in a house with people I love, instead of a rathole of a dormitory. My chores mean something to me—to me, not some professor. Everything I put into my life comes back a hundredfold. Little things and big things. I remember the day my daughter first walked by herself as vividly as I see you two now. Her brothers witnessed the whole bit; and they were so excited."

"Do you make grilled cheese and tomato sandwiches?" asked Little Kiwi.

"'For tomorrow may bring sorrow,'" she repeated. "How does the next line go?"

I told her: "'So tonight, let's all be gay.'"

"Brace yourselves," said Dennis Savage, looming over us. "The Six Hamiltones are going to sing."

We scarcely had time to connect Dennis Savage and Susan Drinker and get him ensconced on the couch with us before Jensen Drinker was calling for silence and attention. As the party wafted back into chairs and against the walls, he welcomed us, joked at us, and marshaled our reserves of sentimental recollection. He held up an old yearbook so we could look back at the Six Hamiltones in their and our youth, so we could split the difference between then and now and feel . . . perhaps not younger, but less adult, less wise, less finished. A buzz ran through the room as old hands murmured, "The *Sex* Hamiltones" to each other. We laughed, relaxed.

Throwing off your bad, mean wisdoms is a hard trick; but the trick was taking.

As the blazer men slid into their first selection, "Hello, Young Lovers," I tried not to harp on the thought that, had they been gay, they could hardly have brought the original sextet back for an encore twenty years later. Some of them would be dead.

Dennis Savage was thinking no such thoughts. He was misted in a dream. Susan Drinker was smiling her smile and watching her husband lead the music. Little Kiwi whispered, "This is nice."

Three songs then followed, to warm, even thrilled applause, all favorites from the Hamiltones' old repertory. However, for their final number, they offered a contemporary song in a new arrangement especially for us, here, tonight. So memory renews itself. Maybe. And at the first strains of "Kiss today good-bye," Little Kiwi was up and moving, and by the line "The gift was ours to borrow," he was standing right up there with the Hamiltones, his tenorino lightly tracing the melody as confidently as if he had always lived in the castle, as if there were no enemy.

"Well, now," Susan Drinker whispered to me, "this is one for the yearbooks."

The Hamiltones took it so calmly it might have been part of the staging. The man behind Little Kiwi even put one hand on this young stranger's shoulder, as if to portray the serenity, the sweet clarity of the moment when everyone is happy and well liked.

And Dennis Savage, jolted from his dream, looked upon this picture like Cortés upon his peak in Darien. Like Diogenes finding an honest man. Like a lover seeing love.

But Chad Jeffers was staring at Dennis Savage like someone who just figured something out and dearly wishes he hadn't.

After the singing, the party restruck its cymbals. Everyone rose and refilled his glass and started grouping up again, but I stayed on the couch talking to Susan Drinker till Jensen called her over for something or other. As she left, she made an "I wish he wouldn't" suburban grimace at me. It made her look like a six-year-old fresh from a mud pie session. Then Chad Jeffers pulled up so quickly that I was staring at him before I realized who he was.

And he was talking.

Sitting next to me on the couch. You know: any chum of my chum is My Chum.

Oh, he raved on about the Hamiltones, and asked me what I did, and told me how much he missed the Old Days. He mentioned the playings of *Tosca* in Dennis Savage's room. Pausing now and again to look comely, confidential, sternly bemused, he leaped from topic to topic as a hunter crosses a woodland rapids stone by stone. He always counted Dennis Savage as one of his best friends, even through all the years of separation, because Dennis Savage is *so* smart. Really such a . . . such a *smart* guy. And knowing smart people is the best thing for you, isn't it? The best way to live. The best friends to have.

"Friendship," he said "amplifies our opinions."

Another pause. We approach a difficult stone, slippery, distant, perilous.

Of course, we all have opinions of each other, he

was telling me. Everyone is very judgmental in our society. Some of us are merry; some are earnest. But all of Know What We Know, don't we?

Who's talking here? you ask. Who's judging? Who's on the couch with a very dazzling Golden Boy, his head swimming with the novelty of place, the excitement of encounters, and, very possibly, the vertigo of the brimming cup?

Who was crinkling? Not Chad Jeffers. Golden Boy is concerned about something. Golden Boy is going to tell me what it is. But Golden Boy doesn't know quite how to manage it. Golden Boy's head must be swimming, too. Two men at this party are very wet just now. But watch the cautious passage atop the stones: from *Tosca* to opinions and smarts, back to *Tosca*, thence to opera to I like opera, don't you? and Oh, you do? because I have this wonderful friend, single, pretty, who'd love to meet you, would you like me to give you her number or no, I could give her yours how about?

And the hunter has made it to the far bank of the rapids.

Now, years ago, when various relatives would do this to me, I had an answer all ready: "Anyone you'd have access to, I'm not interested in." The rudeness deters them from ever doing this again, and also bounces their boring straight fascism back in their surprised asshole faces. Okay, that's very satisfying—and how can it be wrong if it feels so good? Besides, if I were straight, it still would have been true. Eventually, however, I began to feel I was letting my side down by not dealing with the question directly. The issue was not (only) They are trying to manipulate me. The issue was I am gay. So I developed a new answer, and I revived it in conversation with Chad Jeffers.

Let's do this again: *Tosca*, amplifies, pretty friend, can I phone number . . . and I said:

"No, but does she have a brother?"

I believe that's what Chad Jeffers was waiting to hear. His eyes lidded over—the opposite of crinkling, no doubt—and his head hung heavy, and he gasped. I'm wrong, aren't I?, to play Show Them How It Feels with Dennis Savage's special friend at Dennis Savage's alumni reunion. But hypocrisy shatters the soul.

"Anything else you'd like to ask?" I said. "Because I need another drink."

I was already rising, but Chad Jeffers got up with me, his hand on my arm.

"I'm sorry if I . . . intruded," he said. "The . . . young man . . . with the card deck. He came with you tonight. Is he your . . . Is he?"

"Friend. My friend."

"Yes." Chad Jeffers nodded. "Quite a fine fellow. He was up there singing with the—"

"Sex Hamiltones."

Chad Jeffers laughed. "He also . . . the young man . . . knows Dennis Savage. I mean . . . doesn't he?"

Over Chad Jeffers's shoulder I saw Dennis Savage watching us. I believe he had been doing so for some time. He looked somewhere between thoughtful and worried.

"What are you asking me?" I said. "What are you trying to hear?"

"The truth," he said, all wide-shouldered and up-jawed. "I want to hear the truth."

"Mister," I replied, "you caught me on just the right drink."

"No," said Dennis Savage.

"You snuck up on us," I reproached him.

"The truth, that's all," said Chad Jeffers softly.

"This is my scene," said Dennis Savage.

Now Chad Jeffers took Dennis Savage's arm.

"It's my fault," said Chad Jeffers.

"You're both blitzed," said Dennis Savage.

"I am *not* blitzed!" I told him.

"What does 'blitzed' mean?" asked Chad Jeffers.

"Drunk."

He thought it over. "Nor am *I* blitzed!" He shook off Dennis Savage's touching hand. "You're gay, aren't you? That young fellow is your . . . your confidant."

"Look—"

"He *is* blitzed," I said.

"I am *not* . . . I simply require some information."

"Tell him nothing!" I muttered.

"Will the two of you please sit down? You're spinning on your pins."

"No, the room is spinning," said Chad Jeffers. He sat down.

"I'm not sitting next to him," I said.

Dennis Savage pushed me down on the couch next to Chad Jeffers.

"Starting tomorrow," I added.

"I'm sorry if I pried," said Chad Jeffers. "I just think friends should trust each other."

"Friends," I offered, "should respect each other's privacy."

"Look who's talking," said Dennis Savage.

Little Kiwi was suddenly looming over me with those cards. "This time," he said, "I've really got it. Okay. First you—"

Dennis Savage closed up Little Kiwi's outfanned deck, brushed the hair back from his forehead, and said, "Would you please go get our coats?"

"Not yet!" said Little Kiwi.

"Yes, yet. And you," Dennis Savage told me, "should be ashamed of yourself."

"Not yet."

"What did he do?" asked Susan Drinker, who must have come up with Little Kiwi.

I tried to stand, but Dennis Savage pushed me down again. Maybe I fell.

"A controlled substance," said Susan. "Tang in the punch."

"Everyone's gay," said Chad Jeffers.

After a moment Susan said, "Well, you'd better make an appointment with Nurse Renfrew, so Doctor can see you and cure your ills."

"I don't have ills," said Chad Jeffers.

"Oh, Nurse Renfrew!" Susan and Dennis Savage called out at the same time.

Nobody laughed.

I guess I was blitzed. Chad Jeffers was even more so. I looked at my watch—we had been at the party over six hours. All that drinking on an empty stomach, fatal every time. Pushing forty and I still can't hold my juice. Don't tell my father.

"'For tomorrow,'" Susan told Little Kiwi when he brought our overcoats, "'may bring sorrow.'"

"Not at our house," he told her, distributing the coats. "I saved these really radical chocolates from the dish that turns around." He put a hand in his pocket and pulled one out. "Oh, they got a little—"

"I just bought that jacket!" said Dennis Savage. "It isn't even paid for yet!"

"He buys clothes for his friend," said Chad Jeffers. "A sports car. A co-op." He looked up at Dennis Savage. "Is that right or not?"

I said, "Everyone's blitzed on this couch."

"What do you want?" Dennis Savage asked Chad Jeffers. "Tell me and I'll give it to you. Because what you want I swear I don't know. I swear it here. Speak. I listen. I'm still your friend. So what is this about? What have you been looking at? Did something catch your eye or were you out hunting? Just tell me. Because I don't know what this is about. And I'd love to. The two of you stumbling around here, like potty old Latin professors battling over the possibility of a sixth declension. And the term is not 'confidant,' it's 'lover.' This man is my lover."

"They didn't really melt yet," said Little Kiwi. "They just started to squish together a little, so—"

"Come on, confidant, help Uncle Bud to his feet."

"Well, it's been terribly *entre nous*," said Susan as we shook hands. "We'll do this again."

Chad Jeffers hung back, still on the couch, staring at us a trifle glassily.

Little Kiwi smooched her hand like a Parisian bon vivant.

"Lord," she said.

She gave me another wink of her bright, sharp eye, and we were off and away and, in due course, home. Little Kiwi went on up to see to the copiously invalid Bauhaus, while Dennis Savage insisted on

accompanying me to my apartment: because otherwise I would pass out in the hall.

This was a bald libel. On the contrary, I was just
getting my second wind. I put on the Gieseking recording of Debussy's *Children's Corner Suite, mol-
tissimo pianissimo*, and steeled myself to talking it
out. Anyway, I had a feeling he had more on his
mind than keeping me from disgracing us in the
hall.

"It was a good party," I began. "Wasn't it?"

"The best of its kind, I'd say."

"Though I was getting awfully tired of all those
blue eyes. Chad Jeffers figured it out, didn't he?"

"He was bound to. The men who liked you the
most when you were innocent have the most to lose
when you grow smart."

"Don't be wise so late at night," I told him.

"I thought I was afraid of what he would think of
me when he found out. When I first heard of this
reunion, that's . . . what I feared. His opinion of me.
Just as I was afraid of their opinion way back when I
pretended I was one of them. When I did what they
did."

He crossed over to the stereo, carefully picked up
the playing arm, and switched off the turntable. No
Gieseking. Something important to say.

"As soon as I walked in," he said, "I realized that
their opinion couldn't possibly matter anymore. Oh,
I . . . yes . . . I liked hearing them go through the
old routines. That Boffer stuff. I always liked that.
Sure I did. And the Hamiltones, too. And those absurd old songs that used to matter so much to me,
God knows why. But in the end this is nothing.

There's no *here* in it. I'm not like them," he said, looking right at me. "I never could be, whatever I thought once. And if I'd gone on trying to be like them, I would have wrecked myself." Right at me, still, this, because he knows that I understand him and that this aperçu matters greatly to the likes of us. "Those straights can go back to that time because that *was* their time. That . . . that Arcadia of self-righteous adolescence. Gays can't go back. Everything in gay moves forward, do you realize that? It's getting out of school so you can reach the city and find your people. Working for political rights, looking for love, hoping for a cure." He touched wood: my desk. "Am I right?"

I nodded. "'And point me toward tomorrow.'"

"Tomorrow—when I was to have had dinner with Chad Jeffers," said Dennis Savage. He sighed. "Well. Something tells me that has been indefinitely canceled. By gentlemen's agreement."

"What would that have been like?, I wonder."

"It would have been an awkward fit, trying to keep his bourgeois order in kilter with my subversive surmises."

"So you admit you want to take over the world."

"I admit I'm trying to claim my place in it." He got his coat. "It *was* a good party, you know. It just wasn't the right party for us."

"The Boffer passes judgment."

"Can you make it into bed by yourself, you back-bench tosspot, or am I going to find you sprawled on the floor in the morning?"

"Just for that, I hope Chad Jeffers shows up to claim his dinner tomorrow."

It was I who showed up for dinner, because Dennis Savage is not only a reliable cook but a generous one, even to drop-ins from the sixth floor in their stay-at-home rags. His apartment was in its full swell of life when I arrived: Little Kiwi, in his bath-towel cape, was running through his magic act to the strains of "Roses From the South"; Bauhaus, his snout caught in the paper packaging material from the *Chorus Line* CD, was scrounging around near the bathroom; and the master was in the kitchen, happily preparing his celebrated (not to say infamous; to which he would snap back, "Then why do you have to *say* it?") Stuffed Chicken with Wild Rice and Mushrooms.

"I hope I don't look as bad as I feel," I told him, parking myself in the kitchen doorway.

He gave me a quick once-over and grinned. "You'll live."

"You always look most content when you're making food, do you know that? Maybe you should have been a chef instead of a schoolteacher."

"I'll admit that I really blew it on career choice," he mused, stirring the mushrooms. "But I believe I did everything else right."

"Well, you certainly know how to run an apartment. This one comes complete with dinner and a show."

"Was that the buzzer?"

"Sometimes, when I'm sitting in my hobbit cave downstairs, surrounded by books and records and gloating in the stillness, I wonder why I never have to give a guest refreshment or keep him entertained."

"Everyone's afraid of your apartment," he said. "People have been killed there."

Little Kiwi joined us, bearing the Mysterious Talking Dice. "Watch this, now."

"Little Kiwi," said Dennis Savage, "did I just hear the buzzer?"

"Yep. Now, watch closely, as La Dolce Pita confers with the Mysterious—"

"Well, who was it?"

"Chad Jeffers. He's coming up."

The doorbell rang.

"Oh, *shit*," Dennis Savage observed in a kind of murmured shout. "Look at this place! Look at . . . everyone. This is like a . . ."

"A homosexual be-in," I said.

"What do we do?" asked Little Kiwi, missing the implications but enjoying the excitement.

Dennis Savage took the mushrooms off the fire, wiped his hands, strode through the living room, and opened the door.

It was Chad Jeffers, all right, a blatant contrast to the scene in his neat suit and splendid chesterfield. He and Dennis Savage stood in the doorway for a long moment.

"Can I come in?" Chad Jeffers said.

"Sure," said Little Kiwi, coming up. "You're just in time for the Mysterious Talking Dice."

Chad Jeffers stepped in and took in the room, its things and people and Bauhaus, still poking about in his *Chorus Line* logo muzzle.

I shut the stereo off.

Chad Jeffers turned to Dennis Savage. "I guess I'm supposed to say that this isn't going to be easy, or something like that. But it's going to be very easy. I should have done this a long time ago."

Dennis Savage was still holding the door open, his body rigid but his face a blank.

Chad Jeffers nodded at the door. "Maybe you'd better close that," he said. Dennis Savage looked at him as if thinking it over, shut the door, and slowly turned back to Chad Jeffers.

"You get used to certain things," said Chad Jeffers. "You expect a way of living from other people and from yourself. It feels right. So when other people don't agree with you, you think they're wrong. You just do. If they're strangers, they're just stupid or crazy. But if they're people you're close to, you resent them. It's complicated. I feel it better than I understand it. My brother Brian—you met him that time you spent Thanksgiving at my folks'. My older brother. I guess . . . you remember him. Because . . . anyway, we were very close when we were growing up. Those old-fashioned kid things like camping trips and . . . we did all that together. And he . . . well, he told me a lot of things. When I got into trouble at school, you know, or how to get around, like, with the girls, making those right moves. See, we had that. We sort of grew apart after college. Living in different parts of the world, and other things. Things that have nothing to do with . . . with like the fact that he's gay. But the gay part is . . . hard. You must *really* hate hearing that, I know."

His voice was grinding a bit, as if he was trying to

show us how rough it feels—not only to hear it but to have to say it.

"But it's the truth. It's not what people expect, and when you give them this instead, it's very hard to take. You try to like work around it, see if you can keep all the rest of it together. You say, Okay, the gay stuff can be a secret. And I know that some of you . . . I mean, some of your people . . . they play it that way, don't they? But Brian is a very football-player kind of guy. He doesn't believe in secrets. That's the way he is, and, I'll tell you, I've always looked up to that. I knew that whatever shit anybody was handing out, anywhere—our father, or at school, *anywhere* . . . I could always count on Brian to clear it up for me.

"So of course he had to clear this gay thing up for me, too. That's Brian, see? He insisted that we talk about it, and that . . . that is the hard part. He said I ought to understand it, and look, I don't *want* to understand it. Why can't I just accept it? Brian says that with just anybody on the street I can accept it, but with my brother I have to understand it."

He looked around at all of us.

"Well, let me tell you, it made a lot of trouble between us, and it got mixed up with everything else there can be in your family, all those feelings that you want to accept without understanding them. I always get afraid that if I understand one thing, I'm going to get mixed up in all of it. That's why I say it's complicated. No one wants to confront all that . . . feeling in there. Nobody else has to, why should you? Like which kid got the better deal. It's not good to go into that, not good for anyone. My whole family knows that I was the favorite child—"

"Me, too," said Little Kiwi.

"—but that doesn't mean that Brian and I should sit down with our parents and talk it over, does it? It's not what people expect. It's just not what they expect. And Brian's always pounding at me about his lifestyle, which is none of my business. And other people do it, too—suddenly this . . . this event is happening to the rest of us. I can accept it, I know I can. And you're probably saying, Big deal, who cares what he can accept? I'm just telling you this, so you'll know. You'll know that one thing drags in another. All hard things. Because . . . because like how come the guy who took me on fishing trips and showed me how to smooth it out on dates and stand up to authority assholes and . . . yes, and play opera records for me and coach me for my chemistry exams which if I couldn't pass them I was going to get the ax from college . . . How come those guys can get so . . . different from me? I don't know what side I'm supposed to be on anymore. I told you saying this is easy. I've wanted to say it for years. But the feelings behind it are hard. It's not what I want, to have to know so much. And that's why I said . . ." Pausing, he gave a little shrug. ". . . Well, whatever it was I said last night. I apologize to all of you. I just didn't expect to have to relate to all those feelings at that party. I just wanted to go back to . . . to . . . before everything got complicated."

There he halted, staring at Dennis Savage for the longest freeze-frame I've ever seen.

Then he said, "Can we shake hands?"

And they did, and Chad Jeffers shook hands with us, too, and Little Kiwi liked it so much he shook hands twice, and it turned out that Chad Jeffers had come to dinner after all, so that's what happened. We had a fine time. Little Kiwi enlivened dessert by putting on his complete magic show, and a few of the tricks almost worked. Chad Jeffers hoped to encourage the budding performer by asking for revelatory explanations, but La Dolce Pita only smiled—for, as he himself has said, if you talk about the secrets, they lose their secret qualities.

I believe this was the true reunion party, most literally a reunion, a rejoining of splintered interests. And I believe that Dennis Savage and Chad Jeffers felt their bond more keenly this night than ever they had in their rash, free youth at college, because they knew better now what their bond was made of. You can grow up and move on and forget almost everyone you knew, but the truest friends are those who teach us something that matters greatly, even something with hard feelings in it: and those friends stay essential to us for life, not only part of our past but of our future as well. Our teachers are always with us.

So I was not surprised to detect a trace of moisture in Dennis Savage's eyes when Chad Jeffers got on his overcoat and said good-bye. He gave Dennis Savage a whack on the shoulder and told him to take good care, and when he was halfway through the door he stopped and turned back and nodded.

Then he crinkled and said, "So long, Denny."

Away he went: and Dennis Savage's college days were over.

"Is that the name?" asked Little Kiwi once the door closed. "That only Chad Jeffers called you?"

"Did you really help him with his chemistry?" I put in. "You who don't even know how much lime to cut into a Perrier?"

Dennis Savage sighed heavily. "He's out the door but two seconds and the fun begins. This is where you mock my most intimate and beautiful memories, isn't it? Humiliate my quaint paeans to boyhood. Expose secrets that I never entirely understood in the first place. Loot my pathetic treasury of recollections. Right? Am I right? Fine. Go right ahead. Won't you please be my guest?"

"Oh," I said. "Not this time, Denny."

I Read My Nephew Stories

OKAY, WHAT AM I DOING on a beach in Massachusetts?

Simple: my brother Ned ran away from home when he was fifteen.

I bet you didn't know I had a brother who ran away from home—also an aunt who committed suicide, a great-uncle who went to prison, and a cousin who dropped out and moved to India. I'm still trying to get the rights to our saga back from the O'Neill estate.

Anyway, Ned not only ran away from home but never came back, which had my younger brothers and me agog, but which my other older brother Jim called A Very Outstanding Event. Jim and Ned stayed in contact, and I would receive periodic, laconic reports. Now Ned was doing bits at Cinecittà, now he was a reporter for the Paris *Herald Tribune*. Presenting the news was Ned's forte, it seemed, for he stayed with it. He even did it on television.

Better, he came home to do it on American television. Better . . . *Huh.* It seemed unnaturally forgiving, like Samuel Beckett coming home to Dublin, licking his lips at the sight of the Martello Tower, and crying out, "Champion!" Jim and I met Ned for lunch one day at Clarke's; Ned was up for a transfer from New Orleans to New York. So many distances, voyages, in some people's lives. You notice this particularly if, like me, you stay in one place for entire epochs, enthusiastically resisting all opportunities to travel, even just to Brooklyn for dinner.

Ned didn't land the New York job. He ended up in Boston, which he said he preferred. To what, I wonder? New York? Paris? His past? He was married and had a little boy; and that got me amazed. Here was a man, flesh of my flesh, only three years older than I, who had already set upon his course of leaving his mark upon the world—and I was still worrying over whether I would ever come upon a copy of the Capitol *Pal Joey* with the original cover. We were brothers, but we weren't entirely related, if you see what I mean.

It turned out that even a Boston television anchorman has to come to New York periodically for Meetings, and lunch with Ned and Jim became a regular feature of my life. At one of these, looking toward the summer, Ned invited us up to stay with him on Martha's Vineyard. Jim said no, but I was curious. I wanted to see what else I wasn't entirely related to, Ned's wife and son. I had a good time and went again the next year, and it became an annual visit— more than a visit, a tithe. After three or four of these trips, I felt certain that if I tried to stick out a summer without visiting the Neds, they would hale me into court. I had become a participant in their season, a member of my own family.

A certain weekend would be assigned me, set aside, built around the things I was likely to do and say. Ned was a man of Significant Draw, and the trip's logistics were Advantageous. Zesty, highly inflected metropolitan types, doing this important favor for a friend of a friend of a friend, would pick me up in front of my building, the car packed with cold collation, ambition, and wit. Crowded cars, rigid stages. This is traveling. I hate it but—sometimes—I do it. There was usually one guy too many (besides me), and someone would get stuck with a liverwurst sandwich, and one of the women would want to stop when no one else did, and one of the men would drop a truly ghastly ethnic slur of some kind (no one would say anything, but the silence was a hiss). Then, too, the car trip from Manhattan to outer New England must vie with the Damascus-Peking caravan line for density of tedium. Still, eventually I would land at the ferry slip, thinking of some story I might get out of the car people. Soon enough I would be standing on the top of the boat, and I would see my brother and sister-in-law standing with my nephew. I would wave. My brother, whom I understood very well in our youth but now think of as This Guy I Know, or Mr. Mordden, or even (Hey) Mister, waves back. He is jaunty, confident, always taller than I remember. He's going to age poisonously well. He's even getting just a bit gray; good career move. My sister-in-law points me out to the little boy, and he'll gaze at me with wonder and suspicion and bashful delight.

So that's what I'm doing on a beach in Massachusetts: sitting in their kitchen at the "breakfast bar,"
finishing my morning coffee.

Curtain up, and my sister-in-law says, "I wish you
and your brother got along better."

"We get along quite well for two people so near
yet so far, don't you think?"

"I mean, I wish you acted as if you liked each
other. I know you do like each other, of course."
She rinses out the name mugs: Ned, Ellen, Toby.
How come they can find a Toby and I can't find an
Ethan? "It's just so nice to see him . . . relating?" A
paper towel to dry the mugs. My sister-in-law is
very neat; her theory of eating implements is,
they're either in use or in the cupboards. None of
that wet stuff hanging in the porte cochere, or whatever they call those plastic racks next to the sink.
You wash it, you dry it. You're brothers, you relate.

"Ned really isn't a big relater," I say. "I expect the
television camera has spoiled him. He's gotten so
used to addressing a population, he probably
doesn't know how to talk to one person anymore."

My brother, I gather, is a very hot item among
analysts of the 18-to-49 female demographics, but
we never mention this to him because he has a fierce
aplomb, always did. No wonder he left home without explaining why. Frankly, I don't think he ever
did know how to talk to one person; anchormanning
is perfect casting for him.

Still, he has a perfect marriage: his wife likes everything about him and his son is so young that his

occasional testy rebellions pass for standard-make puerile mischief. I think there may be a problem on the brew there, but my sister-in-law sees the three of them as a gang of fun-loving pals. She is very proud of Ned's fame, too. She sends me his clippings. She used to accompany these with warm little notes, trying to explain why she is doing this. Then I told her that in publishing, where time is the first concern, we just write FYI ("For your information") on something and send it off. Amused, she has made it a household joke: she will hand me a bowl of rice pudding, indicate the whipped cream with a spy's nod, and murmur, "FYI, friend?"

Anyway, I already know why she is doing this: loyalty and love. She's terrific, but she feels too hard. "You know," she begins, "last night . . ." She looks away, looks back at me.

"Okay, yes," I say, "but please don't cry."

I always know when she will. It's not really crying; she leaks for joy. It's like those sudden, momentary thundershowers in London, when you look up and see the sun right through the rain. It'll be over shortly. But you still get wet.

"It was just so nice," she says, "to be all together. And Toby loves it when you read to him. He won't let anyone else, you know. We have so much trouble getting him to bed in the city. It's different when you're here."

"It's always different where I am. It's in my contract."

"Now, don't make a joke of it. It was so sweet. And I know you know that, so don't look away, either. You and Toby look so cute together, too. And you read so well." She is leaking.

"Toby and I aren't that great a team," I put in. "He's very tough for six. I only read to him so he won't grouch at me."

"Oh, that's not true." She gazes happily around the tidy summer kitchen: the mounted utensils, the standing machines, Toby's watercolors on the wall, Smurf stickers on the fridge, all their little heads carefully cut off. "Grouch at you? It's family! We've got to be our own best friends!"

"I wish you wouldn't enthuse just after breakfast."

"When he has a nightmare . . . of course, he doesn't often. But when he does, do you know he speaks your name? As if he's worried about you? I've heard him."

"Toby speaks my name?"

"Not Toby. Your brother."

Alarmed, I head for the beach. There's not much else to do out here but eat, sleep, and bake on the sand. You'd think an anchorman would be at a loss here: nothing but individuals to swank around for, at, with. What a waste of an act.

And God knows, Ned's got one. The first time we were alone together as adults—at lunch at my neighborhood joint, the Mayfair, at Fifty-third and First—he broke a copious silence by telling me a sure way to fascinate a woman: immediately after, read her a story. He recommended *The Velveteen Rabbit.* He said the combination of the aggressiveness of cock and the sweetness of the fairy tale overwhelms them. Wrong. It isn't the combination—it's the paradox of the aggressive and the sweet working for and against each other.

But he's definitely onto something here. Sometimes I try to visualize Ellen lying next to him, listening to him read *The Velveteen Rabbit*. I can see it. I can see it more easily than I can see myself on this patch of beach among—forgive me, Ellen—strangers. Still, I'm a game guest. I bring a quart of Johnnie Walker Red. I make my own bed, first thing up, even before the toothpaste. I spell them in looking after Toby. I take us all out to dinner on my last night. And I read my nephew stories.

It started by chance. One evening after dinner, three or four years ago, I happened to pick up an ancient Oz book lying next to me on the couch. As I leafed through it, Toby came up and said, "Mine." His father looked over from six newspapers, including the *Manchester Guardian*. "No, Toby, that's mine," he said. But my name was written on the front free endpaper.

"Read," Toby urged me.

I demurred with some evasion and he hit me.

"Better read to him," my newscaster brother said, not unamused.

I did read to him, and he listened carefully. All three of them do; and they watch me as they listen. It's like reading one's work in a bookstore. They even unplug the phone. After a while, Toby puts his head in my lap, and after a longer while he falls asleep. Then I carry him upstairs and his parents follow, his mother to dote and his father to stand in the doorway, framed in the light from the hall as if he had moved from the news to a suspense series. It's film noir; it's coming too close. Sometimes Toby murmurs reproachful excerpts as I put him to bed— "Why didn't you tell me the secret?" or "You are not playing fairly." Surely these are not meant for me, precisely. Not precisely. By then, my brother has moved into the room to put his arms around my sister-in-law from behind. These soft noises there, as I tuck Toby in. He likes to be tightly wrapped, like a present. Then I turn to face them, hugged together as they are, and for a moment I fear they won't let me out of the room.

The beach is always quiet here, nearly deserted on weekdays. I open my spiral notebook and pursue the tale of the moment—about, as usual, things I have seen, done, said. I have got to try writing *fiction:* about the encounter of Nabokov and Tolstoy in heaven, perhaps "The Goblin Who Missed Thanksgiving." I do not want to write anymore about people I know, people with feelings that I have been tricked into sharing. I should write books like those I read to Toby, set in fabulous places among bizarre creatures. You can say anything you want to in such tales and no reader will wonder who you are. You could be the Velveteen Rabbit.

My sister-in-law comes along after a bit with Toby and several tons of beach equipment. There are flagstaffs to stick in the sand and pails of two sorts, the metal kind decorated with merry scenes and the plastic kind with a side pocket for the toting of a shovel. There are rubber balls, a Slinky all coiled up in itself, picture books, drawing tablets, and remnants of a hundred miniature zoos, forts, shopping centers, and such, the pieces recombined in Toby's imagination to form the characters of some dire cosmopolitan epic.

I burrow deep into my notebook as my sister-in-law pulls out the old Modern Library Giant edition of *Ulysses*, the orange jacket encased in plastic. She maintains the reading level of an academic, but is hurt if you ask why she doesn't do something besides be married to my brother. Or she would be hurt if I dared ask. I've delved into *Ulysses* so often I recently took it up in Italian to keep the quest venturesome. (*Ulisse*, translated with astonishing resourcefulness by Giulio de Angelis. It comes complete with notes and commentary, just as I do.) Yet my sister-in-law knows it better than I, can even recite the chapter titles in order. She holds absolutely still when she reads.

Toby ignores us, digging, patting, piling. A grand, circular moat. A lump of sand in the center. Flags at the perimeter. Soldiers, rustics, exotic animals, and Hollywood extraterrestrials lining up to get in. Toby growls to himself as he works, like a dog fussing at a sock. "I'm making a sand tower," he announces at one point.

When my sister-in-law excuses herself to ready dinner, Toby and I dart suspicious glances at each other. He waits till she disappears over the dunes, then says, "Do you want to help me dribble?"

"Sure."

He hands me a pail and leads the way to the sea. "Look out for octopus," he warns.

He's going to grouch at me, I know. He always does.

"You fill it with water," he says. "It has to be just right. Not like that!"

He keeps pushing me.

"Like this," he shows.

◆ 140 ◆

It takes me eight dips to satisfy him; apparently the water has to fill the pail tight to the rim without spilling. How often in this life one must negotiate a walk along the blade when the topic at hand is absolutely nothing at all. How often one plays one's life for trivial stakes. With certain people, everything matters.

"Now, watch," says Toby.

This is dribbling: you ease the bottom end of the pail upward, leading the water to plop onto the sand, creating a mason's effect on the walls of your fortress. You decorate your power.

"Now you," says Toby, with a sense of challenge.

"Why don't you show me? I don't have the feel of it yet."

Growling, he grabs my pail and throws it off to the side. "I didn't like that water," he explains.

I return to my story, a sad tale of growing up and pulling away in a small southern town. Toby busies himself with his dribbling.

In the city, the scene is fury, speed, and ice, sheer ice. Holding your own, you may accidentally alienate one of the four or five most influential people in your professional or social or romantic life, and you may spend years working off the blunder. But on the beach, nothing happens, and everything is forgivable. The happy time crawls past. You can't go wrong.

"Hey, Toby," I ask, "what's on for dinner?"

Toby looks out at the sea. "No, there won't be any dinner for us at all. Can birds swim?"

"Why won't there be dinner?"

"My daddy is mad at Mommy and they aren't

going to feed us. I heard them crashing last night, so that means they're mad at someone. Do they like you?"

"Your mother does."

"Is she your sister?"

"No. Your dad is my brother."

"I don't think he likes us."

Toby's dog comes snorting up the beach from the west: a large, wirehaired terrier who moves with the frozen despair of an old man and the mild curiosity of a baby, named, by the child, with a child's logic, Tober.

"Get away, Tober!" Toby screeches. "Get away, you sneaky hound!"

The dog gently investigates the sea, sniffing at the waves. Toby's father, my brother Ned, cannot be far away. He is always walking the dog, possibly to see what stir he can inspire with his fame.

Possibly.

This is a sophisticated beach, the cream of Boston hip (if there be such a thing). He would be in no danger from autograph crazies. But people would surely recognize him—"as seen on television," the ultimate American credential—and buzz like wasps in a pancake house.

I see my brother in the distance, walking slowly around the curl of a dune, his hands in the pockets of his shorts, the long-thighed light brown kind you only see on straight men, brothers and fathers.

Tober noses up to Toby, who stares at him for a bit, then gives him a push.

"You aren't very nice to your pet," I venture.

"He comes around too much. And he snapped at

the doorman. They bought a muzzle for him. But you know what? I hid it in my toy chest. Sometimes I wear it in my room. Tober isn't really mine, anyway. He only likes my father."

My brother is almost upon us now.

"Hey, Tober," I call out. "Here, Tobes."

Tober looks at me, starts over, halts. It's not always easy to know what you're supposed to do in this family.

Toby eyes the beast with disgust. "Make him nap," he says.

And Ned arrives.

"How are you coming, my friend?" my brother asks me. He doesn't act like a newscaster, but like a man who might know a few.

"I'm doing just fine."

"Good man. Toby, did you remember to put water in Tober's dish this morning?"

This means Toby didn't, but the boy has unconcernedly returned to his sand tower. "He didn't look thirsty."

"I hate to think that a poor dumb animal is going without water because a little boy was too lazy to bother with him."

Toby and I glance at the dog, quietly settled on his haunches, looking far out to sea. A handsome, suave animal, not the kind to dance on your leg or suddenly begin howling when company comes, like a certain dog I know.

"He was naughty yesterday," says Toby. "So I'm not giving him water for a month."

Toby's father kneels to reason with his son.

"Toby," he begins, "you can't punish a living creature by depriving it of food."

Toby looks down, but resolutely. "You took my allowance away," he says.

"That's just money."

"I was going to buy candy with it. Candy is food."

Toby's father grasps Toby's little child's shoulders and tells him, in the voice that tolerantly introduces those irritating responsible opinions of the opposing viewpoint, "Listen here, Toby, have I ever deprived you of nourishment? Have you ever gone hungry?"

"Yes."

"No, you haven't."

"Last week," Toby insists, "you didn't take me to the puppet play."

"That was nearly six months ago, first off, and second, if you remember, you weren't taken to the puppet show because you got chocolate all over the television."

Patricide.

"Toby," he goes on, "look at me when I talk to you."

My family is made of those who demand to be looked at when they talk to you and those who look away when they hear. My brother started as a looker away; now he has to be looked at. No wonder he became a newscaster. An entire city must look at him when he talks. I visualize his television audience sitting before their sets in high chairs, wearing bibs discolored by strained prunes. Their faces are sad as they are reproached and reasoned with.

"Hey," I put in. "Why don't you tell Toby about the time I pushed you off the roof?"

My brother ignores this; Toby looks up.

"I think you'd better take Tober up to the house," my brother goes on, "and see if—"

"What roof? Our roof? Did he push you off that high?"

"Toby—"

Toby looks at me. "When did you push him? Was I there?"

"No. But I was thinking of you at the time."

"What's that supposed to mean?" my brother asks me. "We were kids then."

"I knew you'd have a child someday. I did it for him."

"Thanks a lot."

"He broke his arm," I tell Toby. "I broke your father's arm. He had to wear a cast for a month, and they threw him off the football team." I ask my brother, "Remember?"

"All right now, Toby, you march straight up to the house and assume some responsiblity for Tober. He's your dog."

Toby claps his hands like a pasha, and Tober meticulously gets to his feet, capping the motion with an elegant stretch of his spine, from rigid neck to apologetic haunches. With half this finesse, Bauhaus would be almost acceptable.

"Tober, come here!" Toby screams. "You mental case!"

"Not so loud," my brother directs. "Go on up, now."

"Keep watch on my sand tower," Toby warns us. "Don't let the other people come and wreck it."

"There are no other people," my brother tells

him—one of those apparently aimless statements, mere punctuation from the sound of them, that, on the contrary, burst from the heart. Who but a fifteen-year-old runaway would get so much out of the statement "There are no other people"?

As Toby and the dog proceed up the beach back to the house, I appear engrossed in my work. I am writing gibberish in order to look inaccessible; a useless defense against a man who remembers what you were like when you were eight.

"Ellen says you brought her a present," my brother offers. No one is inaccessible to a newsman. Impenetrable, maybe: but approachable, absolutely.

"I got both of you a present."

"A mayonnaise jar, was it? Sounds very handy."

"It doesn't just hold mayonnaise. It helps make it. The recipe is printed on the glass. Bloomingdale's."

"She really likes you, you know."

Out come the weapons. We estimate our worth in the quality of the people who like us—as witness the hearty bantering that goes on on news shows between the features and the commercial breaks. A Boston friend taped some of my brother's programs for me, and on one of them it seems to me—it *seems*—as if the other newspeople turn their backs on him and cut him out of their banter, leaving him to shift his papers and chuckle at imaginary colleagues out of camera range.

"Toby says you aren't going to give us dinner," I say as my brother kicks shells and pebbles down at the waterline. "He heard you and Ellen quarreling."

"Toby's doing a very awkward time nowadays. You shouldn't encourage him. It's hard enough to keep him in line without you telling him stories about brothers throwing each other off roofs."

"Why not? You did it to me and I did it to you. It was the great moment of my childhood. I wanted to share it with him."

My brother works his way onto the crest of the tide flat, kicking gusts of sand as he travels. "You know how easily he gets stirred up," he goes on.

"It's funny how cool you were as a child, and how high-strung Toby is. I wouldn't think it would run in your family."

"He's just a kid so far." My brother is kicking up whole wads of sand now, aimlessly, business on his mind. "What'll you do with that writing piece when it's done? Does it go in *The New Yorker*?"

"Why are you stamping around in the sand like that?"

He shrugged. "High spirits. Why even ask?"

"Because you've even kicked Toby's sand tower to bits."

My brother sees what he has done.

"I'd hate to be in your sneakers when Toby gets back and sees what you did," I exult. "He takes his beach sports very seriously."

"So do you."

I have to laugh at that. "I envy Toby his enthusiasms," I say. "He gets such a thrill out of everything, whether he loves them or despises them. He *feels*. Were we ever like that? Puppet plays and candy?"

"I wasn't," my brother says.

"How come you ran away from us?" I suddenly ask. "Do you expect Toby to run away from you?"

He is speechless.

Barking and shouting from across the dunes signal the return of Toby and Tober. They race down to us like a circus on a four-a-day booking. Toby is heading for the water, but his father catches him as he passes, pulls him up, and tosses him into the air as easily as if he were confetti. Toby says, "Daddy!" with delight as he comes down; only this, but this is enough.

I pet the panting dog.

"Toby," says the newscaster. "Listen to bad news. I wrecked your sand castle. Accidentally. I was kicking at the sand without thinking. I'm sorry."

Openmouthed, Toby turns to me.

"I didn't do it," I warn him.

"What if you get a spanking now?" Toby asks, turning to his father, looking up to find him, taking hold of his hand. "Or no dinner?"

"We don't punish anyone for accidents, Toby," his father lectures. "You know that."

"Yes," Toby agrees. "I have to go finger-paint."

"Okay." His father turns to me. "Okay, my friend?" Why do I have to render an opinion? My brother slaps Toby's behind lightly and the child runs up the beach, Tober dragging decorously after him.

Okay, he says. Look, don't waste a smile on me— but my brother does, a television smile suited to a quaint human-interest feature, perhaps a convention of street-food aficionados in south Boston. "See you at dinner," he says.

I go back to writing my story. Bits of the day flip into the text, a field expedient. Bits of every day; it makes people nervous. "You snitched!" a bag lady cried at me once, on Park Avenue.

"No, I didn't," I said; but I was thinking of some story.

"You told how I made a commotion with a cigarillo in the no-smoking section of the Carnegie Cinema show!"

"Never."

"No?"

"No," I repeated.

She shrugged, looked away, and coughed. "So what happens next?"

On the beach, next is always a meal. You pay out a certain number of minutes and then comes food, the four of us at table, all eyes aimed at some imagined central point of contact. But I ask you: Who imagines? Who directs the aim? When we gather at the board, I babble, dispersing the attacks. I am like a bag lady in the scattered energy of my references. I speak of Louise Brooks, of *The Egoist*, of Schubert's song cycles. They nod. They ask Intelligent Questions. They feel they must encourage me, my sister-in-law because anyone she is related to becomes wonderful by rules of love loyalty, and my brother because it is not entirely useless, in his line of work, to be connected to a writer, even a brutally honest one. Still, he'll never quite be able to see me as anything but an infant rebel, reckless, bold for his years, but ultimately ineffectual. He treats me as someone who may have to be soothed, even humored, perhaps disarmed, at any moment.

This only exacerbates my defiance, of course. From the moment I enter the house my brother lives in—to my sister-in-law's welcoming half-smile, as warm as one blanket too many on a surprisingly balmy November night—I am at war.

My brother cuts greens for his Caesar salad, which, for some reason, is genuinely cordon bleu. But then Ned was always a stickler for High Style in everything he did. I hear, from secure sources, that back in Boston notables of the local great world stare over his shoulder as he prepares it. Oh, it looks simple. Who can't make a salad? They can't—not like his salad, anyway. Theirs is correct; his is superb. They come back again and again to watch him and he pays them no heed. He acts as if no one should be able to do what he does.

From Toby's room comes the festive din of the Walt Disney versions of *Snow White*, *Pinocchio*, and *Alice in Wonderland*, on a tape I made for him last year. Occasionally, Toby sings along. I idly glance in at the door. Toby and Tober are sitting on the floor, engrossed in the act of listening; both of them are wearing cowboy hats and neckerchiefs.

When I return to the kitchen, my sister-in-law hands me a glass of white wine. I take it outside to watch the sun burn red over the water. I try to think of my latest story and all this real life. How inconvenient that work merges with truth. I was planning to model myself on Evelyn Waugh, not Thomas Mann. Yet even Waugh turned Mann in the end. Writers have a hundred dodges but a thousand revelations. Every so often, some of my friends ask pettishly why I never write about them. "But I do," I respond, as nicely as possible.

Then they grow uneasy.

Amazingly enough, I enjoy these summer visits up here, so far off my proper turf. I like the break it makes in my city rhythm, the sense the place gives me of owing nothing to everybody—professionally, of course. If only I owed nothing to absolutely anyone socially, emotionally, and historically, I would be white clean free.

A family forms around me as I sit on the deck. Something licks the back of my hand: Tober, a relief from the incessantly dilating Bauhaus. My sister-in-law joins us. A breeze animates the scene. Now Toby is here, querulously asking about the parentage of Donald Duck's three nephews. He knows they have none, but he wants to see what he will be told. His father comes out, balancing his hand on Toby's head as the twilight deepens.

I do not need to look at them to know how it appears. She is gazing upon my brother and he is gazing down at the boy and the boy is gazing at all of us, one after the other. For a moment, I luxuriate in the sentimentality of knowing that, whatever else happens, he will be raised in love. How terrifyingly important that is. Then I feel manipulated by this frenzy of feeling and swear to avenge the dishonor by styling all three of them as villains in my most scabrous stories.

My brother takes my wineglass to refill it, and Toby sits next to me, holding a juice drink poured to resemble a cocktail. "Now you could tell me more," says Toby, "about when you pushed my father off the roof."

"I don't think I ought to."

"Why?"

"That's a good question."

"Then why did you tell me before, on the beach?"

"That's an even better one."

"Tell me a story, anyway."

"Once upon a time," I begin—for these are the easiest stories to invent and the most comfortable to tell, set hundreds of years ago among perfect strangers—"there was a little boy who lived all by himself in a great sand tower in the middle of a forest."

"What was his name?" Toby asks.

"He had none. He had lived all alone as long as he could remember, so he had never needed a name. One day, a knight rode by on a beautiful black horse, and the knight was encased from head to foot in resplendent silver armor."

"What was the horse's name?" Toby asks.

"Toby, you shouldn't interrupt the storyteller," his mother gently chides, her doting look slipping from him to me and back.

"The knight's armor shone so brilliantly in the sunlight that the little boy, looking down from the window at the very top of his tower, could actually see himself. It was the first time he had ever done so, for there were no mirrors in his tower. None whatsoever. There was nothing to look into, no reflection—"

"Did he have Cinemax?" Toby asks, absently yawning.

"Hush. Now, the little boy was surprised to see the knight. But he was even more surprised to see himself. And from his window high above the forest he called down to the knight, 'Who are you?'"

"Here you go, my friend," says my brother, returning with refills of the drinks.

"But the knight thought the little boy was speaking to his own reflection, and so he said nothing. The little boy was consumed with wonder, for he suddenly realized that he must be lonely in his tower. He longed to go down and say hello to the knight and find out some things about the world. But there was no way down through the tower. Nor was there any way for the knight to climb up to him. The little boy felt very sad."

Toby stretches out with his head in my lap.

"The knight was sad, too, for he had been wandering in the forest for many days, having lost his way. He feared he might wander forever, for this forest was so big that no one who strayed into it from outside ever found his way out. But there was nothing for the knight to do but move on, and he spurred his horse to pursue his journey. The little boy again cried out, 'Who are you?' But this time the knight happened to be passing behind a great oak tree, which hid his armor from sight and thus cut off the boy's reflection. So the knight assumed he was being addressed this time, and he thought he should answer the question. He should tell the little boy who he is . . ."

Toby has fallen asleep.

"This tyke is all tuckered out," I tell his parents. "He didn't even wait for dinner."

"Did . . . did Ned read to you?" my sister-in-law asks. "When you were boys?"

"He didn't have to. I wasn't grouchy."

"Did he?"

She is looking at him and he is looking at her.

"Well, my mother didn't, and my dad was away a

lot . . ." Now they are looking at me. "I suppose somebody had to do the reading."

She takes his hand. "*Did* he?"

"Please don't leak."

"Don't . . . what?"

"When the little boy asked the knight who he was," says my brother, "what did the knight answer?"

I look at him for a moment. "He answered, 'I have the same name as you.'"

My brother frowns. "Unusual repartee."

Toby stirs in my arms.

"I have the same name," I observe, "as all of you."

My sister-in-law smiles. But my brother, puzzled once too often this day, looks at me as if he does not know who I am.

Beach Blanket Mah-Jongg

DENNIS SAVAGE FINALLY broke down and bought a VCR, and Little Kiwi was in heaven with a new toy. As winter dwindled into the coolly clever, touchy, mercurial season that we New Yorkers call spring, Little Kiwi began assembling what he touted as "this superscope collection of classic cinema." However, the titles he collected ran to the likes of *Abbott and Costello in the Foreign Legion, The Nutty Professor*, and eight versions of *Heidi*. At that, Little Kiwi somehow never mastered the fine art of taping by timer. On a number of occasions, he herded Dennis Savage, Carlo, and me into the living room for, in his words, "the local world premiere screening" of some hapless old movie, only to unveil, to his flushed befuddlement, *Strike it Rich!* or *Modern Farmer* reruns—even, most useless of all among the likes of us, *Sermonette*.

Carlo didn't mind; he thinks anything a sexy man does is sexy. I was wry about it; you have to be wry at just about everything Little Kiwi does. But Dennis Savage, who has become as much Little Kiwi's father as his lover, would get up and patiently go over VCR mechanics again, which made me twice as wry because Dennis Savage knows less about machines than Little Kiwi does.

"Instead of giggling and fooling," Dennis Savage told Carlo and me, "why don't you help him get his movie collection together?"

"Make up a list," I advised Little Kiwi. "Put down all the films you'd like to tape and hunt them down. Structure your project."

"A list!" Little Kiwi thrilled; he always finds the glamour in the mundane. He immediately got a pad and pencil to start his list, and the rest of us fed him suggestions.

"*The Broadway Melody*," I offered.

"*The Grapes of Wrath*," Dennis Savage added.

"*The Boys in the Sand*," Carlo recalled.

"And *Tigers in Connecticut!*" said Little Kiwi.

The company was baffled. Even Bauhaus, Little Kiwi's incompetent dog, appeared bemused.

"That one where Katharine Hepburn has a tiger and she loves Cary Grant," Little Kiwi explained. "So then she wrecks his dinosaur."

"*Bringing Up Baby*," said Dennis Savage.

"And it isn't tigers," I added, "it's leopards."

"That one goes *right* on my list!" Little Kiwi cried. "This is a pad of classics, you know." Enthused by a thought, he told Carlo, "And guess what else!"

Carlo just looked at him, his thoughts unreportable even to an all-male readership.

Little Kiwi turned to me. "How about *Cabaret Lady*?"

"What's that?" I asked. "A Lotte Lenya musical?"

"No, Hildegard Dietrich."

"Blonde Venus," said Dennis Savage.

"And it's Marlene—"

"Oh, this is a swank list, my boys," said Little Kiwi.

Little Kiwi got so caught up in the provisioning of his library of classics that from time to time he would venture downstairs and knock on my door, eager to have someone come up and admire his latest acquisition. It was still spring, those two or three days that New Yorkers get between the chill and the boil. Dennis Savage wouldn't be free from schoolteaching till late June, and I was handy and agreeable and only two floors of apartment building away. Actually, it was fun watching Little Kiwi show off his technical dexterity. When he tried to fast-forward, the sound would mute; when he pressed the mute button, the tape would rewind; when he summoned rewind, the television would go off.

One day, as I sat at my desk wondering if I should take an eighth work break without having done any work, I realized that Little Kiwi hadn't been dropping in lately. Who's he been showing his tapes to? I thought. About three days later, I found out: I heard a knock, opened the door, and laid eyes on an unknown teenager, younger and shorter and fairer than Little Kiwi.

"Virgil," he said, "wants you to come up and see our show."

Startled, I stared.

"I'm Cosgrove," he explained.

He led the way up to Dennis Savage's, and after a while I began to feel like the head of a day-care center. Apparently Little Kiwi and Cosgrove had put together an entire mixed-bill program: main features, coming attractions, cartoon, newsreel, and second feature. There were still kinks in the system—the coming attractions bit was simply network hype for *Dallas* and the "newsreel" was a slice of the evening news, mostly of commercials. At least the cartoon was a Mickey Mouse, though Bauhaus got frightened and had to be locked in the bedroom.

"This is just like a Saturday kiddy matinee," Little Kiwi was raving. "Isn't it?"

I said, "It's very nostalgic."

Cosgrove was looking at me as if wondering if they even had movies when I was a kiddy, much less Saturday matinees, and I was looking at him as if ready to haul out his blanket and woolly panda for nap hour, when Dennis Savage staggered in from another day of improving the minds of the American young.

"Those cretins," he muttered.

"Which?" I asked. "These or yours?"

"Oh, they're all mine," he sighed. "Hello, Cosgrove."

"Hello."

Dennis Savage shot me a look of amusement, which I shot right back, and Carlo dropped in, so Little Kiwi went into the kitchen to make everyone grilled cheese and tomato sandwiches, Cosgrove assisting. Every so often, Little Kiwi's voice would float into the living room, with "Slice them real crunchy now, Cosgrove" or a "Cosgrove, let's serve half-sour pickles as a side order today."

"Sounds like Little Kiwi's found an even littler Kiwi," I said.

"One of the neighborhood kids," said Dennis Savage, unpacking his valise. "He dropped out of school and his parents more or less threw him out. Or so they tell me." He was shifting papers about, showing us the official kit of his hard work. He seemed distracted. "One of those gay stories, I guess."

"Are those book reports and Latin tests?" Carlo asked Dennis Savage. "You would surely have flunked me if you were my teacher, wouldn't you? You would have stood me in the corner."

A rare half-smile elegiacally unfolded the line of Dennis Savage's mouth. Usually, he's either chuckling or grouching. Especially grouching.

"Go easy on me," said Dennis Savage. "It's been a heavy day."

"Now I'd be pounding the erasers," Carlo went on. "Sharpening the chalk sticks. I'd always be in dutch."

Cascades of giggles from the kitchen.

"If this were 1955," Dennis Savage opined, "that kid would have to straighten out with a wife and a job and make a whole new generation miserable. But Stonewall City has places for boys who are always in trouble."

"Yeah," I said. "He gets to adopt a buddy and revel in a VCR."

Dennis Savage nodded, sorted his papers,

shrugged. "They're quite inseparable. The kid does everything but sleep here."

Carlo shifted position and I cleared my throat. We traded glances. Then we grinned at Dennis Savage. As the Germans say, *Luftpause.*

"What's with you two?" asked Dennis Savage. "Are you totally zonked out from a hard day of loafing and goofing off?"

"He doesn't get it," Carlo told me.

"Give him time," I said. "He's totally zonked out from a hard day of reading and writing and 'rithmetic."

"Taught to the tune," Carlo agreed dreamily, "of a—"

"Give me time for what?"

Carlo and I performed a mock innocent-guilty whistle.

"All right, you jokers. What's the game?"

"'The kid does everything but sleep here,'" Carlo said. "It sounds so truly innocent."

"Two dear little play pals," I chimed in, "with their VCR and their alphabet blocks."

Finally catching up to us, Dennis Savage expostulated with the strenuous resistance of the sighted blind. "You think those two kids are . . . You dare to suggest that Little Kiwi would cheat on me with some . . . some—"

"Some beautiful blond kid?" I said. "Why not?"

"Terrific! Just terrific! You see a perfectly innocent little friendship and all you can do is . . . ravage it with Circuit innuendo. Dishqueens of the world, unite!"

Carlo and I bowed to each other like mandarins.

"It's not funny!"

"Jesus, can't you take a joke?"

Dennis Savage was calming down. "It's not fit comic material," he huffed. "You should tread gently in the sacred wood."

At which Carlo and I laughed so hard we had to hold our stomachs; and Cosgrove, helping Little Kiwi serve the food, eyed us with bewilderment. Little Kiwi, inured to such exhibits, ignored us, and we quieted down, but then Cosgrove tucked his napkin into his shirt collar like a five-year-old, and Carlo and I had to look away to keep our faces straight.

Summer beckoned to us from the Island of Fire, but Little Kiwi moped at the notion of having to abandon his beloved VCR. Finally Dennis Savage agreed to drag the equipment out for the season, and Little Kiwi was in heaven again.

Cosgrove was still around—more than ever, if possible. It was not clear where he went and what he did when he was elsewhere, but he, too, was certainly in heaven when he was in the company of our gang, the typical bourgeois youngster who has evaded a reproving family for a troop of males who accept him as he is. This is called Why Boys Leave Home.

Cosgrove's attachment to Little Kiwi was virtually absolute, and Little Kiwi liked it that way. Once Little Kiwi had hung back in the shadow of Dennis Savage; suddenly Little Kiwi had a shadow of his own, to instruct in the ways of the great world. "Cosgrove, do you think that's a good tie for the eighties?" he would say; and Cosgrove would immediately lose the tie. Or "Cosgrove, your grilled cheese isn't quite as *grilled* as it should be"; and Cosgrove would beg to put the sandwich back on the fire.

Cosgrove even functioned as Little Kiwi's secretary. One evening just before Memorial Day we were sitting around at Dennis Savage's as Little Kiwi updated his list of classic films. He paced the room like a tycoon giving heavy meeting while Cosgrove, with the pad, watched him like a hungry puppy.

"A nifty video collection," said Carlo, "should have lots of horror movies."

"*Razor Fingers With Main Street!*" cried Cosgrove.

"*Knife Man,*" Little Kiwi corrected, "*on Main Street.*"

"*A Nightmare on Elm Street 2,*" said Dennis Savage. Cosgrove noted it down.

"And what about that one where the guy goes downtown," said Little Kiwi, "and then everybody does things to him?"

"Yes!" said Cosgrove. "*The Statue Boy in Soho!*"

"No, Cosgrove," said Little Kiwi. "*Soho Nights.*"

Carlo and I looked questioningly at Dennis Savage.

"*After Hours,*" said Dennis Savage, patiently.

I chuckled.

"While you're at it," said Dennis Savage, "why don't you get my favorite—"

"*The Breakfast Lunch!*" cried Little Kiwi, jumping up.

"No, *Don't Play the Music!*" said Cosgrove, bounding around him.

Carlo and I looked at Dennis Savage. "My favorite is *Love Me Tonight*. And that's *The Breakfast Club* and *Can't Stop—*"

"How do you know what they mean?" asked Carlo.

Dennis Savage shrugged. "I've been watching television and going to the movies with them. I know what they've seen."

"Is *Love Me Tonight* your favorite?" I asked. "You have good taste."

"I always go for the good things," he said. "Don't you know that by now?"

"Cosgrove," said Little Kiwi, "maybe I should alphabetize our list."

"Oh, could I do that?" Cosgrove threw a look of such opulent need at Little Kiwi that Carlo and I furtively nodded at each other, as if swopping answers on an SAT exam. I'm positive Dennis Savage saw us. But he made no remark.

"Do you think it *is* a joke?" I asked Carlo. "About Little Kiwi and Cosgrove? I mean, isn't it—"

"They are truly close now," said Carlo, looking it over in his mind. He likes to pretend he misses everything but who's hot, yet he's as observant as a writer. He doesn't see things; but he sees people like nobody's business. "When two sexy little boys are close, well . . ."

"Well?"

He nodded. "Don't they fuck?"

"Who would be top man in that combination? Aren't they both natural catchers?"

I had decided to paint my kitchen; I think it very restful. Carlo, who had found himself hungry and came over to see about some lunch, ate a red delicious apple and watched.

"Everyone's a natural catcher with someone who's a pitcher," said Carlo. "But two catchers always figure out who's the most natural catcher, and the other guy gets to do the pitching."

"Actually, they could go to bed without fucking, couldn't they? Princeton rub, and so on. Would that count as adultery?"

"Well, I truly think Little Kiwi is fucking that Little Cosgrove."

Shocked, I stopped painting.

"Just like so?" I said. "You describe the infidelity of the era as if it were the tricking of a pair of exchange students in the NYU student union."

"Somebody's got to cheat sometime," he said. "Otherwise, you'd have nothing but people who love each other."

"Somewhere in Stonewall," I said, "I got the idea that *that* was the idea."

He tossed the apple core into the garbage. "Fruit is a good dessert," he said. "Instead of jello."

"What do you think Dennis Savage would say if he knew Little Kiwi was cheating on him with Cosgrove?"

Carlo looked at me as if I had asked him what a condom is. "How could he not know?"

I put down my brush.

"Just a minute there," I said. "Are you telling me that you believe that Little Kiwi is doing the sidestep with Cosgrove *and* that Dennis Savage accepts it?"

He looked at me for a bit. "So what do you believe?"

"I believe Dennis Savage and Little Kiwi are as attached to each other today as they were when they met nine years ago."

"In their feelings, yes, I truly know that. But in bed, too, all this time? Is that what you believe? And with Dennis Savage away all day, and those two alone up there, watching the videos and getting very serious about making little bowls of tuna salad just right. You don't believe there comes a moment in there when those two little boy bodies suddenly can't concentrate on anything but the sound of the other one's breathing, like that, and then the next thing, which is they take turns slowfucking each other?"

"Little Kiwi isn't a little boy anymore. He's twenty-seven."

"Even better," said Carlo. "He'll know how."

I left the kitchen, shaking my head. "I just can't feature Little Kiwi suddenly turning into a couch artist after having been so reticent all these years. He still blushes when someone cruises him too blatantly on the street."

Carlo was staring at the lipstick office tower that replaced the brownstones that used to command the corner of Fifty-fourth and Third. "Look at all those people in there," he said. "Office workers. Do you think they wish they were like us? When they see us fooling around while they're working?"

"Carlo, what would you do if you were Dennis Savage and you knew that Little Kiwi was sidelining with Cosgrove?"

He smiled. "I'd let him get it out of his system. A boy that nice deserves a chance to prove that he can be top, too. Everybody needs a Cosgrove some-time."

"What does a Cosgrove need?"

"He's a beautiful young dude, isn't he? The squirmy kind. If he was my type, I'd surely gobble him up. Anyway, you know how young kids are. They hang around waiting for someone to show them how, don't they?"

"Well, I'm just amazed," I said. "I'm fabulously amazed."

"Young kids need a lot of attention. They really need to be hugged and spanked and screwed pretty nearly every day. I wouldn't have the energy. Maybe that's why I like big guys. They sort of take care of themselves." He settled into my desk chair. "Let them do the spanking and such. A really big guy is so good at that, somehow. So very truly good at that sort of thing, you know."

"I've been your friend for some fifteen years now," I told him. "And you still shock me."

"A really big nice guy," he said. "To hold me when I'm sleeping."

I let Dennis Savage and his Dingdong School get themselves settled in at The Pines before I came out for my visit. If Dennis Savage has had a chance to miss me a little, he doesn't get grouchy as easily as he does in town. Besides, I was running a deadline.

So it was late June before I got out there, and I felt full of the devil, as I always do when I touch base with the only part of the world that is so gay that, for once, straights are the neighborhood problem. For a joke, I left my bag where the boardwalk gave onto Dennis Savage's house and sleeked inside to materialize as if by magic. One of my Pines routines.

No one was in sight, though it was near cocktail time; yet I thought I heard an odd sound somewhere about, as if someone were calling for help from very far away. Following the sound to the doorway of the guest room where I usually stay, I saw Cosgrove on his back, his legs dangling over Dennis Savage's shoulders, the pair of them gone from the world in the dangerous clarity of Buddy Position Number One.

Silently I backed away, left the house, and took my bag back to the harbor. I let a few ferries dock, traded a pot or two of dish with comrades, and finally heaved myself back into gear and returned, whistling, coughing, and stamping the last few feet like the country dolt in an antique melodrama.

Dennis Savage was occupied in the kitchen area. Overhead, I heard the shower going.

"Well, well, well," he said.

"Well enough," I told him.

"Deep as a well."

"Oh, was it?"

"I thought meat loaf and those roast potatoes you love that no one can make as good as your mother."

"I have to admit," says I, setting down my bag, "she is unrivaled in her specialties. Everyone should have a few, don't you think? Specialties, I mean."

The shower was turned off.

"How's the city coming along?" he asked.

"Well, it's still there." I fixed myself a drink. "So are you, I see."

He laughed.

"You usually say, 'What's that supposed to mean?'"

"I'm feeling frivolous today," he replied, washing vegetables and briskly drying them. "I'm running on mellow."

Nothing from me.

"What, no banter on that? No saucy sortie?"

"I haven't seen you this jolly in quite some time. What's your secret, old pal?"

He was about to answer, but stopped as Cosgrove came along the second-floor walkway wearing a bathrobe so oversize that it looked as if the Ringling Brothers had sold him last year's tent.

"Hey, big shot," I said to Dennis Savage.

He was watching Cosgrove come down the stairs; and Cosgrove was subdued.

"What's your secret, big shot? I want to be jolly, too."

"Did Virgil come on the ferryboat with you?" Cosgrove asked me.

"He isn't here, then, is he?"

"He had a job interview," said Dennis Savage. "To be a receptionist at a women's magazine. Apparently they have a policy of hiring—"

Halfway along the stairs, Cosgrove lost his footing and slammed down to the floor on his ass; and I was so tense I laughed.

"I'm sorry," I said, racing over to him. "I'm terribly sorry, Cosgrove."

"I'm okay," he said, just sitting there.

"Anyway, Little Kiwi didn't come out with me. I didn't even—"

"His interview," said Dennis Savage, "was for four-thirty, so he probably—"

Cosgrove burst into tears.

"Oh, Jesus," said Dennis Savage.

"No, I'm okay," Cosgrove repeated as I picked him up and held him. Carlo's cure. "I just got hurt a little on my bum-bum."

At which I could not restrain another shock of giddy laughter even as I patted his back.

"Where did you get that bathrobe?" I asked him, to stir the place up a bit, steer past the trouble.

"It's mine," said Dennis Savage.

"You're not this big, are you?"

"Who says I'm not?"

"Okay, okay," I told him. "Don't flash your eyes at me."

Footsteps on the walk heralded Little Kiwi's arrival, and Bauhaus, who would probably have dozed through the Battle of Stalingrad, suddenly decided to seem useful and barked once from the porch.

"Hey, I think I just got a new position," said Little Kiwi. "And Cosgrove," he added, opening his bag, "look at what I brought out for us for Sunday night: that superclassic gangster flick with James Cagney and Jean Harlow—"

"*Machine Guns and Mothers!*" Cosgrove exulted.

"*The Roaring Twenties?*" Dennis Savage guessed.

"*The Mean Old Slums!*" Cosgrove decided.

"No, Cosgrove—"

"The Public Enemy," I said quietly, gazing at Dennis Savage.

I don't know why I felt so scandalized—even betrayed—by finding Dennis Savage and Cosgrove together. I should have been prepared for it by Carlo's theory, which runs, roughly, "Gay men are always going to think of something hot to do, then they'll go do it." Anyway, surely it's Dennis Savage's relationship to worry about, not mine.

However, I've grown terribly used to this coterie we have, used to playing uncle to Little Kiwi and big little brother to Carlo and whatever I am to Dennis Savage, for which no word has yet been coined. I just don't want anything shaking up the procedures here.

Things calmed down considerably by dinnertime. Dennis Savage does make a first-rate meat loaf (one of his few accomplishments) and the mustard-dill sauce that accompanies it is to die. Now that my folks have moved to California, it's thoughtful of Dennis Savage to complement the entrée with my mother's celebrated roast potatoes, an arcane delicacy of Luzerne County, Pennsylvania. (He came out for a summer day of R & R when my parents were still living on Long Island, in 1972, and was so taken with the potatoes that he asked for the recipe. Mother shared it, but reluctantly, and she retaliated by calling him "David Savage" for the rest of the evening. It made him sound like a Broadway chorus boy.) Wafted on a wave of vodka, I forgave everybody, and doted upon the "kids," merrily lapping up the meat loaf, potatoes, and broccoli as kids do, utterly unconcerned with the relish and gusto of the gourmand. Good food is not delight; good food is to eat. They even raced off before dessert—raspberry sherbet topped with fresh blueberries and drenched in Grand Marnier—to prepare for the evening's entertainment. Little Kiwi and Cosgrove don't just show a movie: they *present* it, like the proprietors of a jazz-age picture palace.

Dennis Savage and I, in sweaters, took our coffee onto the porch and gazed at the ocean.

"How did you know?" he asked me, after a while.

"I saw what you did. I sneaked in to surprise you and . . ."

"You got surprised."

"It's none of my business," I said. "I have no right to an opinion," I said. "I'm a little threatened and that makes me judgmental, so I'm sorry," I said.

"It just happened," he told me. "You should know that. One time," he said. "One slip, that's all. There is no affair. No . . . ongoing calculation. I lost control and I feel terrible about it, but that . . . incredible little boy came up from the beach in those little swimming togs of his and he . . . I just . . . I went for him. Do you know how many, many moments it's been now, having that little darling around and not being allowed to make myself at home? I can't have him, I can't ask him to leave, and I can't loan him out, can I? He's always there. He's going to be near me, right here like this. Go hale me up for rape. Any jury would let me off."

"Was it really rape?"

"You know it wasn't."

"What are you going to tell Little Kiwi?"

He said nothing.

"Yes, good," I said. "One of those old-fashioned relationships. Just like our parents."

He said nothing.

"Maybe it's for the best," I observed. "Why ask for trouble? Forget it. Time will pass. Things happen, this and many other things. Little Kiwi counts his offenses, too, God knows. Then one day you and Cosgrove will be together again with no one else around and *pow*."

He said nothing.

"Just to satisfy my innocent writer's curiosity, would you be willing to tell me how it was? Because you always go for the good things, I know."

He said nothing.

"*That* good, huh?"

He turned to me, tears running down his cheeks.

"Oh, Christ," I said, my hand on his shoulder. "What the hell is going on around here? Where is everybody going?"

"Okay, it's all set up!" cried Little Kiwi, bouncing in with Cosgrove at his heels, as Dennis Savage furtively wiped his eyes.

"Friday night at our free movie show!" Cosgrove added.

"Guess what we've got for our surprise feature!"

"*Gentlemen Prefer Blondes?*" I asked. "*Dr. Jekyll and Mr. Hyde? My Little Chickadee? Love From a Stranger? Nothing Sacred?*"

"*Strange Interlude*," Dennis Savage pleaded. "*An Innocent Affair*."

"Oh, no," I corrected. "*Greed. Golden Boy. A Fool There Was*."

"*Charade,*" Dennis Savage insisted.

"*Idiot's Delight,*" I went on.

"*The Night of the Hunter,*" he said reproachfully. He meant me. "*The Informer.*"

Little Kiwi and Cosgrove were staring at us like chipmunks who come home from a day of frolic to find all their acorns have been stolen.

"Or your favorite," I noted, sure of my climax. "*Love Me Tonight.*"

"No," said Little Kiwi, bewildered. "It's *The Awful Truth.*"

"Ah," I said. "*My* favorite."

"Curtain," said Dennis Savage. "*Please.* Okay?"

The Right Boy for Cosgrove

"Look, I'm telling you,"
Dennis Savage is telling me, "Cosgrove has simply got to be farmed out.
I'm sorry, but someone's got to take him out of here.
I can't have this . . . this apprentice sweetheart underfoot all the time."

Not to mention on the end of your cock, I thought; but I said nothing, for Dennis Savage's moment of weakness was to be our secret, his and mine. No one must know of his adultery—better, no one must know of adultery, no matter whose or why, tomorrow and tomorrow and tomorrow. Not even Carlo, who would forgive Hitler an act of sensual self-enhancement if his partner was hot enough. Not even Little Kiwi—especially not Little Kiwi—the victim of the adultery but also the person responsible for it, as the one who brought the young man known as Cosgrove into our circle.

In the event, Little Kiwi agreed that Cosgrove ought to find a place of his own. "He's been living in our socks, almost," Little Kiwi observed.

"He likes it here," said Carlo, biting into a Granny Smith apple, his latest food discovery. (He likes to sample the stuff in your fridge, and sometimes it changes his life. One dinnertime Dennis Savage and Little Kiwi came out, amid a great deal of hushings and fa la, with a chocolate soufflé for dessert; but Carlo said, "Can I have one of those tart green apples that Bud buys?" and Dennis Savage was ready for the straitjacket.) "That cute little Cosgrove," Carlo concluded, "has a hateful family and no other home but this."

"That's just it," said Dennis Savage. "We have to get him one. He needs a place to move to. His parents have virtually thrown him out. He doesn't have a job. But he's marketable, let's face it. All we have to do is find him a good home."

There was a pause as we faced it. I felt Dennis Savage looking at me, then Little Kiwi looking along, and at length Carlo joined them. All three were grinning. A home for Cosgrove.

"Nothing doing, you bum Samaritans," I cried. "What is this, the Fresh Air Fund?"

"He could be very agreeable, running your errands," said Dennis Savage.

"I'm not taking your refuse."

"He loves your Victrola," Little Kiwi urged.

"That's his problem."

"He's a beautiful little honeystuff," said Carlo, and we other three looked away in bemusement, the usual condition when you pal around with Carlo. "One solid paddling every morning, and he'd—"

"I don't want a roommate," I said, with intense conviction.

"All right," said Dennis Savage, "all right," waving a soothing hand. "All right, but he's got to go. He has to . . . find someone to live with." He shrugged. "My nuclear family is big enough as it is."

He was looking out the window, but his feelings swept the room, and for the tiniest moment something very crucial and abstract became almost intelligible; I couldn't grasp what the something was. It moved so quickly that you'd have missed it if you blinked.

Little Kiwi missed it. "Just when I taught Cosgrove," he sighed, "how to make Baked Beans à la *Whorehouse*."

I guffawed and Carlo chuckled.

"It's a gourmet delight," Little Kiwi told us, somewhat hotly, "whether you're laughing or not."

"Oh," I said, "I'm definitely laughing."

"What goes in that?" asked Carlo, trying to look serious.

Still at the window, Dennis Savage turned back to us. "He opens a can of B & M beans and puts raisins in them."

"And minced onions," Little Kiwi added. "That's what puts the crunch in Baked Beans à la *Whorehouse*."

"Why à la *Whorehouse*?" I asked.

"He named it for the night we met," said Dennis Savage. "At *The Best Little Whorehouse in Texas*. The show."

"Boy, that was a long time ago," said Little Kiwi.

Dennis Savage nodded. "Nine years."

"Cosgrove," I noted, "was only eight then. A child."

Again I sensed an unnamed feeling doing a riff on itself. Something in the room with us.

"Why don't you give one of those Pines dating dinners?" Carlo asked. "We'll bring over all the eligible bachelors and set Cosgrove up."

"How are you going to explain that to Cosgrove?" I countered. "You might scare him into—"

"We don't tell Cosgrove," said Dennis Savage. "We just give the dinner."

"Then how will he know he's supposed to charm everyone? Put his better foot forward?"

Carlo smiled. "Do you really think a kid that sweet has to do something to make guys wild for him?"

"You aren't wild for him, I notice."

"Little kids aren't my type. You know that."

"Kids aren't his type," I said to Dennis Savage later, when we were alone.

"Well, they aren't. He likes to get on top of dark, shaggy monsters. What do you like to get on top of?"

"I had a feeling we'd get to me sooner or later."

"Well, it *is* rather notable that this perfectly cute little . . . honeystuff—"

"You get so urbane when you quote Carlo."

"The Voltaire of the Circuit," he dryly notes. "So this kid becomes available and our Cocktail Dandy, who maintains no other berth that I know of, refuses to—"

"Why don't you let me be the judge of what is honeystuff and what isn't?"

"You listen to me," he begins, getting into his Uncle Know-it-All frame of mind. "He's a very strange character. Okay. But somewhere in there is a nice kid who got strange because of what his family did to him. He's not smart. He's wild and he's young and he hasn't been around much. But he's waiting to fall very loyally in love with the first man who's willing to be kind to him. And he'll . . . be kind to you in return. Couldn't you use some of that, now?"

Keep talking, my friend. Let's do a little scene here.

"I've seen his sort before," he goes on. "They just want to fit in somehow. If they're actors, they fall in love with their director. If they're writers, they fall in love with their editor."

"I never did."

He puts his hand across my mouth. "And if they're houseboys, they fall in love with their host. Remember that old man and that incredible hunk at the Pines ferryslip?"

I sometimes think that Dennis Savage and I are coasting on dire memories more than we are living in the present. Things seen, heard, or read will set off a chain of reminiscence—and suddenly we are twenty-two or so and it's the early 1970s and no one has to pay a price for being alive.

"Remember?" he urges.

I nod.

"It was just after they had redone the Sandpiper, and we were waiting for Lionel's ferry. You had some atrocious jingle you wanted to sing him."

"'Cock full of nuts is that heavenly coffee,'" I sing.

He reacts exactly as he did back then, with that bossy rationalism that Little Kiwi finds sportive, Carlo finds picturesque, and I find endearing. "A cock," he declares, "*cannot* be *full* of nuts."

"Cock next to nuts?"

"*As you recall,* one of those dreary old fat queens was going back to town and he had what was obviously a hired cohort with him. Describe the cohort."

The tester tested. Sartor resartus.

"Tall," I say. "Straight dark hair. Twenty-five. Boyishly handsome. Very gymmed. Very style. Very smooth and opulent. An extraordinarily true man."

"And what was he doing?"

"He was holding the old man, and caressing him, and asking him to stay on the Island."

"Now the old man."

"He was . . . appreciative. He offered to stay, but then the hunk said no, you have affairs to settle in the great city."

"And what did they pass to each other?" he pursues.

"What is this, my SATs? Little endearments. Rash glances. It was a bit much, truth to tell."

"Truth to tell, you were mesmerized. If they hadn't been so intent on each other, the hunk would have punched you out for Aggravated Eavesdropping."

"*You* went out for a snow cone, I suppose."

"I was as dazzled as you were." He rose, crossed the room, looked out the window again. "I want to know the same things. But I always believed in them. You have to be shown over and over, don't you?"

"Shown what?"

"That the hunk-host partnership can be as magical, as real, as any. That a beautiful man can show an unbeautiful man attention, and suddenly, one day—"

"The beautiful man runs off with the household cash."

"*One day it's love*, you unsavory gasbag. It's love, can you bear it? Now, will you please take Cosgrove?"

"No, I'll take the hunk from The Pines that day at the ferry."

Still at the window, he is contemplative. Maybe the tiniest shrug.

"This is where you really shaft me, right?" I say.

After a while, he says, "This is where I vividly recall seeing those two men embracing right in front of everyone. Because their emotional bond was so strong that they had to celebrate it."

"They were celebrating a business deal."

"That gorgeous hunk *loved* that old man!" he insists, advancing on me. "He loved him! Can't you see anything, at long last?"

"Where are they now?" is what I see to say.

So he stands stock-still in the middle of the room, then he nods and demonstrates a quaint little shudder. "'Where are they now?' Right. And that's it for love and Cosgrove."

"Well, that's it, I would say, for the promotion of love and Cosgrove. You can't arrange these things, you know."

"Now you'll run to Carlo, and the two of you will pick it apart and decide that Cosgrove isn't *man* enough for the likes of you. Isn't that how the two of you operate?"

"Terrific: Dueling Types. The kid versus the clone. Why don't you just leave Carlo and me out of this and get your dinner together and give Cosgrove to someone who can appreciate his type?"

"Because I feel guilty." He sits next to me on the couch. "All he wants is to move in here and become Little Kiwi's little brother. And I'm going to sit him at a table with a lot of intimidatingly worldly men and tell them, 'Hello, this is Cosgrove Replevin and one of you gets to—'"

"*Replevin?*"

"That's his last name."

"Replevin . . ."

"So who should give the dinner? Kern Loften? He loves making couples. Perhaps because he never—"

"Jesus, I thought you were joking."

He shook his head. He not only *was* serious, he *looked* serious. "Cosgrove has to go."

"Cosgrove Replevin."

"It's your last chance, Bud. Take him or someone else will."

"Round up the hungry parties," I tell him. "I'm staying innocent on this one."

So the dinner was on, and Cosgrove had to go. As the days passed, Little Kiwi began to wane in his support of the project. Coming home from a literary lunch, I found him moping on the sidewalk in front of our building, the tethered Bauhaus, Little Kiwi's thuggish dog, lying on his back in a trance.

"All set for the big dinner?" I asked him.

He eyed me as Isaac should have eyed Abraham. "If Cosgrove knew, I don't think he'd be glad about this."

"You're the one who wanted to find him a home."

"I didn't know we were going to auction him off like a slave of olden times," he said, dragging after me into the lobby. As we rode up to Dennis Savage's, he was silent, almost sulky. It isn't easy to have to yield up a disciple.

"Look at you in a suit," said Dennis Savage to me as we came in.

Little Kiwi handed him Bauhaus's leash and marched without a word into the bedroom.

Dennis Savage shrugged.

"So who's on tap for the gala?" I asked.

As he recited names and eligibility credentials, I thought back to similar dinners he and I and others have given over the years. And yes, sometimes they do take, not unlike a bitter medicine: because sometimes somebody gets the idea that this year it's Love or Die. But, as I say, you can't arrange these things. Chemistry observes its own schedule.

"You're still determined not to tell Cosgrove?" I asked.

"I didn't tell you when I gave *your* setup dinner, did I?"

I was startled speechless.

"When was that?" I got out, at length.

"The summer of 1977." He was smiling, enjoying my surprise. "You don't remember, do you?"

Bauhaus, haunted by a vision, ran snapping at Dennis Savage's home entertainment center, jumped at the television, fell backwards, and slunk off to the kitchen with a resounding fart.

"While you're getting rid of Cosgrove," I suggested, "why don't you throw in Bauhaus for a package deal? A boy and his dog."

"It was at Lionel's house. When he was still in the Grove."

"No wonder I don't remember it. I usually block out Grove dinners."

"The median income was one hundred thousand dollars," he said. "They were all witty, spry, and nice. A very contempo crowd." He was virtually reciting; he might have been saving this up for years.

"You did this for me?"

Bauhaus stole back into the living room, panting.

"You got drunk," said Dennis Savage, "and started fights with everyone. Lionel was beside himself. You pushed Bill Swanson into a cake."

"Probably for some very good reason."

"He said he didn't like *A Little Night Music*."

"*See?*"

Bauhaus stared at the television screen.

"Nothing's on," I told him.

"Such fine men, too," Dennis Savage went on. I was not going to brisk my way through this one. "Fine young stalwarts of Stonewall, even if it was in the Grove."

Little Kiwi came out of the bedroom, his attire changed from dog-walking pullover and chinos to go-everywhere shorts and a *Me and My Girl* sweatshirt.

"It's cold in here," he said.

"No, it isn't," said Dennis Savage.

"Thank you for giving me that dinner," I said.

"You're welcome, ten years later."

"How come no one around here calls me Virgil, when I ask so nice?" Little Kiwi cried. "Why doesn't anyone listen to me ever?"

Cosgrove arrived, and Little Kiwi sat him down before the television, where the two of them and Bauhaus screened *Alien*, Little Kiwi morose, Cosgrove, obeying his chief, carefully subdued, and Bauhaus whining during all the alien's raids.

"Everywhere you go," I noted, "some monster's coming to get you."

Little Kiwi, his face a mask drawn too tightly around the mouth, put an arm around Cosgrove; it was not an affectionate but a defensive gesture. No one, it said, is taking this treasure away from me.

I went into the kitchen, where Dennis Savage was sprucing up an old beef stew with last-minute infusions of coriander and plum jam. This is what I call "Bloomingdale's cooking."

"Little Kiwi's in a really sour mood," I said.

"He'll get over it."

"I'm not sure he will."

"Don't give me grief."

He poured a bit of red wine into the stew pot.

"I smell bay leaves and lima beans," I said.

"You smell the rapture of the visuals and the tremor of the stories, and the holly and the ivy and the running of the deer. But can I tell you?"

"Why not, after such a poetic outburst?"

"I'm handling this operation. Okay?"

"Okay, captain."

"So do me a favor—*help* us land this kid some-where. Don't hinder. Please?"

"You talk about him as if he were a subversive you're trying to deport."

At one of those "something's happening" shifts in the atmosphere, he and I turned. Little Kiwi stood in the doorway. "Can I take Cosgrove to buy a new bathing suit?" he asked.

"It's almost dinnertime," said Dennis Savage.

"Yes, but this is *very* important."

Dennis Savage contemplated his lover for a bit. "It's not that important," he said finally.

Little Kiwi stamped back into the living room.

Dennis Savage poured a bit more wine into the stew. He put the wine down. He waited. He corked the wine. He started to put it away, dropped it on the counter, retrieved it, and put it in the fridge.

"What's the matter?" I asked. Something in the room again. Some feeling, some idea.

"Here," he said, offering me a spoon of stew gravy. I tasted it. "Nifty," I told him. "I love lima beans in stew."

"Cooking is one of my virtues," he said. "Big, simple meals."

"Little, simple kids."

He covered the stewpot.

"What was all that with the wine bottle?" I asked him. "What's going on?"

He didn't say anything for a while. Then: "On top of all this, I have to give a banquet and feel guilty, and that kid will still be around unless we set him up with a Tibetan monk."

Now it was Cosgrove in the doorway, staring at us for who knows how long before.

"I'm hungry," he said, oh so quietly, to us.

Kern Loften threw the utmost in Pines glamour at our disposal for the Cosgrove husband-hunting dinner, and between him and Dennis Savage a *carte des invités* was assembled to rival the elite at Catherine the Great's coming out ball. One odd note in all this: Little Kiwi brightened up suddenly, without explanation, as if he had decided to walk along with us. Cosgrove, as always, seemed to have no opinion. As long as he was among friends, he was happy.

The natural condition of gay. All friends. So, good; fine. The day of the dinner approached without incident, though we celebrated the avid intention of the feast by riding the hydroplane out to the beach, at my insistence. (The train is filled with straights, and the bus has become unreliable.) Dennis Savage doesn't like spending the money, but I like saving the time. Then, too, Cosgrove couldn't afford his ferry fare, much less a ride on the wind. We compromised: Dennis Savage paid for Cosgrove, and I paid for Little Kiwi. That's what I call an uncopious compromise.

But that's family life; even when you're in the process of cutting loose an excrescent relation. Dennis Savage had promised to supply dessert and salad—unnecessary, for Kern Loften is virtually made of parties—and he spent all the Saturday of the Cosgrove dinner working up to the dressing of the Caesar and the baking of the pies, fastidious, imperious, and audacious.

"Will there be hand-baked croutons," I asked, watching him at work, "or cheesy consumer-ready boxed croutons for this restorative yet divisive banquet?"

"There will be a cheesy author, and in about three seconds I'm going to—"

Footsteps on the deck dissuaded him, and a friend, grade six, materialized. On a scale of one to ten, grade nine is "I always wanted him," grade seven is "I feel better when he's around," grade four is "Intolerable after an hour," and grade two is "May he be refused admission to a disco in Fort Lee, New Jersey, on grounds of looks, style, and happiness quotient." Grade six is "I don't particularly care, but he's too nice to snub," so Dennis Savage and I gave him refreshment and fielded his questions till a clamor of giggles out on the deck warned us of the official closing of the beach for that day: Little Kiwi and Cosgrove had come home. By house rules, they were supposed to wash the sand off their bodies with the usual Pines hose, leave their beach toys on the deck, and come into the living quarters like gentlemen of quality. But by habit their return usually comprised a hose war, playing bullfight with Bauhaus, the knocking over of all the deck furniture, and the sneaking of various scrofulous beach toys into the house. This day, we got an extra: a chorus of one of Little Kiwi's new songs, "The Ballad of Fauntleroy." It's one of his weakest compositions, but Cosgrove loves it. Conversation in the house faltered as the two of them, wearing swimming trunks and canteens, paraded in in full chorus:

Fauntleroy was a funny clown,
Went to school with his panties down;
Out of luck in an old dump truck,
So they call him Fauntleroy!

"Little Kiwi," said Dennis Savage patiently, "the pails stay outside."

"Yes, but this time it's our unparalleled shell collection," Little Kiwi replied, mounting the stairs. He gestured: "Cosgrove, if you please."

Cosgrove, who apparently had been rehearsed, solemnly held up a shell for us to admire.

"Yes," I said. "That's a shell, all right."

Our guest, grade six, entranced by Cosgrove, asked, "Do you . . . do you know the names of all your shells?"

Cosgrove said, "This one's Herbert."

"Come now, Cosgrove," said Little Kiwi, moving on, "we really ought to change for dinner."

"Can I wear your dark blue sweater?" Cosgrove asked him. "With my khakis?"

"That's an important combination," said Little Kiwi, leading Cosgrove along the second-floor walkway. "But only if you'll be a good boy at the dinner."

"I'll be very good," Cosgrove promised as the two of them went into the bedroom.

"Tell me," said our guest, with the oddest smile on his face. "Is someone around here married?"

Someone was going to be, as the local intelligence ran. But I couldn't help noticing how enthusiastically Little Kiwi pressed his Kazootie Koolers upon us at cocktail hour. Dennis Savage, intent on his pies, missed a nuance here; I thought the usually abstemious Cosgrove was imbibing rather resolutely, a questionable act for a young man on the verge of his engagement party, even if he supposedly didn't know that's what it was. Questionable, too, was Cosgrove's intake of wine at the dinner itself. At the slightest provocation, Little Kiwi would suggest, "Let's drink to that, Cosgrove!" and Cosgrove drank.

What about the flowers? you ask. The decor, the tone, the stirrings of the place. Well, it was the usual Kern Loften A-list do; I'll let him identify the flowers. I'd call the decor late-middle beachfront attitude palazzo soothed by a pride of bodybuilders who act as if helping get you through the night is their essential deed. I don't know where Kern finds them. Anyway, there we were: four lawyers and doctors or so, three physiques of death, a writer, a schoolteacher, two little kids, Carlo, and Kern Loften; and Cosgrove got blitzed from all of Little Kiwi's "Let's drink to that" toasts and began to chortle, waver, and fade. He was leaning on Carlo's shoulder, calling him Mr. Smith in a dreamy manner, and Carlo, who does not comprehend such behavior but thinks it's probably hot if you like little kids, patted his head as if he were a poodle. Finally, Cosgrove's eyes closed and he went slack in his chair, so Carlo picked him up and laid him on the couch.

"So much for the *jeune premier*," said Kern with a merry shrug.

"He had a very heavy day," said Little Kiwi.

"Of what?" Dennis Savage asked.

"Of being asked to go away," said Little Kiwi. "Of everybody doesn't like him enough."

"What delicious pie," said a lawyer.

"Sweet," said a doctor, "yet I seem to taste no sugar."

"As sweet as sweet can be," said Little Kiwi, furious. "As very sweet as they make them. If only certain people knew that at the table."

Cosgrove was asleep, and the party went on without him. It was a fine party. The intellectuals poured forth, the sensualists listened well, and the friends did a little emotional squeezing. Then it was over, and everyone went his way. Cosgrove had not been connected. In fact, Cosgrove had totally passed out. I thought he'd have to stay over at Kern's till Carlo offered to take the boy home.

"That's fine with me," said Dennis Savage.

Little Kiwi was sitting at the table, the last diner, holding his arms around his chest defiantly.

"That's fine with you, too, isn't it?" I asked Little Kiwi.

His eyes tightened aggressively, but his face tried to stay impassive. This is like Joan of Arc trying to stay peaceful. I wanted to tell him what I knew, and how much I sympathized with him; but that sympathy was disloyal to Dennis Savage. Cosgrove had to go.

Kern, Dennis Savage, and I went on cleaning up, and still Little Kiwi held his post. I believe he was on strike of a certain kind, telling us in his immobility that he hated us, at least for tonight. I busied myself with the tape deck, sifting through Kern's old party reels, some of which I, in my penniless youth, had effected. Dennis Savage and Kern were clearing the table.

"I," said Little Kiwi, "am not moving from this peculiar spot."

Dennis Savage's eyes tensed, but Kern, sponging up the bits, laughed and said, "Well, you're such a nice-looking youth that you can do whatever you want around here."

Dennis Savage gave Little Kiwi a searching look but went on with the cleaning up, helped here and there by one of the bodybuilders. Finally the dinner was over and everyone was long gone, and nothing had been accomplished. This sometimes happens, even with the dearest intentions. Little Kiwi left the table and we all went home, where Dennis Savage fiddled with the pie tins and I made a drink and Little Kiwi scoured the house. Then he announced, "Cosgrove isn't here."

For which he got nothing. Not just silence: *nothing.*

"Carlo was supposed to take him home," Little Kiwi went on. "This is home."

"Maybe he's at Carlo's home," I said.

"Why would he be there?"

A fair question.

"I'm going to go find him," said Little Kiwi—but Dennis Savage put a hand on his shoulder and looked at him.

"Well," I said, "we probably should figure this out." The two of them glaring at each other. "Where Cosgrove is just now."

"So go find out," said Dennis Savage, turning away.

Carlo's house is way on the other side of The Pines, on the sea to the west, filled with suave, rich, grey-haired men on weekends and empty on weekdays. It was silent and dim, but Little Kiwi purposefully pushed in and I followed. He stood there for a moment, listening. Then he walked to Carlo's bedroom.

And there he froze.

I waited for a bit; I don't know why. The whole caper was running past me, somehow, like those ideas, those feelings, that flew by me in rooms filled with my friends, ideas of déjà vu mixed with feelings of the avant-garde. When I drew up to Little Kiwi, over his shoulder I saw Cosgrove lying in bed next to Carlo, the boy's arms wound tightly around the man. Cosgrove was sleeping, but Carlo was awake. Wasn't he? It was hard to be sure in that odd light. He was looking at us, I believe. And we looked at him, certainly, for quite some time. Then Carlo did something I found unforgivable yet beautiful: he ran his hand through Cosgrove's hair. Cosgrove said, "Please." And Carlo said, "Yes."

Just that.

I couldn't tell whether Carlo was smiling or just being there, just having screwed Cosgrove, just knowing who Little Kiwi is and who I am, just being able to point to us if he is ever challenged to produce friends.

Cosgrove said, "Please," again.

I gently pulled Little Kiwi back through the house to the boardwalk, both of us silent.

Until Little Kiwi said, "Everybody takes advantage of Cosgrove."

"'Out of luck in an old dump truck.'"

"You can just see how much he needs love, and that's how they lure him into the trap."

We walked on.

"And you know how handsome he is," Little Kiwi added. "So they're going to start grabbing for him. They think he's some little punk, so it doesn't matter what they do to him. But I know that he has feelings just like the rest of us, and you have to be very careful with Cosgrove."

"Were you very careful when you fucked him?" I asked.

Yes, he was shocked, but he kept his cool. We were passing the harbor, to some the most romantic part of The Pines, a great horseshoe of welcome scooped out of the sand, where boatloads of mythical figures would sail up before one, standing there on a Friday evening on the verge of perhaps the major weekend of one's life. To others, the harbor is the scandal of The Pines, the straight section, where abrasive owners of little cabin cruisers would rend the serenity of a Saturday trading atrocious gobbling noises; and where the mainland kids invaded in the evenings.

I have very mixed feelings about the harbor. Sometimes I try to believe that it is merely one of the places I have frequented over the years, like D'Agostino's or my roof. A location, no more. But this is hard to believe. The Pines harbor is where, in my twenties, I first realized that in coming out of my former life of lies and excuses, I had caught a fabulous adventure by the tail, its danger no less intoxicating than its exuberance. This is what my friends and I call "the rapture," and I feel it acutely every time I pass the harbor, even if only on an errand to the grocery—even now, in the midst of trying to trick A-list dish out of Little Kiwi, wretch that I am, sleuth and storyteller that I call myself.

"I knew that Cosgrove was unsure," said Little Kiwi. "I had to be protective of him. That's what I knew."

The thing about Little Kiwi is, he cannot lie.

"Poor little Cosgrove is not what you think. He's very unknowing. And he always says please."

"Did he say, 'Please love me'?"

"He said he would die if I didn't take care of him. I couldn't just shove him away, then, could I? When he was holding on to me, and he even cried?"

I cleared my throat. "So, did you in fact—"

"And poor Cosgrove is so dandy when you're nice to him. You and Dennis Savage don't know that, because you never are. You just laugh at him."

"But did you and Cosgrove finally—"

"Oh, it did him no good, did it, at the dinner? All those rich men around the table. It was like a meeting of a fancy club."

"Well, he got blitzed rather quickly, didn't he?"

Little Kiwi said nothing.

"And not," I went on, "by chance."

After a bit, he said, "I had to do something. You guys were turning the whole place back on us. You were giving us plenty of worry." He shook his head. "I told Cosgrove to drink a lot so we could push them all away." He sighed. "My poor little Cosgrove."

We walked on some more. Then: "So did you," I asked, "or didn't you?"

Long pause. Long, long, long pause; and we were almost home.

"Well, everyone's so mean to him but me. I was the one who had to make him happy, because he's my pal. So what else could I do?"

"So *what* . . . did . . . you . . . do?"

"Well, he wouldn't let go of holding me, and he kept saying please. And Cosgrove is so little when you hold him like that, and he gets scared so easily. So then . . ."

"So then *what* then?"

He thought about it for a long time. "I made him happy," he replied.

That is all he would say on the matter, and all I was ever to hear, but now I knew two secrets about Cosgrove, one from Dennis Savage and one from Little Kiwi. And by then we were back and Dennis Savage said, "Well?"

"When Carlo offered to take Cosgrove home," I told him, "that's exactly what he meant."

"You've got to be kidding."

"It's all over but the retrospectives."

"Carlo and *Cosgrove*?"

"Why not? I've known stranger pairings to occur in the misty elegy of a Pines nighttime."

Dennis Savage suddenly got busy poking around in the fridge.

"I don't feel so good," said Little Kiwi quietly, sitting alone in the center of the couch. "Something didn't happen right."

"What didn't happen?" asked Dennis Savage.

"Cosgrove went to the dinner," Little Kiwi began,

tripping over his thoughts the way little kids do when they don't know how to center an all-pervasive complaint. "He went to it, and then he was afraid and went to sleep."

"Afraid of what?" I asked.

"Everyone's bigger than Cosgrove. He isn't smart enough yet. I was going to teach him. Now he'll always be afraid. Poor little Cosgrove."

"Poor little Cosgrove?" I said. "He just got a date with the hottest man in town. He's surrounded by loving friends." Then: "*Deeply* loving," I added, tossing it to Dennis Savage.

"I don't know that he is that well loved," said Dennis Savage, facing me down this time.

"He's not," said Little Kiwi. "He's lonely in the crowd." A tear ran down his cheek. "What will Carlo do to him? I know that Carlo is kind, but he's a big fellow and Cosgrove is very delicate." Another tear appeared. "He doesn't know anything. He's just Cosgrove."

"Not anymore he isn't," I said. "He's one of us now. He's a buddy, staying over in the best little whorehouse in The Pines."

"I'm mad at everyone," Little Kiwi blurted out. "My feelings got hurt!"

Dennis Savage pulled him up, held him for a moment, then let him go. "Get on upstairs," he said, putting his hand lightly on Little Kiwi's head, right there on top. "I'll be up in a jiffy."

"All right," said Little Kiwi, wiping his eyes as he started for the stairs.

"Boy," I said to Dennis Savage, as that oddly confidential but remote feeling pestered me again, begged me to know what it meant to me and my friends. "Back there, an age ago, when you first came to New York, did you have any idea all this was going to happen? I mean, that all this was possible?" Now, the feeling nudged me; yes, it urged; forward, it says. I wonder if at just that moment Dennis Savage felt it, too—he was looking at me in an indefinably certain way, as if he had just forgot something terribly important, or just remembered it.

"Could we have French toast for breakfast tomorrow?" said Little Kiwi as he trudged upstairs. "With powdered sugar on mine?"

"Have we ever refused you anything?" Dennis Savage replied.

"You didn't let me wear my mesh T in the parade last year," Little Kiwi told him.

"That parade is perilous enough without you in your mesh T."

"When I was very young," said Little Kiwi, pausing as he reached the second-floor walkway, "I asked my parents that since there was a Mother's Day and a Father's Day, how come there was no Little Kiwi Day? And they said that every day is Little Kiwi Day."

"Well, today," I announced, "is Cosgrove Day."

"Now they tell me," Little Kiwi said tragically. And he went into the bedroom.

"Poor kid," I said. "He lost his devotee."

"Everyone's been losing out on something in this adventure," said Dennis Savage. "Except you, as usual."

"I have nothing to lose."

"Stop rehearsing Cocktail Dandy lines on me." He

started upstairs. "Go take a walk in the misty elegy of the Pines nighttime. That always revives you."

"I was planning to, actually."

He stopped halfway up. "What was it like at Carlo's?"

"Scary." I pulled on a hooded sweatshirt. "Cosgrove was saying please."

"He always says that."

I looked at him. "Always?"

"I mean, he said it to me that time."

"Did he, now?"

"It'd be funny if Cosgrove couldn't walk around for the next few days after . . . you know, after Carlo. He'll be limping around with his legs crossed and falling all over the place."

"We could rent him a golf cart to ride around on."

"Tell me something. What exactly did you see there?"

"Two people becoming."

"Becoming what?"

The feeling roved through the room. I felt it very powerfully. I felt haunted. I felt inflamed. I felt daring and reckless, like a child playing war games with, yes, nothing to lose. I felt so free I could have been generous to my worst enemy that night. I felt grateful that there were still things to be comprehended, even discovered.

"Becoming what?" he repeated.

I shrugged. "I'll tell you when the story is over."

He went upstairs and I took a walk.

Strolling the beach at night does revive me; I suppose I feel stimulated by the dense rustling of the curtain as it falls on another day in the life of the gayest address in the world. Maybe I just need the solitude, the peace. Heaven knows, it's quiet there on the edge of the sea. A good place to think about your feelings.

The lights were on around the pool at Carlo's house, and I caught the firefly of a toke moving softly in the dark. It was Carlo, surely, smoking the day's last joint, and I walked up to his deck. This is what is known as the *scène à faire*, the obligatory confrontation in the well-made play. All the world's a stage, and this is the end of the story.

"Well," he said, "I truly thought you might be along soon enough."

"I know two secrets."

"Yeah, you're always around when someone's life is falling into little bits, aren't you?"

"How's Cosgrove doing?"

He exhaled deeply and proffered me the roach. I shook my head.

"You always have to do everything your own way," he said. "Beautiful kid's up for grabs, you don't want him. Someone's smoking, you don't smoke. The trouble calms down, you're collecting secrets."

"Don't blame me. I'm not a snoop, I'm a confidant."

"You're a snoop."

"I've been a good friend to you," I said. "Haven't I?"

He relit the reefer and took another puff.

"I just noticed something," he said. "So here's another secret for your collection. Unless you already made your quota for the day."

"Carlo, I'm not a snoop."

"Did you ever wonder what guys are really after when they have sex with someone new? A hot time, you'll say. Sure. Some guys, now, that's very true of them. They want pleasure. Sex is a pleasurable thing. That's very true of sex. But some other guys want something besides that. What do you believe they want?"

"Tell me."

"They want a friend, some guys, now. They want a friend so bad they don't even care is the sex good or not, precisely. Not as long as they can know that other guy as close as it gets, know him to death." He stabbed the cigarette out. "But then there's another kind of guy here, and what he wants is to be taken care of. That's what I just noticed. You'll say, sure, that's what kids are like." He shook his head. "No, sir, my friend. I've seen kids'll top you so hot they make Big Steve look like a seven dwarf or something the like. Some little twerp thing. No, there's kids who don't need a friend, don't need someone taking care. It's not kids versus men. It's not the size of a man anymore now, it's the shape of his feelings."

"Was Cosgrove afraid of you?"

"Secrets," he breathed out. He waited a bit, looking around at the night. Moody man. Then he said, "What do you mean, afraid of me?"

"I mean, he's very nearly a virgin, after all."

"The hell you say." He laughed softly. "Let me tell you about was he afraid of me. Let me tell about that. I've never been with a real little kid before, so I played like Big Steve does. You know that scene, on the lap and so on? I toyed around with him, and I whispered sweet talk in his ear, like Big Steve loves to do. He's really good at that . . . cajoling stuff. He can make you anything he wants, turn you into something he thinks will look real cute on you. I asked that Cosgrove, Has he been a good boy? He said yes, he was always good. And I said, What about how you drank more than your share tonight and got pissed and went to sleep? And he admitted he was not a good little boy tonight. So I asked him what he thought we should do about that, especially because he has such a beautiful little butt which is all ready to take a very heavy whipping."

"I don't want to be shocked any more tonight."

"Well, now we truly see that some secrets are too much even for the secret man himself. But there's one thing for you to know about now, and that's what this Cosgrove here wants out of sex."

"Then you can tell me what you want out of it."

"That's *just* the kind of fucking thing you always have to do, huh?" he shouted, grabbing the front of my sweatshirt. "When do we hear about *your* secrets, you son of a bitch?" He pushed me back so hard I lost my balance and fell off the bench. "How about I pound you pretty good now, and you can figure out what that means, huh?" he growled.

"Didn't you get enough of that already," I said, getting up, "with Cosgrove?"

With a coarse shout, he jumped up and shoved me against the deck railing, looming over me as he forced my head back. His breathing sounded like an avalanche. I tried to ease him off me, but he wouldn't yield. Carlo has a violent streak, I know, but he only gets into fights when he has been attacked.

Physically, I mean.

We were locked there for quite some time, not moving, silent, just looking at each other, as his hostility—not his anger—died away. Finally he let go of me, stepped back, nodded his head once, twice, put his hand on my back, gently pressed me over to the bench, and sat me down. He sat next to me, looking away, back toward the house. I was shaking, I have to report, but that strange nameless feeling slipped alongside us, both of us, and put an arm around my shoulder.

"I'll feel like heck about this tomorrow," he said. "But right now I'm not going to apologize. You have been a good friend and all, and I shouldn't have done that. Except you . . . you truly have to stop doing this."

Now he looked at me.

"Yes, you have to. You go around and watch everyone and you know too much and it gets on everyone's nerves. Because no one gets to watch you. You don't want anyone knowing about you. So you and me, we're very much alike in that, see? Very much alike."

He was silent for a while.

Then he said, "You remember when I was hustling for Dave Direnzi, way back a time there? You and Dennis Savage got all on my case how I was taking a chance with doom and like that, but my unemployment ran out and I needed the money. And most of the guys I did the calls with, they didn't want much from me. Anyway, you gave me some advice, at least, just in case. Remember?"

I didn't do anything in response. I wasn't remembering; I was looking forward.

"This was it: If the door opens, and there's two of them, get careful. If there's three of them, get worried. And if there's three of them and they're grinning, run like hell. You remember that?"

I remembered.

"Okay, I went to this one gig, and just as the door opens this flashpop goes off right in my face and there's this old guy with a camera. And behind him is this huge black muscle dude, not a stitch on his build. And in the corner there I see a young guy in a sailor suit. And everyone's grinning."

He laughed quietly.

"So what did I do, huh?"

He laughed again, a warm rolling sound.

"I ran like hell."

That feeling put an arm around my shoulder again, and now so did Carlo.

"I'm ready to apologize for what happened before," he said—but just then Cosgrove came out of the house, holding a blanket around himself. He stood on the porch, watching us, then approached.

"He calls me Mr. Smith," said Carlo.

Without a word, Cosgrove folded himself into Carlo's lap and Carlo held him.

"This young boy is one of the ones who wants to be taken care of. Maybe it's time for me to try some of that. I've been playing around for so long. Now I'm forty, and maybe I should get serious about this. Sometimes when we're all together, I believe I am thinking of something. Something real important. I'm never sure what it's about."

So Carlo feels it, too.

"Maybe this is what it's about, here." Carlo stroked Cosgrove's hair and the two of them turned to me.

"See, it's us watching you now," said Carlo.

In the pool lights their eyes blazed like the fierce embers of a fire that won't go out no matter what you do to it. They had become, Carlo turning from boy to man, Cosgrove from orphan to son. One day it's love; and so the story ends.

"He's not afraid," said Carlo.

Cosgrove took one of Carlo's hands and opened it up.

"He has nothing to be afraid about," said Carlo.

Cosgrove placed his little hand inside Carlo's great paw and folded it around his own.

"He's not the one around here who's afraid of me," said Carlo, pulling the boy close so the two of them could tremble together and feel that keen, brash moment at the start of love when the heart speeds.

I left them then.

Because of course Carlo is right: Cosgrove isn't the one around here who's afraid of him.

I am.

The Dinner Party

I<small>T IS A TRUTH UNIVERSALLY</small> acknowledged that a gay man in possession of a fortune must be in want of an oceanfront house in The Pines. And I *told* Colin: east of the co-ops is the chic quartier. But no. No, he found what he wanted so far west that when we're still, we can hear people coughing in Hoboken. But we are seldom still this weekend, for the usual Pines reasons—a lot of guests, a lot of dropping in, a big dinner planned, and there has been another death. Greg was diagnosed, went right home, and decided to choose in a no-choice situation. Heroin overdose.

Are you with me so far?

Greg's family hadn't known he was gay, I was told—but isn't this just another of those euphemistic concepts designed to protect straights from seeing the world too well? A markedly unwise and unobservant family might honestly mistake your sexuality even into your late teens. But Greg was twenty-nine or thirty and uncloseted. He never spoke of his life to his parents or siblings, apparently—but surely by this time they must have Known. They just didn't Speak of It.

This left them with little to say at the funeral, when they met the people of Greg's life. Straight sons are survived by a wife and kids, not by a porn star, an opera impresario, an ad man, and an airline pilot.

Guillermo, Luke, Stephen, and Cliff.

They had all (or mostly) been boyfriends—Stephen and Greg, Cliff and Guillermo, Guillermo and Luke. Eventually the five of them passed into a second honeymoon of casually devoted friendship, a state unique to gay—penetration without sex, you might say, penetration of the feelings. They were always together, dancing, planning a surprise party, dining at the Tiffany Coffee Shop after the gym, breezing into The Pines atop a ferry—Stephen and Cliff waving, Luke grinning, Guillermo solemnly charismatic, Greg drumming restlessly on the boat's wooden ribbing. It was not my circle, particularly, but I went to college with Luke and was an old Eagle buddy of Cliff's. A fellow traveler, they called this, back when the subversives were political rather than sexual.

In a dream, my fourth-grade class, at a carnival, beckons me to come along, flourishing cotton candy and Pokerino prizes. I hang back; someone behind me needs help. I turn: and everyone I have known for the last fifteen years is lying in a heap of corpses. We are all children in this dream.

A porn star and an opera impresario, you say? An ad man and an airline pilot? And Greg himself was a professional sweetheart, a "houseboy." It's a questionable coterie, no? What is a striped-tie-and-vest ad exec doing in the company of a man whose work clothes are chest hair? What did the opera maven and the pilot talk about? Ah, but was not this very sophistication of identities one of Stonewall's revolutions? Have we not made the received bourgeois discretions of status and culture irrelevant? Sex outranks status. Friendship purifies culture.

And these men were good at what they did. Greg took his liaisons so seriously that he held his employers' hands as they strolled the boardwalk. He wasn't, he felt, hired for ecstasy, but for affection. Guillermo may have been the best-known pornothespian of the late 1970s, strenuously pacific, opulently brooding, known to the many under a Colt code name I daren't reveal because he'd get mad and brood at me. Luke rose to dominate the American opera scene, most adept at casting. Once I challenged him to cite ideal casts for the three most obscure operas I could think of, Casella's *La Donna Serpente*, Delibes's *Jean de Nivelle*, and Auber's *Gustave III*. Luke not only did it, he cast *Gustav* entirely with artists of the Prague National Theatre, for a *bonne bouche* of expertise. Then I hit him with a fourth challenge, describing an unperformable grand opera by D'Indy that doesn't exist.

Luke knew it didn't. His eyes narrowed as he leaned in, the scent of the kill strong in the room. "No one living can sing those roles," he said, "so I'll cast from the Golden Age." Out came Melba, Ponselle, Nourrit, the de Reszkes—a night, in all, of some twenty stars. I was about to crow, "You left out the Page"—those old grand operas always sport a trouser part for a page—when he said, "I'll have to cut the Page's scene. Even Marietta Alboni couldn't get through that."

Because they were a circle, a set quintet, I gave them nicknames. Guillermo was El Macho Muchacho. Greg was The Boy. Stephen was Eyes—his were green, and a man once told him, "I'd love to take a dip in your eyes." Luke was Il Divo. I could never reckon one for Cliff, but he came up with one for me: The Human Typewriter, because he knew the source material for some of my stories and was amused that I plunked things and people in from anywhere. He said everything I see and hear goes right to the typesetter.

It's time he went, anyway. I've been saving him up, because I'm a little apprehensive of him, of his slashing moral clarity, I guess, or the questioning fervor of his conversation—brunch with Cliff is as exhausting as the Royal Shakespeare *Nicholas Nickleby*. Or perhaps it's just the way he slams out when he doesn't like what he hears.

Cliff was not only good but downright radiant at what he did—flight, friendship, education. He flew planes, befriended gay men, and educated the ones he loved. He was a gay success story, a Washington Stater who came east and made the scene in all its appetite, intellect, style. His thrift-shop special, screw-you attire was a fashion defeating Fashion. His rash wisdom was mission irresistible. The first time he and I talked at length, I told him I didn't like the word "homophobe" because the stem had been incorrectly applied in the word's invention. "Homo," from *homos*, denotes "same." A homophobe hates what he is. Thus, a homophobic lawyer would hate not gays but lawyers.

Cliff and I were sitting, this particular night, on a couch at a party, his thigh pressing mine, his arm around my shoulder. He had this way of . . . what? Militantly relating.

"You will use this word," he told me, "because it's our word. So we defy them, see?"

"Them?" I asked.

"Breeders."

He's the only man I've known who used the word consistently.

"Writers are useful," he said. "Publicizing the lingo, doing it along."

"I don't want to be useful," I said, "except to myself."

Wryly pensive, he replied, "In revolutionary times, everyone contributes. Everyone inside."

"Inside what?"

He smiled, but his eyes were blazing. "Give your hand here, ace," he said.

"Why?"

He took it, clapping it between his two, and he laughed, watching me, as he pulled it around into a stalwart shake.

"I want to be your friend," he said. "Inside the ghetto."

This was 1976, the age of High Attitude, and I had never met anyone who behaved like this. Under the abrasive gambado, Cliff was ruminative, intellectual, a historicist. Others said, first thing, "How are you?" Cliff said, "What have you done this year?"

He would look at you as if reading the caption under your likeness in some chronicle. "One day," he constantly predicted, "they'll write about all this."

He saw *long*. He lived as if inhabiting an era, a locale, an ideology. A little smoother, gentler, he would have been a star; he acted as if a man with energy and dedications shouldn't be handsome, as if perceptions made hot unnecessary.

It was shocking, then, to wander down a hallway at the Everard baths and realize that the Swedish lifeguard who just stalked past you had, three brunches ago, discussed *The Soft Machine, Intolerance,* and antihumanist tendencies on the *New York Times'* editorial page. It was Cliff, of course. His head was so intense that he looked different silent and undressed. He was better than handsome or sexy: he was exciting. I accepted his not saying hello; one didn't observe punctilio in a bathhouse. But then Cliff sidled up behind me, to point out an absorbing hunk often seen in the Eagle but never elsewhere.

"Off his turf," Cliff murmured. "Uncertain, disconnected. What mores obtain here? Is he supposed to have sex? Is he not supposed to have sex?"

Indeed, the Eagle avatar did look confused.

And Cliff, who is simply not afraid of anything, called out, "Hey, buddy!" And he said, "This is where," and the Eagle guy went into Cliff's room and Cliff had him shouting for joy, and a small crowd pulled up to know more about this, and the Eagle guy came out literally staggering, goofy with pleasure. Then Cliff stood in his doorway and said, "Big cock, slow fuck, deep intention." He laughed at the way everyone stared at him. "It's slick," he said, I swear to you.

So he was a star, in the end. But primarily he was a comrade, tending his relationships, heartening his mates with his copious, impatient affections, holding them when they ached and congratulating them when they prospered, lending them money and giving them holiday dinners and musing fondly on their capers. He kept them warm. One flaw: he was not always gentle enough; but he could only be gentle with the wounded. He complimented his friends by treating them like soldiers, barking when they broke formation. "Solidarity," he would urge, even before there was a Poland.

The left-out gay writers who have to publish in porn slicks or local newspapers of occult circulation try to cheer themselves up by hating what they think of as the Pines School of Fiction: all about good-looking men finding themselves, so to say. And yes, I can see why tales of men getting men threaten them, because they don't get anything. (A homophobe hates what he is.) However, the primary theme of my particular Pines fiction has been friendship. Not sex: a kind of eroticized affection. Not cruisers: buddies. Men such as Cliff, Guillermo, Luke, Stephen, and Greg. This is where, I swear to you; and knowing of such men and their sense of fraternity must be even more threatening to the left-outs than a simple Pines travelogue, because good friendship is harder to find than good sex. And you can live without sex, but you can't live without friends.

And this: I've known men who made wonderful lovers but terrible friends. But I never met a wonderful friend who couldn't also be a wonderful lover.

I tell what is.

So it's the last weekend before Labor Day, big dinner promising, and I'm staying at Colin's for a change of company while Dennis Savage enjoys a last chance to entertain some deserving city-bound friends. It's Saturday, and I still can't get the hang of Colin's coffee-brewing machine. Or anyone's. At home, I make it cup by cup, fresh-ground, hand-poured water, the works. On Thursday here, I didn't put enough water in. On Friday I didn't put any coffee in—and Colin, viewing this pot of hot water and intent on soothing anxious guests, observed, "That'll be very handy for tea," which no one in the house drinks. Today I must have pushed the wrong button—everything that Colin owns has eighty buttons, a timer, and a musical attachment that plays, for instance, "Nessun dorma"—because the machine uttered atrocious noises, shuddered, then was still: and *nothing* came out.

Colin appears, sees me glaring at his coffee machine, and says, "You know, I can always get a new machine."

He is what is softly known as "well off." I try to redeem myself by vacuuming the living room for the big dinner tonight, but Colin has to explain how the vacuum works.

"You never used a vacuum before?" he asks, incredulous. Think of the dinner parties I must have given, with more dust than *The Grapes of Wrath*. "Didn't your maid ever cancel on you?"

"What maid?"

He passes over this lurid confession in a soigné

manner, and, to the barking of his malamute and Akita, Luke and Guillermo arrive. (Actually, the Akita, Nijinska, does most of the barking. The malamute, Dame Margot, barks here and there out of formality, but, fed up with Nijinska's commotions, often growls at or even nips the Akita, as if to say, Enough is enough. We call her Miss Manners.) Luke is playful; Guillermo, off sure turf, is wary. Colin is festive and impeccable. Now Stephen breezes up from the beach, signaling more barking from Nijinska and some heavy chiding of Nijinska by Dame Margot.

The gang's almost all here. Ensconced in the living room with notebook and pen, I simply wave at everyone and pass up the usual convening chat by the pool. Anyway, I know (and dislike) what they're talking about: reincarnation. I suppose that belief in an afterlife makes it easier for them to bear a world in which important people are missing. Important to us. This is the last weekend before Labor Day, nearly the end of the summer, but it feels much more final than that, like the end of an age.

Of course, the summer doesn't end all at once for everybody. Colin comes out whenever he wants, because he owns his house, and even some renters take leases that last till Columbus Day. There's always someone left after everyone else has gone. But the essence of a Pines summer—the Rhine music, so to say, if gay life were *Der Ring des Nibelungen*—is the bonding of the crew as a whole, the circles of friends intermingling, corroborating the theory of erotic platonism, even if only by a hello as merry strangers pass on the boardwalk. The summer needs everybody, to claim this place for us, not just porn stars and houseboys but opera impresarios and airline pilots.

Cliff suddenly plops down next to me. He has crept through the house and, tousling my hair, too roughly as always, nods toward the voices down at the pool and says, "The Human Typewriter furtively delineating. Round up the usual suspects."

"Hey, Cliff."

"So many breeders on the walks. Why do they have to go where we are? Why don't we make it uncomfortable for them, like they do for us?"

"Did you hear about Big Steve? He goes out after dark and when he meets straights, he throws them off the walk. Almost all his old boyfriends are ill or dead, and he's so angry he—"

"Good man. Give it to them back."

"I talked him out of it. It's good therapy, but he'll get into police trouble."

Cliff nodded. "Still. Get some action going, maybe, and Big Steve would be prime soldier stuff. That boy must be the biggest thing in New York, huh? I was always a little afraid of him."

"You're not afraid of anything," I told him.

Given pause, he quietly regarded me.

"The Human Typewriter," I went on, "sees and knows." On my fingers, I ticked off the storyteller's four essentials: "Experience, observation, retention, imagination."

He shook his head, half-smiling.

"The day you're afraid of something," I concluded, "will be the end of the world."

He nodded again, his mind speeding through

agendas—emotional, cultural, sociological. "Get some action going," he murmured. "Do some fight, some taking. Even it up." He turned to me, his eyes keen as searchlights. "They talk about boycotts. What if we boycotted the closet? We all know a few sneaks." His term for closet gays. "Across the country, right?, everyone writes letters to parents, bosses, friends. Reveal those suckers. Push them out. What are the breeders going to do, ace, fire twenty million men? Disown twenty million sons? Make them see us, ace. Make them know."

"Pretty heavy artillery."

"What are they waiting for?" he asked. "How can they stand living like that, sneaks? Do they think they're going to be spared the roundups because they're such good liars? What you are is what you see."

"That's just it—what you are is what *they* see. The sneaks will be spared. They *will*. Because it isn't homosexuals the straights hate. It's gays. They don't mind if you have a secret. They don't have to deal with secrets. Secrets aren't there. It's that hammering home of the truth that enrages them, the *exploding* of the secrets."

"So why? Tell me why."

"Apparently their whole civilization stands or falls on the fucking of women."

"Jewcatchers," he says. "That's what the closet creeps are. In Berlin in the 1940s, because some Jews were still hiding out, the Nazis had platoons of Jews temporarily free of the Hitler death camp. Why?"

He points a finger at me, warning, showing, this is the world. A little history for me here.

"This is why: they stroll through Berlin looking for old friends, for non-Aryan faces. And they follow them home and alert the SS. Because the Nazis can't rest as long as a single Jew is still alive. The *hatred*, ace! It's as if nothing matters to them as much as this one thing, this murderous hatred of . . . what? Of *what*? Of people who are very different from them and almost exactly like them. Can you comprehend this hatred? Can you understand a Jewcatcher?"

"We'd be Jewcatchers if we blew the whistle on all the closet gays, wouldn't we?"

"Roy Cohn, ace. There was the king of Jew-catchers. A gay man, listen to me. Yet he helps McCarthy root through the government for gays to hound." Hating what you are. "Aside from count-less other crimes." He closes his eyes. Being Cliff is hard. It's endless. "Ace, the greed of these people. The implacable hunger to destroy what they can't own. The unlimited debauchery of the closet, the breeders' conspiracy of silence, the . . . this Gulag guardhouse of fat-cat ghouls. But he died gay, didn't he, that Cohn bastard?"

He wants me to see the history, comprehend the grid of patterns. In cafés, discos, bars, I would spot this athlete of ideas lecturing to boys who just wanted to party for their lives. Do you see it, you must read, let's consider, get off the drugs, stop dancing. If he couldn't talk you around, he'd reform you with love, and if that didn't work, he'd get mad and beat you up. It worked with everyone but Greg.

"What do you think Roy Cohn will be in the next life?" I ask. I'm joking, but even Cliff has been toy-ing with the possibility that dead souls return. He is not remotely convinced, but some of his friends are, for they need something to believe in besides Cliff— he is somewhat beyond love, beyond touch and sentiment and kidding around. He can be unforgiving, like the Old Testament God; and asks too much of them, like the New One. He mustn't be loved, only feared and admired. Greg once told me that life with Cliff was like being found innocent at a show trial.

Colin comes in to ask about lunch. He fends off Cliff's controversies with a disquisition upon the versatility of the Cuisinart. I don't know what his politics are; but he doesn't like anger in any cause. I got in trouble with him some years ago for blowing up at dinner.

Colin proceeds into the kitchen and Guillermo comes in to change his outfit and make his standard lunch, an arcane preparation of Bumblebee solid white in water. Guillermo changes his clothes every time he does something: there's one kind of Speedos for sunning, another for beach parade, one fashion of tank top for napping, another for tea. Luke and Stephen amble in, and after a moment's hesitation, Guillermo decides to fix his lunch in the running shorts he bought at a boutique in the harbor on the way here.

"I think they will match the blue T," he says, heading upstairs to change.

"When the going gets tough," Luke remarks, "the tough go shopping."

Cliff, encased in thought, is an age away, assembling analytical contributions: Socrates, the Taiping Rebellion, pink triangles.

Now Stephen joins us, completing the set; and

dead Greg comes with him, for their affair was the longest and deepest transaction in this circle, the sexiest of the romances. Stephen sits, listening to Luke and me trade opera quips, then says, "Everything just goes right on."

We turn to him, Cliff with the grip of a hunter at point.

"I mean," Stephen explains, "just because someone dies, that doesn't . . . the whole world doesn't keel over. Nobody stops doing anything. We pick up where we were, same difference. So we go to the funeral and we stay alive."

Luke cleared his throat opera-style, a lengthy, grinding rasp like the windup before the pitch. Some high notes coming up.

"We stay alive," Stephen repeated. "Sure. No matter how many of us die, nothing is going to change. Well, so rip out a few pages in your address book, that's all. So what? And you know what they're saying? They're saying the ones who get sick had the best sex. That's what they're saying."

"Leave it to The Pines," I sigh, "to come up with plague prestige."

"Sex doesn't give you AIDS," said Cliff. "Breeders give you AIDS."

Went the day well? After lunch, Cliff and Stephen returned to their houses, Luke and Guillermo sunned at the pool—Guillermo turning at precisely regular intervals—and Colin and I went to the harbor to assemble the dinner. The guest of honor owns an art gallery in Soho, *the* art gallery in Soho, really;

he also owns Soho. He and Colin are not close friends, not playfellows, confidants, comrades, God forbid buddies of a shared Stonewall mission, the chosen people without a God. We chose ourselves. Yes: so why is Colin going to such trouble over this party? We ransack the grocery, denude the liquor store of choice wine; there will be Tabasco chicken wings in sour-cream–bleu-cheese sauce for cocktails, the thinnest veal cutlet the world has ever seen with tortellini in a prosciutto sauce, plus condiments in fetching little crocks and two astonishing desserts. This is world without end, but what world? This is metropolitan life: only gays would take it along to the beach. Colin and I even sock in a little container of nasturtiums, a flower you can eat. It goes on one of the desserts.

There are a lot of straights about, I notice, as we regroup with our bags at the harbor. Are they going to take The Pines away from us if we don't Big Steve them down? I look at the gays standing there with us, chatting, meeting the ferry, heading for the grocery. A lot of muscle there; but what do they do when some mainland straight kid mutters "faggot" as he passes? What's muscle for?

Who was it who said, "Extremism in defense of liberty is no vice"? Oscar Wilde? Eric Blore? Richard Locke?

Another dream: I am lying wounded in the middle of Third Avenue, and a troop of straight doctors, thin-lipped and as savorless as dishwater, line up to cut me open and rip out my vital organs. As I scream for help, they brandish their accessories— scalpels, clamps, catheters, bedpans. The first one kneels. It is George Will. Following a drawing in a textbook, he drags an electric can opener down my torso from neck to waist.

The house is silent when we return, but for momentary elation from the dogs. Luke and Guillermo are off visiting.

"I don't know why I'm doing this," says Colin as we unload, referring to if not answering the question I myself have raised. "Every time I give a dinner, somebody loses his temper." He describes the last three parties, all superbly planned fiestas and all, in the end, drunken brawls. The trouble with Pines dinners is, they start so damn late. What do you expect at a ten o'clock starting time but maniacs and bums, pugnacious on booze and frantic with hunger?

We unload. Colin starts cooking and I walk the dogs along the beach, the Akita straining on her leash to attack every dog we see. The wind has come up and almost everybody has gone inside. I run the dogs along the water's edge. I worry. A lot of that lately. At the access to Colin's beach walkway— PRIVATE, DO NOT ENTER—I turn and survey the view. I have seen amazing things here over the years; I am postulant, celebrant, town scribe. I told what was. If Stonewall were a sentence, this summer is punctuation. Comma, semicolon, period? Maybe it is world *with* end.

Amazing things. You mean, the poignantly restitutive sight of a talismanic hunk with heebie-jeebie tits and junk of death tersely encountering an elegiacal youth of bracing attributes? No, I mean a flea circus. *Yes*, I mean: of course, I mean. But I've been trying to tell you about something else in story after story; is it taking? I've been trying to tell you that a man-to-man system that doesn't fear sex creates the ultimate in man-to-man friendships. This is what I mean by penetration.

No, *this* is what I mean:

About ten years ago, I took a share in a muscle house, as The Pines terms it: seven tremendous men, a fair passel of free weights, and me. My lease gave me weekdays only, so I seldom saw anyone until August, when everybody started taking vacations. Used to treating me as a sort of flesh-and-blood nonperson, like Oakland without a *there* there, two of my housemates came back from the beach assuming they had the house to themselves. In fact, I had been there all day, away when they were around and vice versa, and now I was in the bathroom shaving while they were in their bedroom changing clothes, with nothing to separate us but what the construction business calls a party wall. Thus I overheard—virtually was drawn into—the end of a long conversation between two men who, it appeared, had had a lot of sex but little personal contact. Not lovers, fuckers. But listen, as I did, to how easily sex slides into friendship.

(I wonder if the heightened sense of comraderie that suffuses The Pines derives from the pervasive lack of privacy. No, that's absurd.)

The two boyfriends in the bedroom were not, from the sound of them, equals on any level. One was older, tougher, smarter; the other, one of those young, know-nothing charmers that the gay world can't seem to get enough of. The youngster was speaking of the family farm in Iowa that he might return to. He said the city was "a hard place," that he didn't know what he was doing "here."

The older man told the boy what indeed he was doing, why *here* existed in the first place, and I heard what amounted to a commentary on, a crusade for, and the national anthem of gay life all at once. Standing at the sink, razor in hand, half here and half there, I stared at the mirror as the man went on with his exhortation. He said he would help the boy with his rent, help him get a job, help him. *Help him*, the italics are mine. And the boy said, "Why would you do that for me?" And the man said, "What do you think I've been stuffing your ass for? For the fun of it? What do you think we've been doing?"

"I . . . I don't know what there is," the boy replied. "I guess I didn't hear the choices."

There was a long pause, then the man said, "It's because I like you. That's what the choice is."

Another pause; and I heard the pair of them head downstairs. A bit later I came out, too, and found them in the kitchen making salami-and-cheese sandwiches. They were much as I had pictured them, the boy clean-cut trash with a delicate mouth and the man a Viking with self-reproaching eyes. They smiled at me, and the boy said, "I'm Greg and this is . . . this is my friend, Cliff."

Watching Colin prepare the dinner, I wondered why someone—Colin, I, anyone—would go to this trouble just because somebody owned the hottest gallery in Vanity Fair. Well, who knows what else

we have in our here, what inducements and loy-
alties a Cliff would find hard to respect?

I kept us supplied with Finlandia on the rocks, savored with cuttings from the special lemon-lime
hybrids Colin has flown in from northern California,
whence he derives. Lifestyles of the rich and famous. Step by step, the menu comes alive, the hour
grows apace, the Finlandia flows . . . and by dinnertime I'm a bit hazy on data. Even a Human Typewriter occasionally jams.

I do remember the arrival of the art gallery owner,
an enraged schmuck with a suave facade, sweeping
in with entourage of aged-queen sidekick and pleasant young boyfriend. The two older men were already so wet they could have been served in glasses.

I remember Luke and Guillermo walking in
straight from tea, Cliff and Stephen following a minute later.

I remember the art gallery guy putting down
everything within reach, including Guillermo—
something about "Well, if you like meat on the
hoof"—and his hand waving, waving.

I remember going into the kitchen and telling Stephen, "These people are dreadful."

I think I remember Cliff looking more pensive
than usual, as if he were in caucus with the
querulous presences of history, propelling him on to
sanctions, rebuttals, orations. Anything, Cliff, but
compromise. I remember tensions rising during
cocktails; I remember the sour-cream–bleu-cheese
sauce. And I remember the art gallery guy, at the
dinner table, going into a eulogy of Roy Cohn, how

misunderstood he was, how fair and smart and delightful.

I was in the kitchen. I glanced at Colin, obliviously ladling out tortellini. I heard a skirmish, gasps, a clatter. Looking around the corner into the dining room, I saw Cliff strangling the art gallery guy.

Strangling him.

I don't remember what everyone else was doing, name by name. I expect some were clearly upset, some went on with what they were doing, and a very few sought to do something about it—as with AIDS, as we do, as we all, as it is. I believe Stephen got to Cliff and smoothed him off: held him and talked to him and made him stop. Cliffed him, you might say. How many times Cliff had got his friends out of trouble like that. There was a lot of yelling then, and Colin materialized, looking stunned with a platter of the most incredibly thin-sliced veal cutlets, and a certain amount of walking out and door slamming followed. The dogs picked up on the tension, and when I tried to calm the Akita she bucked her head and snapped at me, sending me reeling. Stephen said, "You're bleeding," and I went down to the bathroom to find a cut near my eye.

I'm hazy on the details thereafter. I recall staying up to listen to CDs of *Die Frau Ohne Schatten* with Stephen and the art gallery guy's boyfriend. Everyone else had left or gone to bed.

I do remember saying, "We never served the nasturtiums," as I saw Stephen and the boyfriend to the door; then I bundled up to taste some night air before I hit the hay.

The wind was rolling furiously in, great black waves beating the beach, the clouds so rocky they thudded. I was cold in a sweater and sweatshirt; it might have been winter. I was shaking, and I kept thinking, At least it wasn't me.

I sat down at the edge of Colin's steps and waited for The Midnight Rambler, a stranger who, on weekends, uses Colin's walk instead of the public right-of-way, blithely strolling along the decking, sometimes closing an open door, latching the front gate behind him, and marching off into The Pines, somehow never arousing the dogs.

Maybe he'll try it tonight. It's so dark he won't see me, and if he's straight, I, like Big Steve, will toss him off the deck. This is private property. This is Inside.

Now Nijinska barks, and someone does come along, but behind me, from Inside: Cliff. He sits and puts an arm around my shoulder. He grips me, he Cliffs.

"How's your eye?" he asks.

"Okay. I can feel a bump there."

He samples it.

"You're going to have a black eye," he says. "We'll do some ice on it."

"I don't want to do ice on it."

His mustache tickles my ear: "What are you going to tell people when they ask where you got that bruise? 'An Akita punched my lights out'?"

He shoves me a little because I won't laugh.

"Who're you mad at, ace?" he asks.

"Not you."

"Take it easy," he says, "and you'll live longer.
Came back to apologize to Colin, and the whole
house is dead here." Then he says, "Listen to the
wind. When I was a kid, I thought wind was the
voice of God. So many nights sitting like this, or on
the deck of someone's bedroom, huh? I'd listen for
the messages. Accusations. Warnings. Best wishes
on a memorable occasion. I don't understand the
right language, though, sure. Back when All This
got started, I would listen really careful, because I
thought . . . well, there ought to be some interpreta-
tion in it, you know? *Purport*. Maybe no purport a
gay man wanted to hear. Nothing we'd like, right?
But something to know. Something that I could hear
most clear here in this place. Something in the wind
out there, ace."

"Go on," I said, for he had stopped.

He patted my head. "I will," he replied. But he
was silent.

We listened to the wind.

"I will," he repeated.

I don't understand the right language, either.

"It was bad enough at first," he finally went on,
"because it was so obvious that there was a plague
on and no one was doing anything about it. And
there we are trying to figure out what the victims
have in common, to know who's going to get it next.
It's from drugs, it's poppers, it's from rimming, it's
in the quiche, it's attitude. Maybe it's in the wind.
Then it's got half the guys you know, so how come
you're healthy?"

He found a rock in the sand below the walk and
pitched it into the black night.

"Neat scheme, wasn't it?" he said. "Infect a few faggots and let their baths and bars and beds do the rest. Excellent mischief, huh? By the time they realize what's happening, they'll all be poisoned, the whole degenerate Stonewall gang of them. Then we pull out the deterrent vaccine and say, 'Oh, look what we just found. Too bad about the queers, but now those perverts are going to be buried up good and tight, sir, yes *sir*! Won't be no Stonewall trouble around here again, sir, no *sir*!'"

Another rock flies in the dark, this one all the way to the water.

"I used to think it was who's going to get it and who isn't," he told me. "Now I think it's who dies first and who dies later."

Just like the *Ring*: everyone is dispensed with. "Good weather," I said, "for *Götterdämmerung*."

He pulled the hood of my sweatshirt over my head, surveyed me, nodded. He likes it when his friends turn into little kids who need soothing. Greg was more a kid at thirty than most ten-year-olds are.

"What should we do?" he said. "We ought to leave something behind. We were going to change the world and all we're doing is leaving it."

"Why don't you write down how you feel?" I asked.

"That's your cure for everything, isn't it? Getting published?"

"If we all write about what we did, and how we felt, who we were . . . we *will* leave something behind. They can't kill books. Even the Nazis couldn't."

"Can a book change the world?" he asked. "Change a guy's life, now?"

I threw a rock at the wind, me.

"What changes lives?" he asked. "I tried to change Greg, you know. Listen to this—I was going to make him a better man. Get him off the stuff, make him believe he had things he could do."

I pulled the hood off my head.

"Do you ever change a life?" he wondered, putting up my hood again.

Two rocks, one each.

"Do you remember," he asks, "that beautiful black muscleboy that Carson Jennings brought here? Way back in . . . must have been 1975 or nearly so. Just picked him up off the street and out he comes here. What was his name, remember? Very sweet man, never opened his mouth. Incredible bod, real big stuff. If you went over there when Carson was in the city, that boy would come over to you and just start making love. He'd be cleaning the pool or something, and he'd see you and smile and just give it to you. Never said a word the whole time. Very thoughtful, any way you liked it."

"His name," I said, "was Roy Deevers."

"He remembers! Good man."

"The reason he never spoke was, when he did, everyone laughed at him."

"How would you know this?"

"He told me. Can I take my hood down?"

"No. So the boy was doing a happy summer on the beach, and sooner or later Carson would close up the house and dump him back on Forty-second Street or wherever he came from. This is changing a life, watch. Because there are halfway houses, right? Community setups? There's placement, sociology, education, all this. Easy to do if you're connected. That's how it works, being connected. Too bad I'm connected with just what I need, but it's in San Francisco. Friend of mine runs a halfway house there. Ran it, I mean." He pauses. "And he changed plenty of lives, I know that. So all we need is the money to get this boy out to San."

"And you can't get it from Carson, because he doesn't want you interfering with his summer-houseboy routine."

"Stet." Let it stand, meaning That's correct. Publishing term.

"I taught you that," I said.

"Everyone teaches and everyone learns. That's friendship, ace."

The Pines-hating leftouts must be screaming by now, because the thing they can't abide is to hear that the love they couldn't get in touch with actually exists.

Scream, you fuckers.

"Changing a life," Cliff went on. "Everyone chipped in five bucks and I got the black kid on a flight as a standby and I took him to my friend's place and I told him to stop screwing everyone he met."

Rocks. Wind. Death by catastrophe as the world looks on.

"How'd he do?" I asked.

"Terrific. I changed a life. He got on to painting apartments. Union and everything. He lived out good."

"Stet."

"Did you ever go over there? To Carson's? For a date with that kid?"

"No. Just dinner."

"Why not?"

"Because that parade of horny Carsonians was racist and exploitative."

"What are you, ace, a saint?"

"In some ways."

"That boy was filled with love. Sharing it with everyone was his way of communicating."

"Cliff, my ace, you are dead wrong. He wasn't sharing love—he was putting out because he thought he had to if he wanted to stay in paradise."

Cliff threw a rock. "Anyway," he said, "I changed his life, right?"

"You changed a lot of lives," I said. "Anyone else, I'd bet, was fishing for this. But you're so busy taking care of everybody you probably never noticed how much care you took. And nobody knows you. They don't know you at all, because there's so much of you. In the baths, they thought you were some hotshot top. At the Firehouse, you were the Great American Organizer. In San Francisco, you're a chance not to loathe New York. At the airline, you're straight. With Stephen and Luke and Guillermo and Greg . . . you're the reason the center holds. Held."

Lighten up, boy.

"At brunches, you're a matinee idol, a little on the robust side, perhaps. But at dinner tonight . . ."

I stopped, out of breath. Jesus, that man is handsome.

"At dinner you were a hero," I went on. "I admire what you did. I've always admired you. When I first came to New York, I was afraid that all the gays were going to be like the ones in *The Boys in the*

Band, full of self-hatred and cultivating phobias. You know what I saw instead?"

He is smiling. "What, chief?"

"You. And the people you knew. They came in every kind going—queens and clones and up-towners and villagers." I wrote in the air: "The ambitious and the slack"; he grabbed my hand and held it for a while. Stop writing, Human Typewriter.

"Okay," he says.

Okay. "That was a whole world," I went on, sensing some distraction in him, something on his mind that he means to hide. My observation chills me, for even here in the darkness his sorrow glows, rigid, unsharable, uncharacteristically not okay. My retention will hold the visual, my imagination fear the worst. That may be one of my problems. Take it easy and you'll live longer.

"A whole world," he says. "I am thinking of that world, ace."

"Your friends all took their sexuality for granted, is the thing," I tell him. "It wasn't a cross to be borne, but their gift. They were great examples for someone like me."

"Where are all the self-hating gays now?" he wonders.

"They're writing book reviews."

"Bet you Colin doesn't admire what I did."

"Colin has a different take on everything," I told him. "He's of the great world. We're ghetto boys. Inside."

"Inside."

"Nobody knows you."

"Right you are, ace." He patted my head, his sorrow a flame. It lit up the beach. I took his hand, and he looked away, toward the Grove—which is also toward Washington State, where Cliff, incredibly, was once a kid who needed help himself, band-aids and love and a paper route—and he asked me, "How come I never scored you, chief?"

"You mean," I said, "how come I never scored you. Because I wasn't good enough. You only go with the best."

Now there was a great space of nothing, and finally he nodded. "Maybe just as well, my good friend," he said. "Because I've got it too, now, and who knows if I wouldn't have given it to you?"

He gently pulled my hood back and put his hands on my shoulders. "I haven't told anyone yet, because . . . I don't know why. Because nobody knows me, maybe. They need me to keep them tough. Stephen was fit for the white coats the night we heard about Greg, you know. He kept asking me why I wasn't there to stop him before . . . stop him in time. Got me so mad I belted him. That's all I do now, get mad. I've had pneumonia already, and now I've got KS. I'm not ready to tell them. I don't want anyone to forget me. I don't want the world to go on as if I hadn't been here."

"Cliff," I began, but he clamped his hand over my mouth.

"Don't sympathize, ace." He shook his head. "Don't be kind to me, don't. Better not test me. This would be the wrong time."

Listen, the wind.

"I thought we were going to achieve a new evolutionary state," he said. "If this was a heart attack or

a car jumped me, I could take it, right? Sure. Because everyone else would be left to remember me.
But if we all go, who's going to be there to know we
were here?"

"I'll be there," said a man standing before us, an
outline in the ink. "I promise I'll remember."

"Who goes there?" I said.

"Do you two live here?" he asked, approaching.
"I've been wondering who does."

The Midnight Rambler!

"My friend Colin lives here," I said, "and he's
very annoyed with you. Why do you use his house
for access?"

"I have dinner with my ex-lover and his wife in
the Grove every Saturday night. How else can I get
home?"

The stranger was close enough now to glimpse.
Thirty-five or so, a woozy preppy with a southern
accent.

"Aren't you Cliff Dickenson?" he said.

"Yeah. How would you know that?"

"Everyone knows you."

Cliff shook his head. "Nobody knows me."

Staggering a bit, the stranger very gently touched
Cliff's face. "If you're Cliff Dickenson," he said,
"how on earth can you be crying?"

"Because I'm going to die."

We were still sitting on the walk, looking up at the
stranger like boarding school truants being chastised
by an indulgent junior master, and he said, "There
was one night in the Eagle. You were standing with
an unbelievably beautiful man. Laughing. And then
you were quiet. Just looking at him. And he opened

up the buttons of your shirt, very slowly. One button after another, right there in the bar. He ran his hand down your chest. And I thought if I could know you, I would give ten years of my life. Just to be your friend."

Cliff whispered, *"Is that what I'm going to be remembered for?"*

The wind tore at us and the ocean thundered. It was like the moment just before a hailstorm, when the sky blots out black and God hates you. It was like earthquake fever, when animals craze and the earth, not yet shuddering, is furtively lurking, ready, avid.

Cliff began to sob, and it was like the end of the world.

The Tale of the Changeling

ᴸATE OCTOBER NOW, ON the mild side, a drizzly Tuesday. I had to come up with a costume and was rummaging through my closets for something picturesque yet flattering when Dennis Savage came down for a grouch session. He was on sabbatical this term of the school year, so he was around all day; but so was Cosgrove, it seems. Thus the grouching.

I had been wrong about Cosgrove and Carlo. That was not love: that was Carlo's soft heart accommodating Cosgrove's need. Technically the kid was still living in Carlo's apartment, but Dennis Savage's place remained Cosgrove's headquarters, just as before.

"I hate to tell you," Dennis Savage let slip, "but I don't even like him. Call me a scandal, do your worst, I don't care. You think he's a cute little number, right? Well, he's a little fiend. A tyke thug."

"He was a little honeystuff, if I recall it correctly,

when you were trying to park him on me a short
while ago at your Pines bride-finding ball."

He takes a deep breath and nods. "Oh, yes. Yes,
you're quite right. I was totally wrong about him.
But it took a while for me to absorb the depth of
menace in that kid. To see through his disguise. He
looks like a homeless orphan, but in fact . . ."

I was trying to assemble the parts of my old Boy
Scout regalia. I had the shirt, the shorts, and the
neckerchief; I couldn't find the doodad that goes on
the kerchief. What do they call those things?

"What are you doing?" Dennis Savage asks.
"Planning to disrupt another Jamboree?"

"I'm trying to decide on a getup for this Halloween weekend thing in Woodstock. Saturday
night is a costume party."

"First, that's not a costume, that's a uniform, and
second, you couldn't get into that today with a six-
foot shoehorn."

"If you're so smart, why aren't you rich?"

"Why don't you go as a corpse? A real one?"

"Boy, Cosgrove really brings out your sweet
side."

"He fucks from the bottom up."

I looked over at him from my hunt for the thing
that holds the kerchief straight.

"Yes, I thought that would get you. A new story,
right? Yes, he's a born catcher—but even so it's as if
he were in charge. In his sad, scared little way he's
always looking for an angle. A hook. So no wonder
he tired of Carlo—there's nothing to hook on to, is
there? But, oh, here's a nice den of bachelors or
whatever you call us, and some of them are lovers

and some of them are friends, and let's just see, shall we? What can we get out of them? Everyone's going to feel sorry for me, right? Poor little me, never hurt a thing, secretly vicious and crazed, but they won't figure that out for months and months . . . oh, *now* what?"

"Well, I've got a few cowboy shirts, the string tie and the hat and the boots. With a pair of jeans I could—"

"That's Village prowling attire, not a Halloween costume."

"Straights think it's a costume. Remember, this is a publishing party—mixed grill. They're not too up on Village prowling attire. Anyway, I can't find the Boy Scout tie thing, so I'll go as a cowboy, *force majeure*. What are you going to do about Cosgrove?"

"I'm going to throw him out of my house."

I looked at him.

"Let him do it to Carlo. Not to me. No more of this from him."

"Do you think Virgil is going to stand by and let you toss that kid into the streets?"

"I'm not tossing him into anything, because he isn't my responsibility to begin with. His parents are the ones who did the tossing—though, for all we know, they're roaming the town right now with lantern and bloodhounds crying for their lost boy. And ho, do my ears delude me or did I hear you call somebody Virgil? *Virgil?*"

I was looking for my boots in the coat closet. "You may as well face it," I told him. "He's not your private little nonesuch anymore. He's not a little anything. He's twenty-eight and he wants a job and he's got his own little something in tow. He may have more whimsy and frolic in him than all of E. F. Benson put together, but he has other things, too. And you can't stifle them. You're going to have to let him be what he is."

"Or else what?"

"Or else your relationship is going to become very troubled." I found the boots and took them to the bed. "He came down here a few days ago and asked if he and I could have, as he said, 'a man-to-man talk.' The gist of it was that he wants me to call him by his real name from now on, and would I please help him to convince you to do the same?"

"*Never*," he seethed.

"Maybe you should try for a compromise," I suggested, trying on the cowboy drag. "He'll let you call him Little Kiwi and you'll let Cosgrove stay."

"You still don't realize what I'm up against, do you? Cosgrove is not the innocent victim he pretends to be. He's the Eve Harrington of Fifty-third Street. Besides, no one who is truly innocent is that expert in bed at the age of eighteen."

"How good can he be?"

"He's not good, exactly. He's *hungry*. It's like making love to a black hole. Debauchery is his . . . his language. The medical problems alone are bound to be overwhelming, somewhere in the near future. I mean—imagine what he was doing before he met us. Imagine with *whom*. And the emotional problems are intolerable. He's a *bad influence*, like some . . . some kid from across the tracks in a fifties movie. A rotten apple. He's corrupting Little Kiwi."

"Oh—"

"I'm telling you! You should see the two of them, singing that idiotic song, like . . . like demons plotting a raid."

"You mean 'The Ballad of Fauntleroy'? It's just a—"

"They sing it deliberately to annoy me. Whenever I leave the room, they drop whatever they're doing and start in, verse after verse of that unseemly nonsense. Grinning at each other and . . . dancing . . ."

"*What?*"

He nodded. "They dance to it. It's like a Black Mass or something. And when they get to the choruses, they put their heads together and lean forward to make their voices go down to bass. It's *indescribably* repulsive."

"Maybe it's a new form of safe sex."

"That shirt's a little tight on you," he gloated. "Cowboy Bud's been hitting the chuck wagon a little heavy."

"It'll pass."

"You should hear the new lyrics they've been putting in. 'Fauntleroy, he was home all day,'" he quoted, "'laid a kid, then he let him lay.' What the hell is that supposed to be? What . . . what could be running through their minds when they sing that? And why do they have to put their heads together and drop their voices? It's so—yes, *you* think it's funny, thanks a lot! You don't have to live with it. Why can't I just have a lover? Why do I have to have a lover who is also a performer?"

"All gays are performers. But is it possible that this tirade is a mere projection of guilt?"

"What guilt?"

"Yours," I said, tugging on a boot, "for taking a taste of Cosgrove. His being around so much magnifies your sense of self-reproach, no? Hem-hem, my dear. George Cukor said that Clark Gable had him fired from *Gone With the Wind* because Cukor recalled Gable from his first days in Hollywood, hustling the gay Circuit for money and notice. Now you want to fire Cosgrove for nearly the same reason. It's understandable, but is it fair?" I rose. "What do you think?"

"Oh, look, it's John Wesley Mordden," he said, somewhat unenthusiastically. "Head for the hills, the savage is loose."

"Well, I've got my costume set, anyway. I'll go back with you and show off to the two buckaroos upstairs."

"That'll make their week."

"Are you going to spend your whole vacation like this? Maybe you should go away somewhere. You haven't traveled for fun since—"

"I'll tell you where I'd like to go: back in time."

We walked the two flights, and even before we reached the hallway we could hear a chorus section of "The Ballad of Fauntleroy" through Dennis Savage's door:

> Fauntleroy,
> Home all day,
> Laid a kid
> Then he let him lay.

Imagining the two boys head to head in the center of the living room, ooching down to deepen their voices, perhaps dancing a bit as well, I tried to look nonchalant. But Dennis Savage's jaw was set as he pulled out his keys.

Even before he had clicked the metal home, the singing cut off, and when we got inside, the two were across the room from each other, sitting and reading. Virgil, bless his heart, held *The World According to Garp.* Cosgrove was deep in the *New York Times.*

"Little Kiwi, I told you to lose that disgusting song."

The couple stared at each other.

"What song?" asked Cosgrove, the third man, with an edge.

"Cosgrove," said Dennis Savage, "go home."

"This is his home," said Virgil.

"This is my home," Dennis Savage snapped back. "Cosgrove, out. Go back to Carlo."

Cosgrove shot an imploring look at Virgil.

"I had some good news to tell you," said Virgil, putting down his book. "I thought you could be in a good mood. The magazine called and they said the guy they hired didn't work out and I could have it instead."

"Have what?" Dennis Savage asked; but his features jiggled a bit and I saw that he already knew.

"The job, remember? That I had that interview in the summer for? They said I can start right after Thanksgiving."

"I'm going to get a job, too," Cosgrove vowed.

"Are you still here?" Dennis Savage cried, wheeling on him.

"Please don't be mad at me," Cosgrove pleaded,

getting up. "I am always trying to be nice. Please let me be nice."

"Don't pull that stuff on me!"

"It isn't stuff!" Little Kiwi cried. "It's Cosgrove!"

"Little Kiwi—"

"And stop calling me that! My name is Virgil Brown!"

Cosgrove got behind Virgil, watching Dennis Savage as if ready to dodge a flying chair.

"Why don't I take Cosgrove down to Carlo's?" I said. "I haven't been out yet today, anyway. We can settle this later."

"*Now*," said Dennis Savage, his eyes boiling.

"I'm going with Cosgrove," Virgil said.

"The hell you are!"

"I won't stay with you if you treat me like this," Virgil told him. "I can go to Carlo's, too."

"Virgil," I put in, "you'd best remain here and straighten it out about your job. Congratulations; and you two have a lot to talk about." I asked Dennis Savage, "Okay?"

"Who the fuck are you to call him Virgil?"

Cosgrove ran for the door, hauled it open, and fled.

"Cosgrove!" Virgil shouted, and began to follow, but Dennis Savage grabbed him by the arm and threw him back on the couch.

"You go fix it up with that little monster," Dennis Savage told me. "I'll handle this one."

"You're the monster," Virgil told him.

As I wasn't moving, Dennis Savage turned to me. "Please," he said.

Fourth man. Carlo, no doubt, completes the

quintet. He's the oldest of us all, did you know that? "Just as long as you're always trying to be nice," I warned Dennis Savage as I left.

Cosgrove, in the hall, was frantically pushing the elevator button. When he saw me, he cried, "Don't do anything else to me, you can see I'm going now!"

"Just take it easy. No one's after you."

We rode down in silence, Cosgrove glaring at me, till the fifth floor, when one of my neighbors joined us.

"Can't the Tenants' Committee do anything about that street trash that's always hanging around?" she asked me. "You never see a policeman anymore."

"We're meeting with the precinct captain next week," I told her.

"Everyone's mean to me," Cosgrove put in.

She glanced at him; then, back to business: "You have those meetings every year and it doesn't do a bit of good. Pushers, dopers, vagrants, and faggots, they must think they own the—"

"Cosgrove!"

No sooner had the door opened than he pushed past us and ran for the street. I caught up with him a few doors east, but he pulled away from me and kept running—and not in the direction of Carlo's. Hunched under the umbrella line, weaving furiously through the heavy weekday afternoon pedestrian traffic, he lost me in no time. I hadn't realized how upset he was. I had also forgot that my costume made me look a little, uh, sightly in the middle of midtown. To the grins of passersby I went back upstairs.

Frost greeted me at Dennis Savage's; these two were calm but unmollified.

"Where's Cosgrove?" Virgil asked.

"He didn't want any company," I said. True enough, however evasive.

"I apologized," Dennis Savage told me, in the tone you'd use for "I confessed under torture by sadistic Mongolian devil midgets."

"Not to me, yet."

"You're both monsters," said Virgil.

"I told him we can go on a trip," Dennis Savage explained.

"But he won't take Cosgrove."

"A new idea," said Dennis Savage. "That's what you have to have every so often. You need a sudden shift of tactic, right?"

Virgil shrugged. "I don't care."

"We're losing something here," Dennis Savage went on. "We're getting confused. Where's our list of goals, you know, to write down and shoot for, like on those long yellow pads?"

"When do I get apologized to?" I asked.

"Oh, please. Once you lead a sit-down strike at the Valley Forge Boy Scout Jamboree with someone, you're brothers for life. You never have to apologize to him no matter what you do."

"Do you by any chance remember what they call those things we put on our kerchiefs, to hold them in place?"

"At this point, I don't even remember what they call Valley Forge."

"I don't want just any old trip," Virgil grumbled.

"How about coming with me to London?" I asked.

Gasps, thrills, fears, and silence.

"Well, why not? My trip's all set and the timing is perfect—mid-November. You won't have any trouble slithering in on my dates at this time of year, and we'll be back just before Thanksgiving, so Virgil can start his job right on schedule."

The two of them treated each other to bellicose looks but said nothing.

"It's a bargain with the hotel tie-in," I went on. "And just think, Virgil's never been to Europe. It's a new idea."

"I want to see the Colossus of Rhodes," said Virgil.

"*Finito.* But you can see Westminster Abbey, Big Ben's tower, and St. Paul's."

"What are they like?" asked Virgil, weakening.

"Fabulous."

"I'm willing," said Dennis Savage. "Anything to escape this glut of arguments."

"Can we really just *go* to London?" Virgil asked. "Like that?"

"Why not?"

"One of us needs a passport," said Dennis Savage.

"This time of year, it'll come in a week. You can apply right at the post office. A mere block away."

"London!" Virgil marveled. "A mere block away! Do you have a map of London?"

"I've several."

"Can I see one? Right now?"

"Sure as Bob's your uncle."

As we left, Dennis Savage appeared to be tidying up in a desultory manner, but he wore the face of a man new-made. I paused at the door and caught his eye; he said nothing, but his face read "I apologize."

True, the Question of Cosgrove was as yet unsettled. The boy did not go back to Carlo's—nor, especially, Dennis Savage's—but he stayed in contact with Virgil. Dennis Savage told me the phone sometimes went dead when he answered its ring; this was almost certainly Cosgrove fishing for Virgil. Dennis Savage also suspected that Virgil was sneaking meetings with Cosgrove and giving him money out of his allowance. Most unpleasant was the realization that I had exacerbated the trouble by letting Cosgrove slip away from me. Virgil must have thought me the blackest of scoundrels. But the subject was so tense as it was that nobody wanted to bring it up again, and we all kept our counsel.

Friday night before Halloween I packed up and went upstairs for a bit of visit before going down to wait for my ride to the publishing-world weekend party in Woodstock. Carlo was there, in a thoughtful mood, darkening what was, as so often those days, a gloomy place. Even Bauhaus, snarling to himself in a corner, seemed peckish, his growls perfunctory and his eyes half-closed.

"Next thing," I told them, "you should pull down the blinds and cover the mirrors and stalk around with veils over your faces like the women in *Vanessa*."

"There's romance blues in this house," said Carlo. "It happens when love loses its mystery."

"How would you know?" Dennis Savage asked

him, almost piteously. "All you've ever had are flings."

Virgil was looking at me, rather militantly for him. "See what everyone is like now, because a certain person went away?"

"Listen, guys," I said, "we all better air our feelings and find some solutions, or we won't be happy again. I've never seen you like this. Like a bunch of sulky children."

"And the dinner," Carlo observed, "was very mediocre. BLTs and potato chips."

"Sandwich platter," I replied, "in The House of Mary Gourmet? Then is there truly trouble in paradise!"

"You're not supposed to make Mary jokes during Stonewall," Virgil told me.

So Carlo winked and said, "Virgil's getting into New Age."

Dennis Savage, who bristled, glowered, or passed a sarcastic noise at every mention of this name, muttered something about not having been raised to be a short-order cook.

Then there was silence.

I cleared my throat. "Okay, gang," I began. "I'm going to start it off and Carlo can be referee and you two just better get this Cosgrove thing wired down so we can all go back to being glad about each other and supportive and so on. Now—"

"How about if you let Cosgrove be your houseboy?" said Carlo. "Then he can be real close to the kid himself here and we wouldn't have to worry about where he is."

"That's a *wonderful* idea!" said Virgil.

◆ 247 ◆

"That's a quite terrible idea, actually," I said, "be-cause—"

"See, I tried to take him in," Carlo went on, "but he truly didn't like it around my place."

"—goes against the sacred beauty of the libertar-ian bachelor plane of existence, besides which—"

"It's feasible," said Dennis Savage.

"I think Cosgrove would forgive you," Virgil told him, "if you let him visit anytime."

"—would really throw my work routine out of—"

"Does anyone know where he is now?" Carlo asked.

"I have a theory that some of us do," said Dennis Savage, eyeing Virgil.

"—not to mention, of course, that I am allergic to being in rooms with people in them for more than an hour or two, three at most, and—"

"Well, *someone* had to make sure that nothing hap-pened to him," said Virgil, facing Dennis Savage down. "He only just turned eighteen and he's very sensitive."

"Oh, he's legal now?" said Carlo. "That's out-standing."

"—couldn't possibly agree to any arrangement that would so to say encircle my—"

"Oh, please shut up," Dennis Savage told me. "It's the only way out for everyone."

"We're trying to be nice," Virgil told me.

"I'm afraid to be nice," I concluded. "And anyway I have to go downstairs and wait for my ride."

"La, the merry dance of New York," said Dennis Savage.

"This is much better," observed Virgil as I went

for my bag. "I don't like it when everyone's mad and Cosgrove is in distress."

"You were worried about that Cosgrove, huh?" said Carlo.

"It's a dirty job," muttered Dennis Savage, "but someone's got to do it."

"I call it a good thing," said Carlo, "to see someone worried about his pal. Come here, Virgil." They were sitting next to each other on the couch; he meant, Come closer to me so I can hold you. Resting contentedly in Carlo's arms, Virgil said, "I just want to make sure he's all right."

"Yeah, I know that," Carlo replied. "You have a real good heart deep in there, and you know what? That's why everybody loves you."

"But how come nobody loves my Cosgrove? He has a good heart, too."

"Well, yeah," Carlo drawled out. "Yeah, okay. But that Cosgrove . . . well, he's run into a spell of bad luck, I guess."

A shadow crossed Virgil's face then, because he knew that Cosgrove was pledged to sorrow far more deeply than this. "I just . . ." Virgil began, and gulped, and was quiet, and Carlo shook his head and held him tightly and said, "You truly goddamn very sweet little kid."

I was at the door, staring, and Dennis Savage said, not unkindly, "So go."

Something fancy happened downstairs as well. It was warm for the end of October, and a great many people were out, rushing and strolling and lurking,

including the usual complement of midevening hustlers, though the plague and its concomitant closing
of most of the local buy-a-kid bars had thinned the
ranks to a large degree. Glancing down the block to
the east, I saw Cosgrove in front of the antique armor boutique.

He was looking at me.

Just then an atrocious fat geezer came up to him
and started talking. Cosgrove made some brief reply, refusing to look at the man, but the stranger
went on with what was obviously a john's sweet-
talk spiel.

Cosgrove shook his head.

The man went on, unperturbed, smooth, rehearsed by experience, and Cosgrove moved away a
few paces, toward me.

The man hesitated, started back to Second Avenue, paused, looked around, and followed Cosgrove.

Again Cosgrove bore the man's come-on in irri-
tated silence, then said something sharply and
moved away again. By now he was almost up to the
garage of my building, about thirty feet from me.

Still the man pursued him.

So I picked up my bag and went over to them. I
told Cosgrove, "Pack it up, 'cause you're all covered
for tonight. Deep-pocket appointment in Yorkville.
Real pretty gig." I don't know the lingo, but I can
invent.

"I was just telling this fine young lad," the man
told me, with oily geniality and a shabby smile,
"about my place on Park Avenue."

I gave him a B-movie once-over and said, "Beat it,
scum."

Luckily, he did.

I put down my bag and waited till he was out of hearing. "Cosgrove," I asked, not gently, "what do you think you're doing?"

He looked down, hands in his pockets. "Just waiting," he said.

"Waiting for what? Money and death? Have you been selling yourself on the street?"

"What do you care?"

Good question. "What do you think Virgil would say if he knew?"

Better question; and Cosgrove was silent.

"He's working his tail off to fix things up for you," I pointed out, "and meanwhile you're turning into street grunge. Nice timing."

Cosgrove looked at me, soft anger there, and despair, and a flash of hope.

"Where have you been staying at night, Cosgrove? Tell me. I won't get mad. Just tell me what you've been doing."

He started to weep. Wiping his eyes, he said, "I had such a nice time in the summer at the beach with everyone. I wanted to go on like that. I don't do anything wrong. Why are people always so mean to me?"

"Hey, Mordden, get your bod in the truck!" somebody yelled, and a horn sounded, and someone else called, "You're missing the trivia championship of the age!"

My ride to Woodstock. Cynically cheery faces at the windows, Cosgrove gazing wonderingly at the car, my bag in hand: the weekend begins.

What would you do? I took Cosgrove to Woodstock.

Even in a packed car, no one seemed put out or even surprised at the extra man. Straights of the publishing world, from senior editors down to assistants in the sub-rights department, generally take gay in their stride, perhaps enjoy it as another aspect of the rebellious glamour of fast-track New York. Granted, the attitude varies from house to house. The corporation-oriented places that emphasize textbook publishing and the tight-assed trade houses that cultivate an air of Ivy League old-boy conservatism both frown on rebellion and glamour, all the more so in combination. But my houses of choice admire originality and eccentricity, and their people are quite used to the sudden appearance of an attractive young man with no word of explanation beyond his name. Of course: this would be the current . . . beau, date, companion. The *trick*. But perhaps that last word should be made outcast; it reaffirms the myth that gays fuck rather than love. You're not supposed to make Mary jokes during Stonewall. In any case, Cosgrove was not my trick but my emergency, charge, friend in need. My charity.

Cosgrove was quiet, afraid to make the move or say the thing that, life had taught him, suddenly and mysteriously turns people against you. Breadsticks and fruit were as plentiful as shop gossip and jokes as we headed for the West Side Highway, yet Cosgrove didn't dare partake of any of it. He was listening, watching the faces to guess how they would treat him; and he was hungry, clearly, because he so carefully tried not to look at the food. I handed him two Granny Smith apples and a box of breadsticks while holding my own in another of those trivia challenge contests we of the great world obsessively hold, trying not to think of what Cosgrove had been doing in the last few days. We were one married couple, two women, and two men; we represented Knopf, Random House, and two magazines; we quizzed Hollywood, Modern European History, and Famous Murder Cases; we piled smarts upon knowledge and wrapped them in put-down drollery; we were good company. But Cosgrove was still, all the way to Woodstock, no doubt in the hope that if he did absolutely nothing, nothing bad would happen.

The merrily neutral acceptance of Cosgrove continued through our arrival, to his shyly growing delight. He stayed close to me, which tells us how unsure he is of strangers: for was I not as mean to him as anyone, laughing at his faux pas and standing by when Dennis Savage threw him out of our lives? Dinner was a big do-as-you-please buffet in a basement rec room, something like the opening night of the opera season blended into a freshman mixer. Cosgrove's eyes searched the room, but he never circulated, and I felt that if I let my hand dangle he would have grasped it like a child on his first day in school.

Everyone was nice to Cosgrove, though no one attempted to trade more than a line or two with him. Discretion? Thoughtfulness? Miriam Sonkin, however, decided to dote on Cosgrove, in her ambiguous, stepmotherly way. The maximum leader of the party, organizer and maintainer of many such expeditions, Miriam has an eye for all kinds of people— but I believe pretty kids with an air of worry most comfortably fascinate her.

Cosgrove was careful with Miriam; but then so am I. He quickly warmed to the attention and didn't hang back when I suggested he refill his plate at the buffet table. While he was there, someone spoke to him and he responded, and soon he was in lively conversation with some PR people from Simon and Schuster. I recalled Eliza Doolittle running her gauntlet at the embassy ball in *My Fair Lady*.

Miriam was humming, any old notes, ironically intoned.

"Do tell," I dared her.

"No, you. Who is he and what is he like?"

"You just met him." Keep it light, lots of footwork. "What's your impression?"

"I want the long view."

"What he's like . . . is raw and wounded. Who he is . . ." I gave her a smile and a shrug. Two for nothing. "He's nobody's boy."

"Wounded. Raw." She sighed, mock-sighed, surely; but who knows? "These are a few of my favorite things."

"I can cover Cosgrove's share in the—"

"Already covered," with a forgiving flat of her hand. "Someone didn't show, can we talk? We collected more than we needed, anyway. You don't mind if I put you in the faggot suite, do you? The only other gay couple is—"

"Don't use that word to me."

Startled, she blinked in retreat, bit her lip as she

regrouped, and stormed forth with, "My brother is gay, my ex-husband is gay, and half my friends are gay. If I can't say 'faggot'—"

"You can't."

Maybe a little humor? "Don't crab my act, buster. I'm breaking par tonight. I'm hot."

"If you were Jewish and I called you a kike, wouldn't you mind it, no matter how sure I was that I'm not a bigot?"

Another hesitation. Maybe we'll fight about it. "I am Jewish," she says, challenging me not to be appeased.

No way, ma'am. "Then you know exactly what I mean."

Perhaps I should say something about this party. It is not typical of the publishing world, or of any world I know of. Weekends around New York tend to run on more intimate connections, and publishing socializes in one-on-one lunches, Friday afternoon booze rodeos at a favorite café handy to the office, and Christmas parties, as a rule. Grandly organized weekends like this one, especially thus centering on a camp holiday such as Halloween, are usually the notion of someone who is eager to attain to a reputation as top madcap and is fearful that no one else's invitation will fulfill it. So Miriam, a major editor in a minor house, gives her own party—fifty bucks a person for expenses, transportation mildly guaranteed, prizes for the costume party Saturday night— at a surprisingly sizable old house in Woodstock, the inherited property of a friend of Miriam's who likes noise and fun every so often.

This is a party for in-house staff rather than for authors, middle-level people at that and not the fabled great of the book world who steal each other's writers over a nosh at the Russian Tea Room. Miriam's guests are young enough to believe in crazy silly weekends built around charades and costumes and free enough to spare the time. Perhaps this is what makes the party typical: the very ambition to pull off a party of this size is New York, as is the availability of a crowd sharp and fast enough to finagle the details of an end-of-the-world costume and to fill out a tournament-level charades match.

I don't like party games. The simple instituting of teams and rules and time limits reminds me, horribly, of the Boy Scouts; I have only to take part in anything involving the supervised activity of a group for my hands to begin tying imaginary sheep-shanks and my throat to choke on the memory of campfire Spam. Old pressures die never; and look, I didn't move to the City to recall the collectivist energies of the Country. Monopoly, where it's every man for himself, is so much more civilized than, for instance, Capture the Flag.

Still, I must admit that Miriam's friends play a wonderfully wild-and-mad, anything-goes charades. Each player puts down on a slip of paper a title, name, or quotation for someone on the other team to try to communicate—yeah, you know all about that, right? But my contribution was Rimsky-Korsakof's opera *Skazaniye o Nyevidimom Gradye Kityezhe i dyevye Fyevronii*. I expected a cry of Foul! from whoever got saddled with this impossible challenge, but no: the player studied the paper, nodded, and set to—and he was gamely plowing through when time was called on him. This is what I call zoom. Most players dispatch their assignments in seconds—this, mind you, in a game that bans the aid of category definitions as amateur style. No mimes of "movie," "book," or whatever for this crowd: you check your slip, call out "Time!" and start in. Now this (for those of you from other places) is New York.

Not everybody plays. Bands of kibitzers gravitated to far corners of the basement hall, and a few people served as spectators for the game and, led by Miriam, cheered us on impartially. Cosgrove chose to play, encouraged by the friendly atmosphere. I fretted. I was certain he could never master the intricate deployment of wit, speed, and body language dell'arte called for: and true enough, when it was his turn at bat—on a quotation from Lord Chesterfield's letters to his son—he had his team completely mystified. Nor was he adept at reading anything in his teammates' mime. But he did realize, quickly enough, that a goodly number of the slips of paper posed movie titles, and he began to punctuate the turns by calling out anything that came to mind, such as "Movie! *Close Encounters in the Third World!*" or "Movie! *Hitler on the Roof!*" This scattershot approach will get one nowhere, right? But then someone on Cosgrove's team was struggling badly, unable to get a single word out of his band. With time running out—this was a "sudden death" round, and you lose five points if you don't get your message across within forty seconds—Cosgrove's

teammate had taken to repeating an obnoxious pantomime over and over, walking and insistently
pointing at his feet.

"Legs?"

"'Cripple Creek Something Blues'?"

"Play: *On Your Toes*?"

"Movie!" Cosgrove happily shouted, *"So Wales
Was My Valley!"*

The actor of the turn stood stock-still, then beckoned wildly to Cosgrove.

"Movie: *How Green Was My Valley*," someone corrected, and the points were saved—the bit with the
feet and the walking was supposed to suggest
"grass," hence *Green*. Cosgrove, quite accidentally,
had made the touchdown, and I watched his eyes
grow wide as his teammates clapped his shoulder
and shook his hand.

Poor guy, I thought. If you hold your self-esteem
hostage to such idle compliments, you will never
know peace.

I was afraid, too, that his success would make
Cosgrove tipsy and lead him into some indiscretion.
But something happened first. The *How Green Was
My Valley* actor was one half of the only other gay
couple at the party, and as he went back to his chair,
he affectionately ran his hand along the back of the
neck of his lover; and his lover, smiling but not looking at him, grabbed his hand and held it for a moment. Most of us scarcely took notice, but Cosgrove
was so transfixed by this little byplay that he said
very little for the rest of the game.

This gay couple, I should warn you, is another of
those "ideal" combinations, both of them hand-

some, firmly built, intelligent, polite, strong and tender, young but on the rise, uncloseted junior editors working in separate houses. I think they're a pain in the ass—like Lanning Kean, the kid down the street from us, who always got straight A's when I barely skidded through math. "Why can't you be like Lanning?" Mother would fume; and of course telling her that she is a rag and Lanning a brownie, though good for the soul, cannot defeat the sensation of Overwhelming Reproachful Comparison. Miriam's gay couple, Jack and Peter, always make me feel like a rolodex in a gay dating service.

Jack and Peter rather impressed Cosgrove. Like Lanning Kean, they went to bed like good little brownies sometime around midnight, while the rest of us continued to play. The wine flowed, sweet music soothed us, and Cosgrove was drowsy long before he and I climbed to the faggot suite.

We can say it. They can't.

Jack and Peter were asleep in their bed; we two undressed in darkness. By now Cosgrove was so tired he could barely stand, yet he stared at Jack and Peter for a long moment, as if trying to place the playful hand-squeeze from the charades game in this utterly pastoral scene, two lambkins intertwined in a misty spring on some farm where no one eats mutton. I was already in bed, and Cosgrove joined me as coolly as a mandarin taking a bow. He knows his business, I thought to myself, as he calmly folded about me, one arm under the pillow and the other around my chest.

"Can they hear us?" he whispered.

"No, they're asleep."

"You know what? I want to be just like them when I'm grown up. Do you think that can happen?"

"I think wanting it is halfway there."

He dropped off then, but came to after a bit and asked, "What do you want to be?"

"Well . . . I'm already grown up."

"Yes," he agreed. Then: "What are you?"

He fell asleep again, this time for the night, so I didn't trouble to respond.

Saturday, almost unnaturally warm, brought on a kind of free-lance field day, with touch football, nature walks, and hide-and-seek. A far cry from a weekend in The Pines, but then this is Straightville. Clothes matter, so Peter lent Cosgrove a black turtleneck and sunshades to go over his corduroy pants from the day before and give him something of a Look. Jack topped it with a Greek fisherman's cap.

"He looks good enough to eat," Miriam told me as the company sashayed into the sun after breakfast. "*Is* he?" she insisted.

"As you asking or telling?"

"You know I don't like mysteries. At least share what you talk about at night."

"He tells me what he'll be when he grows up."

She performed one of those slow polysyllabic laughs that Irene Dunne specialized in. "Gay men always think no one knows anything about them."

Cosgrove ran by us, shouting for joy. He had already lost the hat and the glasses.

"No one of you possibly could know us," I told

Miriam. "We're still working on knowing ourselves."

"What's there to know? We're all the same. There
is only one life. When you're young, you run
through it yelling because you're loaded with sex
and friends. When you're forty-eight, scarred by a
couple of tough romances and terrified your building will co-op and dump you out, you stalk, *stalk*
through your life." She snorted. "So for God's sake,
give me a hug, you!"

Lunch was a hamburger cookout, and if they had
held an eating contest, Cosgrove would have taken
it. I've never seen anyone so devoted to baked
beans. However, he had plenty of opportunity to
run it all off in the hide-and-seek that followed. I
enjoyed it; it must have been well over twenty years
since I had uttered the words "Not it." In the event,
It was a cumbersome art director who had the air of
resenting everything about the weekend, especially
including hide-and-seek. Cosgrove and I smuggled
ourselves high up in an apple tree, and when It
came upon us, in sight but out of tag reach, he
looked like L. B. Mayer screening Joan Crawford's
porn loop.

"You're supposed to hide," he told us. "Not *do*
things!"

The straights' reply to Stonewall.

Meanwhile, in the near distance, we heard one of
the other players cry out, "Allee allee, olsen gee;
everybody tagged is free!" Giggles and catcalls re-
sounded as It turned to see all his prisoners running
loose.

"You goofball!" said Cosgrove.

◆ 261 ◆

Whereupon It grabbed a loose branch and began banging the trunk of our tree in irate frustration.

"Neutrality! Neutrality!" said Miriam, coming up from the house in something like a bridal gown, veil and all. "It's the Red Cross." She took us all in. "Whatever is this man doing?" she asked me.

It complained, "How am I supposed to get them way up there?"

I whistled "Here Comes the Bride," and Miriam responded, modeling her wedding dress. "My motto," she explained, "is 'Be prepared.'" Like a number of straight women who chum around with gay men, Miriam both fears and apes the queen. "You never know what will happen," she concluded.

Two players came sailing by, taunting It, and he ran off in pursuit. "I only hope to give," said Miriam, watching It's progress through the trees, "the truest party ever given."

"I love it," said Cosgrove. "I don't ever want to leave."

"You don't ever have to," she replied very simply.

"Why *are* you dressed like that, anyway?" I asked.

"It's Halloween. I came out to bring you all inside. To save you from things that go bump in the night."

In fact, it was getting dark. We had literally whiled the day away. Miriam held out her arms to us. "Come!" she called. "This is our time!"

She was speaking to us but she was looking at Cosgrove, and he scrambled down the tree and ran into her arms with that peremptory desperation that always shocks the unready. But Miriam loved it; she seemed to understand, all at once, his grief and anxiety, and to want to assuage them.

"Now this is what I believe is a hug," she said.

Nowhere in this weekend was the difference between straight and gay as evident as in the parade of the costumes. Gays spend all of their lives in costume, from the disguises of childhood and the closeted to the dress codes of the ghetto. One's costumes are, in effect, an objective correlative of the role or roles one chooses to play. To straights, clothes are at most an expedient, a convenience, perhaps a sensation: but always supplementary and occasional, varying with the personality rather than attempting to identify it. To straights, costumes are a treat. To gays, costumes are life.

Cosgrove, of course, had no costume. Even if he had had a chance to appoint one, I doubt he could have done so, for Cosgrove was of neither the straight nor the gay world, culturally an orphan. He did not feel left out at the costume ball, however, for Miriam let him and two other noncontenders judge the contest, and the responsibility entranced him. He got a little carried away, asking a Fairy Princess to "turn around all over" and telling Kharis the Mummy to "do a funny dance." But everyone seemed to be taking him for a charming eccentric; and heaven knows they've all had to put up with far more questionable behavior from men they took to be tricks.

The costume ball peaked in an impromptu theatrical, under Miriam's direction. Each of us was assigned to extemporize scenes in the role suggested by our dress. Naturally, Kharis the Mummy was after the Fairy Princess, who blundered, at Miriam's suggestion, into his tomb. We also had a Robot, Jimmy Carter, Snow White, and miscellaneous monsters, and I as Cowboy eventually rounded everyone up and knelt to do homage to the Fairy Princess, while Peter, who for some reason came as Charles Evans Hughes, passed judgment in his Supreme Court robes.

It was fun, though it lacked the demented verve of comparable exhibitions by Stonewall's thespians. Cosgrove, nonetheless, was thrilled. He clapped and cheered like a suburbanite at *Cats*.

"Why do we have to go back?" he asked me when the music came on and the gang took to the dance floor.

"We don't live here."

That's easy for me to say, he thinks: I do live somewhere. Where does Cosgrove live? He looks at me with the wheedling eroticism of Cosgrove the intruder, Cosgrove the hungry, the devious, compulsively begging men to use him in the absurd hope that sex will connect him. It will: but not to what he needs. He wants to be Jack, permanently emPetered, enfolded. He uses sex because love doesn't work for him. It comes too slow, or not at all. It fails to shelter him.

I should reassure him; I have been thinking of what we can all do to rescue him.

"Cosgrove," I say, taking him by the shoulders. "Don't be afraid. You have friends. We won't let you down."

He watches me. Has he heard this before: before he was let down by friends?

"Can we go back to the beach?" he asks.

He doesn't mean physically, but emotionally: can we treat him like a member of the family again?

"Yes," I tell him.

"How?" he poses.

He's not that stupid. Nothing is automatic. Everything must be arranged and agreed upon by all parties.

"We're just going to have to find a way."

"Please," he says. He always says please.

And I think, after all these years, of the narrator of the clown dog story, and I see a version of him in Cosgrove, and I have no choice but to put my arms around him and pronounce the most meaningless two words in English, "There, there." Why *there*? What's there?

Miriam is; she misses nothing, especially the sight of two men who can't figure out what they mean to each other. The party has gone quite well, all told, but it has climaxed. Tomorrow will be a series of farewells, of guests breaking free of Miriam's hold and, for all the good times, probably not returning for another of these so very elaborate endeavors. Sometimes even charm, wit, and good intentions are not enough, and the fun simply dies on you.

"It's all over," Miriam comments, "but the toast and coffee in the morning."

"Every story ends," I tell her.

"What about the story of nobody's boy?" she asks, scanning Cosgrove's face. "How does that end?"

"Is that me?" Cosgrove asks.

"Just the question I ask myself," says Miriam. "Almost every day now. '*Is that me?*'"

"I know a story," says Cosgrove.

"When you're young," says Miriam, "you never have to ask. You don't think of it."

"Once there was a mother and father," Cosgrove begins, "and they had a baby boy. But there was magic, and the Elf King put an elf baby in its place and took the human baby to live with the elf people. And the elf baby seemed just, just, just like the human baby, and ate the same foods and watched television. But the human mother and father were not sure. The mother said to the father, Something is wrong with him, and the father said, He is not what we wanted. He doesn't please us right."

Cosgrove looked at us.

"Even though he did everything to be good. He was out playing, and they said, No, no, no, you clean up your room, you are selfish. So he was inside cleaning everything right up, and they said, No, no, no, you have no friends, you don't act right. And they were mean to him, like making him eat foods he hated and saying he was stupid and probably not even human."

Cosgrove looked at us.

"But the elf child knew that the other children in the family were not good, even though they were always getting presents. The elf child gave presents to his mother and father more than the human children did, because he *had* to, so they would think he was human, too. He gave better presents every time. He gave them high castles to live safe in, and fire that would never go out, and dreams that come true. But the mother and father never cared about it. All they knew was, he was not what they liked. So he ran away and begged the Elf King to take him back where he belonged. But the Elf King said, No, no, no, you must be with humans and give them more presents."

Cosgrove looked at us.

"But no matter what, the boy couldn't make the humans like him. They always figured out that he was an elf, and they would never let him in, because they were frightened of elf stuff. So one day the boy gave them other presents. You know what he gave them now? He gave them clothes that itch and you can never take them off, and scare-you noises coming from secret places, and candy that when you eat it it's like broken glass in your mouth and your blood pours down your chin and everyone screams when you look at them."

Miriam shook her head. "If he does that, the Elf King will swoop down and take him away and shut him up where no one will ever see him again. He has to learn how to live with humankind." She looked at me. "And with straights," she said. "Right?"

Cosgrove looked down, his hands in his pockets. "Maybe he doesn't care after all this," he said. "Because how come he has to give presents and never get any back?"

Everyone else had gone to bed. Alone in the great room, we shuffled about in some halfhearted tidying and then dragged upstairs. Miriam kissed us both good night.

Once again, Jack and Peter, so beautifully interlocked they might have been poured from a mold, held Cosgrove's gaze. And again, Cosgrove slid into bed and fitted up against me as if we had been, like Jack and Peter, doing this for years. For a long while we lay thus, listening to each other breathe, then Cosgrove whispered, "Would you please pet me a little?"

"Pet you?"

"You know."

We played together then, Stonewall-style with a postmodernist edge, circling around the scary parts in our morbid new Precautions for this age of Love Is Death. Even so, cut off from each other at our most intimate, the physical remains the essential communication of our fraternity, the door through which friends long to pass. How else shall we know each other? Compassion, you may say.

But this was compassion.

I didn't care to have Cosgrove till I cared what would happen to him. Selfishly, I suffered a rage of distaste for him because his reckless adventures had compromised my ability to know him: selfishly, because these adventures were the dues Cosgrove feared he must pay, the changeling's attempts to become human, his presents. I squeezed him, all of him, arms and legs, so tightly I thought he'd cry out; I wanted to squeeze the recklessness out of him. But all he said was "Please." I loved him furiously. I hated him dearly, for comprehending the perfect lovers Jack and Peter while having helped to destroy the perfect safety of such love. I was in bed with the Plague—poor thing; it can't help itself. It doesn't love to kill you. It just kills you.

And Cosgrove, beside me, was laughing so quietly that I didn't realize what I had heard till some moments later.

Of course, none of my friends knew that Cosgrove had come with me to Woodstock, and there was great relief when the two of us turned up at Dennis Savage's on Sunday afternoon. Virgil, unable to reach Cosgrove through whatever code procedures they had set up, had been frantic with worry, and Dennis Savage, as The Man Who Sent Cosgrove Away, had been paying for Virgil's discomfort with his own. So, then: a knock, we enter into a moment of dumbstruck catharsis, and Virgil explodes with greeting of Cosgrove and Dennis Savage apologizes to him and Cosgrove, barely able to believe this change of fortune, is telling of his Halloween weekend.

And "Look what we got a copy of," Virgil cries as he shows his buddy the latest videotape, *The Wizard of Oz.*

"It's magic," Cosgrove rhapsodizes.

"It's also missing a chunk of the beginning," Dennis Savage puts in, "because someone in this room decided he couldn't do without a tape of *Pee-wee's Playhouse.*"

"I was just experimenting," says Virgil, blushing.

"Virgil," says Cosgrove, "we had a show last night, and a costume party. I was one of the judges of the contest."

"Was our Cowboy Bud cited?" Dennis Savage asks. Now that he's off the hook he has to catch up on his baiting and teasing.

"I was cited," I say, "for having the worst friends in town. Now come downstairs and give me your ear."

"Sit quietly and watch a movie, children," Dennis Savage tells them at the door. "And no singing."

"If you tell me what is right to do," Cosgrove promises, "I will always do it."

"Cosgrove will be good," Virgil adds.

Dennis Savage has misgivings, but away we go to figure out what to do.

Yes, yes, yes, got it all figured. Cosgrove stays with Carlo till the London trip. Then he house-sits for Dennis Savage and the Katzenjammer dog. We come back and spang! Cosgrove can move in with me.

"Suddenly this?" says Dennis Savage.

But there's magic. We help him get a job, an apartment. One of those share-a-place services.

"Reality says no," he tells me. "What job could that little dope hold down? And somehow I don't see him persuading anyone legitimate to let him live in. The kid's a ditz. He'll just get in trouble again."

No, no, no, we'll help him.

"A terminal ditz—and sorry, but what about the medical problem? For all you know, he may be infected."

We'll work it out. Some dream that comes true.

"What is it? What's happened to you?"

His hand on my shoulder, yes; but no, don't be sage and understanding because you don't know about feeling so sorry for someone that it changes your outlook. I didn't know about it myself. What I knew about was, for instance, someone brings his new boyfriend to a party and you think, Oh, I want that, and somewhere in there the boyfriend is telling you about his job as a waiter and he can't direct a story and he's not articulate and you wonder if he's just being social to please his lover, but what you are *really* aware of is how he leans in *very* close when he talks to you and tut-tut, mon vieux are we slavering and making a fool of ourselves and will our appetites be dish of the week tonight? We all know about that. What we don't know about is being touched sufficiently by someone's pain to want to gentle it.

And suddenly I remember what the Boy Scouts call the kerchief clasp: a woggle!

"He's not a stray puppy," Dennis Savage is warning me. "He needs a great deal more than eats and a mat."

"There is only one life," I tell him. "He needs what everyone needs. One thing. One word. You say the word."

"You're the one who never says it, man of the world."

"Hush, I use it all the time."

"You write it. You don't say it."

"I'm getting to it."

The Woggle

$$\blacktriangleright\!\!\blacktriangleright\!\!\blacktriangleright\!\!\blacktriangleright$$

Virgil was so excited about the London trip that he was packed a good two weeks before we left. Reading in histories and appreciations of the city, tackling Evelyn Waugh and Simon Gray, listening to tapes of Flanders and Swann and music-hall records, studying guidebooks, tracing walking tours on maps, and memorizing key routes on the underground public transportation system, he attacked this novel adventure—as he does them all—with a rash savor.

Well he might. He had never been out of the country before, had scarcely been anywhere but Cleveland and New York. Dennis Savage, however, one of those well-traveled people who become tirelessly sedentary on the grounds that they've Done It All, fell in with my travel plans out of sheer desperation.

"A new idea," he kept saying. "What I need is a new idea."

Taking Virgil to London was it, then: so I called my travel agent and plonked them into my reservations, not only for the same hotel and plane but even in the two seats next to mine for the flights over and back. This is one advantage of traveling in November rather than in the summer's high season. Another advantage is the proliferation of theatre in London's autumn. Summer theatregoers can only pick up the tail end of the previous season. It's a has-been *cartellone*. The pre-Christmas visitor, however, gets to sample a pride of new works, some of which will close before one's theatre-buff friends can get to them in the spring, thus driving them crazy and adding to the fun.

I logged all my London sightseeing decades ago. Nowadays it is enough simply to traverse the streets of this amazing city, or to cross the Thames on Waterloo Bridge and glimpse Big Ben, the Houses of Parliament, and the Abbey to the west, and St. Paul's and (on the rare clear day) the Tower to the east. The London of Christopher Marlowe and William Shakespeare vanished in the Great Fire of 1666 and in any case would have lain eastward, beyond the range of the West End of playhouses, restaurants, and hotels that my tour centers on. But Dennis Savage and Virgil were coming as neophytes, to do what newcomers do and undergo the rites of debutant tourism.

Dennis Savage was not looking forward to it. Grumping and grousing, he counted the days till takeoff as if he were going to the hospital instead of to London. Two or three times a day he would stomp down to my place, leaving Virgil to pore over his touring kit alone.

"Trenovant," Dennis Savage exclaimed, crashing in on the eve of our departure. "Trenovant, okay? That's the latest from our little Brit in residence. If he waves that map at me once more—"

"If you feel that way," I said, "why did you agree to go in the first place?"

He threw himself on my disreputable couch, upholstered in blankets and pillows to keep the stuffing from dripping out through the lining's thousand tears. I feel like that couch myself, sometimes.

"Why?" I repeated. "No one was holding a gun to your head."

He just looked at me.

"It's a new idea," I said. "Right?"

He shrugged. "I'll tell you what I'm hoping: that he'll be so exhausted and homesick after the week is up that he'll be relieved to get back to . . . I don't know . . ."

"Life with you?"

Nothing from him, and a face like a blasted wall.

"You know," I ventured, "lately we've been getting signals of grave misgivings upstairs."

"Well, he's growing up on me. That's the trouble."

"Most people look forward to a trip like this, you realize."

"He's a confident young man. Remember when he was a shy waif?"

"I secured us tickets to the big shows by phone on my plastic—*Follies*, *Kiss Me, Kate*, the National Theatre *A View From the Bridge*, and the new Maggie

Smith–Peter Shaffer comedy. I figure that's all you'll want to see in a week. I'll do the rest of it on my—"

"He's finally figured out," Dennis Savage growled, "that everybody, but *everybody*," he went on, "loves him at first sight," he concluded. "And you know what?" he asked. "He likes it. He knows it and he likes it."

"What's got into you?"

"*He* did, for a fact. Last night. His first time."

Possibly not counting Cosgrove.

"Had you ever wondered about that?" he said. "So now we know."

"How'd you enjoy it?"

"I hate getting done. I've always hated it."

"Okay. How'd *he* enjoy it?"

"He's out of control. He's all over the place now. Take your eye off him for a minute, he's going for it somewhere. He used to be afraid to walk the streets of this town, took me years to train him how to keep an eye on the scene, watch out for trouble. If he can't be alert, let him pretend to be, right? So he pretended. The wide-eyed kid who sees nothing. Oh, and that worked fine for a few years. Now you know what he does? He cruises. He's wide-eyed all right."

"Come on."

"He watches men, just as we do. A few weeks ago, when I was coming back from the grocery, I spotted him about thirty yards ahead of me. I was just catching up to him when a man came out of the hardware store—big fellow, the rangy, lean type. I didn't see his face, but he was wearing bright red corduroy pants, and he had the most incredible butt, the sort that was put on earth to be admired in corduroy pants. And our little boy there, he just stared at this man, drinking him in as they walked together a few paces in front of me."

Shaking his head ruefully, he paused there, letting his headline news sink in: UNSPOILED KID TURNS INTO RAVING WHOREMASTER LIKE ALL THE REST OF US.

"Just think of it," he went on after a while. "How long before one of those corduroy dreamboats turns around and sees him and picks him up?"

"So he'll cheat on you. Everyone cheats sometime."

"Yeah, he'll cheat. He'll cheat again. Then he'll happen upon a devastato with a great job and a house in the country and pots of money and charm of death, and Little Whatshisname will ask himself, What do I need with that broken-down Dennis Savage when I can start all over again with the real thing? Because, in case you haven't noticed, the world is full of incredibly nice, alarmingly handsome men."

"Why are you suddenly doing this? Why *now*, I mean? If he was going to leave you, he could have done so long before. New York has been nice and handsome for quite some time."

"He needed me before. He . . . he wanted raising. I was his teacher. Now it's been nine years. For every couple, gay and straight, that's the danger time."

"I just don't see Virgil picking up street meat. Everything with him is social. If he was to leave you, he'd choose someone like Carlo or Lionel or even Big Steve."

"Never. They're like uncles to him. He'd as soon go with . . . with Cosgrove or someone."

We are all fools.

"No," he went on, "I think he's ripe for the romance of the surprise encounter. He's finally reached that epiphany of Stonewall that we all had a hundred years ago, when you realize that the world is full of marvelous men and all you have to do is jump out and connect with one." He sighed. "'Only connect,'" he added, quoting E. M. Forster. "That's the whole opera, right?, right there. Isn't it? That's all that matters to anyone."

I said nothing.

"You know I'm right. A feeling comes over you every so often that you've got to put your arms around a certain man and be held back—held tight, I'm saying—and feel the hardness of him, and the hair of his head, leaning against your head. And you can't do it with just anyone, oh, no. A *certain* man, waiting somewhere out in the world for you to come and take hold of him like an apple on the bough. Ah, but what if you never find the man I so pathetically and embarrassingly describe? What then? Can I tell you? This then: nothing that you do in your entire life is ever going to matter, not hardly at all."

He got up as if to leave but he just stood there. "Trenovant," he said at last. "He wants to rename Bauhaus Trenovant. Do you know what Trenovant is?"

"The legendary ancient name of London, if you believe the tale that it was founded by survivors of fallen Troy. Totally spurious, of course. One of those majestic bygones that cities sometimes dress their histories in."

He nodded. "I figured you'd know all about it."

Well, I do know a lot; but I am yet capable of surprise. I had remarked Virgil's steady maturing as a man of the world, an authentic gay New Yorker. Still, his childlike love of games and frolics had never deserted him, and it obscured the densely gathering articulations of his coming of age. Brought up short by Dennis Savage's talk, I stopped to take a clean new look at Virgil—perhaps as a parent does, one day well along in the course of life, to see the dear pieces of the child all fallen away in the bursting forth of the adult. For years I had taken Virgil for granted as a member of my family. Now I actually felt proud of him. I had helped raise him, after all. There was something of me in him.

My family: an odd notion for an outsider to accept, no doubt. And even some of our own initiates, boys and girls, might take us three for no more than a house party, two queens and their weekend guest. Certainly a lot of my tales deal with people being taken for something they aren't. I wonder what the craggy-featured, Scots-accented British Airways steward took us for as he flirted shamelessly with Virgil, even *over* Dennis Savage and me, because Virgil had insisted on taking the window seat so he could mark his first view of London from the air. It is widely known that a substantial fraction of the airline steward, uh, community is gay; why is that? A bartender once told me that the salient one-up of his

profession was "You get to see everyone and everyone gets to see you." This is true of stewards, certainly. But you know what?

It's also true of writers.

Virgil accepted the steward's attentions with a
mild amusement, and as soon as the man passed on
to take the other drink orders, our little tourist tried
to imitate his speech. Virgil was juggling two
guidebooks and three maps, wearing a headset,
chattering about the quickest route between
Trafalgar Square and our hotel, and balancing the
expediency in concentrating on different sections of
town on different days or on steaming through the
place in a mad medley—all this, remember, put
forth in the sketchiest of haggis twangs.

He's a silly boy, but he has great charm. And he
does command, in astonishing quantity, one of the
most significant virtues: loyalty.

Dennis Savage was patiently floating along with
Virgil's lecture, putting in his oar at the odd moment. I sometimes think that he gets along so well
with Virgil because he doesn't have to work as hard
with him as with our more intellectual friends. Like
Carlo, Virgil needn't be constantly entertained or
amazed; he brings his own theatre with him. I was
scribbling away in the aisle seat as the merry partners plotted their sightseeing campaigns, and so the
time passed, broken by the dinner break, the movie
show (*The Untouchables*), and the continued flattery
of the Scots steward. We had taken a late-night
flight, and long before the film was over, most of the
passengers were asleep, some stretching across
three seats, empty in the calm of off-season. I can't

sleep on planes, but Dennis Savage made some fitful stabs at a doze, and Virgil, depleted by excitement, went out like Samuel Pepys's candle. I had put my notebook down to do some thinking, and the steward, passing, paused to look upon us and smile.

I smiled back.

"Can I gaet ye anythin', ser?" he asked.

"Another of those little bottles of white wine," I replied, "would do me nicely."

"Wus it the dry German ur the French?" he said, admiring Virgil.

"The German."

"Yur brother is fast asleep, I sae," the steward noted, his voice lowered. "It's a peaceful picture."

"Wait till he hits London. It'll be about as peaceful as the Blitz."

"I'd be glad to know him then," said the steward, and I half expected him to slip me his phone number to give to Virgil. But he went off to the galley, and Dennis Savage, his eyes still closed, snorted.

"Do you believe that?" I whispered.

"'Your brother,' huh? Your lover. Your project. Your hustler . . . What do they call hustlers in England?"

"Rent-boys."

"Your rent-boy." He opened his eyes and looked over at Virgil, deep in dreams. Looked, I dare say, for quite some time. As the steward came down the aisle with my wine, Dennis Savage closed his eyes again, murmuring, "Tell him it only works in bright red corduroy pants."

Upon arrival we took a cab to the hotel and moved in. I conquer jet lag with extra infusions of

Shaklee Vita-Lea multiples and an iron will. Besides, I had the rest of my theatre tickets to buy. But Dennis Savage proposed a nap.

"I'm tired," he told us. "I'm done in. I'm dead or dying."

"How can you be tired?" Virgil asked. "London is outside."

"How can I be tired? How about an eight-hour plane trip, not to mention getting out to the airport and hanging around waiting for our flight?"

"But all you did was sit there. You didn't do push-ups in the aisle or anything."

Dennis Savage was already pulling down the bed-clothes.

"Well, *I'm* going to see London," said Virgil; and away we went. We walked down prim little Gower Street to the Shaftesbury Theatre, where I had to pick up the *Follies* tickets I had ordered by phone. Here the southwestern tip of Bloomsbury opens up on a more metropolitan London. Here, suddenly, were men in business suits, scorning overcoats despite the nippy weather, and the unique black taxi-cabs and the red double-decker buses. The streets grew broader, the buildings soared, the town began to clatter, dashing and seemly as it is. And Virgil stood stock-still and took it all in.

"Are you going to be okay?" I asked him. "You won't get lost, will you?"

"Are you kidding?" he said, brandishing his nineteen maps at me.

I might have said something about . . . well, I don't know. When are you coming back? Will we see you for dinner? But he is a man now and needs no looking after. Just as I was about to enter the

Shaftesbury Theatre, I turned back—oh, just in case, you know—and saw Virgil authoritatively pointing a passerby off toward Oxford Street. Apparently the man had asked him for directions to somewhere.

Apparently Virgil, now, could give them.

Well, I proceeded from the *Follies* box office to the Cambridge Theatre (for Lulu in *Peter Pan*), just re-opening in a new coat of white paint after three years in the dark. The Cambridge is my favorite London theatre because the unsuspecting can never find it. Most London playhouses are named for where they are: the Piccadilly, the Aldwych, the Strand, the Savoy, the Haymarket. The Cambridge is named for where it isn't: Cambridge Circus. The Palace, where *Les Misérables* is playing, is in Cambridge Circus. The Cambridge itself is two blocks away in Seven Dials, a crossroads of seven streets. This reminds us that things are not invariably sensible or fair. We need to be reminded, especially as we near our forties.

I went on gathering tickets into the late afternoon. This is always a choice time for me, as my trip takes on its shape and color. This tour took in the World War II musical *Girlfriends*, the drag artiste Dame Edna Everage in her one-man show, *Back With a Vengeance!*, *King Lear* and *Antony and Cleopatra* at the National Theatre, the new Simon Gray play *Melon*, with Alan Bates. Thus a world opens up in a week— history, parody, wit, poetry. Of course, just being in London opens up a New Yorker's perspective— somewhat, I think, as age enlightens youth. One cannot help but learn here, in the very shadow of the history of Western democratic civilization; and the intelligence and politeness of the people is quite a lesson after the lawless rages of New York. London does not teem with madmen on a spree, with desperadoes hungry for an order of mugging to go, with crowds of the homeless, tossed into the gutter as if they were literally human garbage. Nor does London challenge you with bizarre, un-provoked assaults from waiters, bank clerks, and such, as New York insistently does.

All this is London. But there is something more, and very important: the people you run into are not only courteous and sensible but *pleasant*. Dealing with them even in the most impersonal and formal capacity gives one a lift, adds a sweet breeze to a warm day. Shocked, a New Yorker finds himself easing up his defensive postures and enjoying his encounters with strangers.

It's a high. It's like dropping ten years from your age or lucking into a dynamite apartment. The dif-ference between New York and London is like the difference between being alone and being in love.

My ticket buying kept me so busy that I didn't have time to go back to the hotel. I had dinner out, took in *Peter Pan* with a house full of children, and, just beginning to fade from fatigue, went home and crashed. So I didn't catch up with Dennis Savage and Virgil till the next morning. Our typically En-glish hotel offered the typical bed and breakfast, and when I entered the dining room I found Virgil con-versing with a middle-aged Australian couple. He was telling them all about England in a wildly coun-terfeit English accent, something like David Frost trying to talk with Piccadilly Circus in his mouth. On the table close to Virgil stood a little metal copy of the red London Transport bus, the first of what was to prove a caravan's worth of souvenirs.

I joined this improbable trio, saying as little as possible: who wants to crab an act as fetching as Virgil's? Certainly the Australian couple were enjoying his company. The man sat on the quiet side, with a touch of wry, but his wife avidly pumped Virgil for sightseeing tips, and she virtually had to tear herself away from the table when her husband rose to go.

"I say," Virgil observed in his voice of a thousand monocles as they left, "a rather posh couple, anyroad, don't you think?"

"So what did you do yesterday?" I asked, working on my typically English runny eggs and raw bacon.

"Oh, I saw everything!" he cried, losing the accent. "I was on the tops of buses and I went into Westminster Abbey and across the river on some bridges! Guess what I found! Refrigerator magnets of London street signs! I got you one that says Covent Garden, because of opera."

"Was Dennis Savage in on any of this?"

"That old fogy. He was still sleeping when I got back, so I went to a pub for a pint of the best and some—"

"You went to a pub? By yourself?"

"Sure, my dear chap, old bean. I found some really nice people, too. They have neat names here, you know . . . Simon, Rupert. And Gillian, of course. She's Rupert's bird. Topping sort. I wish we had food like that at home, like this stew you get inside a pie. Only they don't give you any napkins. Rupert and Gillian are going to invite us to tea."

"Wait a minute. You just walked into a pub and
. . . I can recall when you were afraid to go into a
bar. Suddenly you're having tea with Rupert and
Gillian? *How?* I want how."

"Well, Gillian said how cute my little bus was, especially in a pub just like that, and then she thought
I might be American, so I—"

"She *thought* you *might be*—"

"Well, I gave them a little of the old-boy pi-jaw,
don't you know."

"Listen, you—"

"All the comforts of home," said Dennis Savage,
sitting down. "Everybody's fighting." He noticed
the bus with a silent groan but pressed on. "What's
in store for us today, skipper?" he asked Virgil.

"Knightsbridge, Harrod's, the Royal Albert Hall,
and the Albert Memorial in the morning," Virgil told
him, pulling out a map as Hannibal might have
shown his elephants their route to Rome. "Lunch.
Then—"

"Are you along with us on this?" Dennis Savage
asked me.

"No, I've got a matinee at the National, and the
traditional Checking Out of the Record Stores."

"There's a Tower Records," Virgil informed me,
"in Piccadilly Circus."

"So I've noticed."

"If Bud doesn't have to go," Dennis Savage asked
Virgil, "why do I?" But he paled at Virgil's look of
bewildered disappointment. "I'm joking, of course."

"We'd better get started," said Virgil, grabbing his
bus. "This is going to be a crowded day."

"Don't forget we've got *Kiss Me, Kate* tonight," I said.

"At the historic Old Vic," Virgil rejoined.

"If I live that long," Dennis Savage put in.

That last little exchange might be our trip in miniature, with our boy centering on the theatres, Virgil on tourism, and Dennis Savage on sheer survival. And I have an illustration to fix this paradigm in its visual truth, from that same afternoon, when I was walking back across Waterloo Bridge after my National *Antony and Cleopatra*. I had reached the traffic light at the Strand end of the bridge, and a man approaching me on the walkway called out, "Some bloke's tryin' to twig ya, mate." He pointed at a bus. I turned just in time to see Virgil waving at me in a grin of innocent devilry in a window of the upper deck, Dennis Savage asleep next to him, his head a-loll against the glass.

"You aren't traveling hard enough," I told Dennis Savage later in my hotel room. "You're sleeping your way through London."

"I don't even know why I came."

"Perhaps to shake up the settled routine of your existence with a little adventure."

"This is too much adventure. He's had me in and out of every attraction between William the Conqueror's bedpan and Virginia Woolf's outhouse." Sitting on the edge of my bed, he threw himself back to stare at the ceiling. "What am I supposed to be getting out of all this? St. Paul's was so thronged with tourists it was more like a D'Agostino's than a church. And Poet's Corner—what a thrill. A bunch of tombs and plaques. He was falling all over himself and he doesn't know who half the people were."

"Why do you keep calling him He? Is it too much for you to ante up with his name?"

Slowly he pulled himself back up. "What is this," he asked, "the Face the Music Hour? Whose side are you on?"

"Ours."

"Oh, you very clever, feeling man. With a best friend like you, who needs mid-life crisis?"

"Is *that* what this is?"

"I'm tired," he said. "I'm old. I've lost my looks. I made crucial mistakes. I'm not content. I didn't get to do what I wanted to do."

"What did you want to do?"

He looked at me for a bit. "Carlo's had a nice life," he observed. "Wouldn't you say?"

I didn't say.

"True, he has reduced all human existence to one essential act," Dennis Savage admitted. "But within that limited compass, he did hit all the points, didn't he? Or even Big Steve. It's a simple way of life, I grant you—he doesn't go to brunches, or the theatre, or London. He goes to the gym. But he gets up when he likes, and he works when he likes, and he dresses as he likes. And when he walks down the street in summertime, lovely boys tremble with a terrible joy at the sight of him. Even now, and how old is he? Forty-five? And while we're on the subject—stop me if I advance overmuch upon our intimacy—why aren't *you* miserable by now, like most of us?"

"Maybe I did what I wanted to do."

He gave me a shrug.

"What, no riposte?" I said. "You must really be down."

"I really am."

He got up.

"I really, really am."

"Maybe a change in wardrobe would cheer you up. What do you look good in?"

"Winter."

"Has it occurred to you that you'll only make things worse by going around in this . . . the stupor of doom? Why don't you fight back?"

"What is there to fight? What's there?"

"Inside you, I mean."

"No." He shook his head. "It's inside him. It isn't happening to me. It's happening to him. So let it happen."

"You don't want to try outwitting it? Forestalling it?"

"Oh, please," he said as he passed through the doorway. "You are what you are."

Still, Dennis Savage did seem to energize his manner after that, if only for the sake of style. He was always an arbiter of gay manners, one way or another, and disdained defeatism as surely as an incorrectly soiled T-shirt or balcony seats. "How many times have I told you?" he would tell me. "You don't go to the Village in a suit."

"I came from the opera," I explain.

A hand weighs on my shoulder, the hand of probity; and I looked up to him then, because he knew more than I did. Also, he's taller than I.

"You're supposed to go home and change first," he would say.

I try not to give the past more than a backward glance, for it can be dangerous to recall days when one had few cares, no stomach, and all the time in the world. But this London trip kept forcing a retrospective mood on me, as if we had come to a watershed of some kind.

I ignored it. I banded with my two friends to see the town. We became tourists, disintegrated from the place we were in and thus made to become complete unto ourselves.

It was easy to do. Gay men do it, in fact, every day of their lives. No gay can ever be a part of his nation unless he gives away something of himself, his self-esteem, perhaps. We are always disintegrated from the status quo, always complete unto ourselves. In the straight world—in the world—we are tourists till we close Them off behind our doors.

At least New York is filled with us. London's gays blend into the scene. One notes none of the gym development and dress code of gay America—virtually no visibility of subculture, unless one counts the posters and stills for the film *Maurice*, playing at the Cannon Shaftesbury, which we often passed on our way back to our hotel.

Only connect.

Virgil invariably stopped to examine the *Maurice* pictures and ask about them. As so often with him, he knew none of the background—E. M. Forster as closeted novelist with the closeted novel, this same *Maurice*, that only came to light after his death. Yet Virgil sensed something extraordinarily relevant in the logo shot of the confidingly secretive Maurice, in the photographs of Maurice and his . . . chums. In a city devoid of bomber jackets and loaded glances, a picture of two men lying asleep in each other's arms was a high-concept visual.

"I'm going to have to see that movie," Virgil told us as we hustled him up the road. It was a Saturday, two days before our flight home, and we had stuffed the day with events. I squeezed a used-bookstore rampage between two shows; Dennis Savage and Virgil had taken a bus tour to Windsor Castle and Oxford University. We met in Chinatown for a late dinner and were taking a slow walk through the West End to our hotel. A light fog had set in; strangers would not approach but suddenly materialize before you—cause for terror in New York but a bemusing novelty in London, the most graceful city in the world. Venice is more colorful, Paris more elegant, Vienna more beautiful. But London has an ease, a logic, a sense of fairness, that has no rival.

I don't know how much of this struck my friends as we strolled the last few blocks home, the two flanking me, Dennis Savage's steady tread to my left and Virgil, watching, pausing, and absorbing, to my right. But I definitely sensed, from both of them, the blithely stimulated romanticism of the true traveler, who comes into the exploit for its own sake, not to find anything in particular: just to look. You cannot learn without first observing.

It has been a success, perhaps, I told myself.

When we got our keys at the porter's desk, there was a message for Virgil.

"Who's Rupert Duttson?" asked Dennis Savage, looking over Virgil's shoulder.

It was Virgil's pub companions, inviting us to tea tomorrow at four o'clock.

"Nifty," I said. "London's dead on Sundays, anyway."

"Rosebery Avenue," said Virgil, reading from his paper, his eyes aglow as he savored the single *r*: another place to look up on his maps. "It says we have to take the Number 38 bus from the southeast corner of Bloomsbury Square."

"We'll just cab it," said Dennis Savage.

"It's more scenic on the bus," said Virgil.

The bus it was; you have to get up on the top deck of things and *observe*. I went down the hall to their room the next afternoon to fetch them. We were to leave London the following morning, and there were signs of incipient departure, most directly in the full-scale display of Virgil's souvenirs. These now included, besides the bus and street sign magnets, a little black taxicab, an underground map mug, a Prince Charles–Princess Di dessert plate, an Old Vic T-shirt, a *Follies* sweatshirt, teaspoons adorned, at the handles, with miniatures of Big Ben and the Nelson column, metal mockups of the Tower beefeater, a bobby, and a Buckingham Palace guard, matchboxes decorated with postcard views of Great Britain, and a tiny Union Jack.

"Wrap up a set of spoons, please, shopkeeper," I said, "and a box of soldiers. You take VISA?"

"Very funny," said Virgil.

Dennis Savage was chuckling.

"Nice to hear you laugh, pardner," I told him.

"Guess where we went," said Virgil.

"The only thing you haven't seen that's open today is the British Museum."

"Which has not, despite the song, lost its charm," Dennis Savage put in. "Now let's go to our first authentic English tea party, and that's the trip, and then we're all going home."

"Don't rush me," said Virgil, fussing at his exhibit. "My spoons are crooked."

"Many replies come to mind," said Dennis Savage, getting him into his coat. "Many replies of a drastically soigné nature. But we're on vacation from all that."

"Teatime, everyone," I called out at the door.

"I can get my own coat on," Virgil complained.

"Yes," Dennis Savage agreed. "But it's more fun this way."

"Come on, Dick Whittington," I said as we gained the hallway. "We're going to Islington."

One odd thing about London is that while no one lives in the city center—as we may in Manhattan—everyone ends up with a house rather than a flat. It's like one's Brooklyn friends, with English accents. Rupert and Gillian's house was small, but it was a house; and they had an instructively wide circle of acquaintances. The party took in a baby and a grandmother. The baby was Otto and the grandmother was hard of hearing.

("All she needs is an ear trumpet," Dennis Savage whispered to me, "and the curtain could rise on a veddy English play, old sport.")

Virgil greeted his hosts as if he'd known them all his life, a swank of bravado they clearly were not used to. But I must say he was right in there, taking stage, as they say in the theatre. Dennis Savage and I were so busy balancing our teacups and sandwich plates—not to mention trying to eat cake with our hands, in the English teatime manner—that it was quite some portion of the party before we could take part. By then, of course, Virgil had established himself as Our American Cousin, fascinating the company with accounts of life in the United States.

"The main thing," said Virgil, "is that there's a constant supply of napkins."

"Eh?" cried the grandmother.

"And the streets are bigger and the heat never goes off. And we dress warmer than you outside."

"Yes, I must say," Rupert agreed. "You can always tell an American in winter by the astonishing amount of sweaters and scarves they wear."

Simon arrived with Graeme, clearly—to the practiced eye—his lover. This unelaborate mixing of straight, gay, and family was utterly unlike what I'm used to in New York, where gays party either among themselves and trusted fellow travelers in a distinctly gay atmosphere, or among outsiders on the outsiders' terms. Seldom if ever in New York have I seen a gathering that merely included gays yet *took gay for granted* as naturally as it accepted a baby and a grandmother. But then, one expects it of travel to develop a long-term view of one's home life, to see one's routine with extraordinary eyes. A good voyage sends one back a little wiser, maybe a little younger as well, with a renewed sense of mission.

Of course, one has to have a mission in the first place.

Speaking of that: no one did speak of missions at this tea. In New York, one's profession is a key tack of conversation. In London, it isn't done to ask for or volunteer such information. Work is a private matter, a clue to self not to be exposed to strangers. Work is like sex. I wonder if Rupert and Gillian— even Simon and Graeme—ever realized that their three American visitors were gay.

"One thing we never get enough of back home," Virgil was saying, "is cucumber sandwiches," biting into what was probably his first ever.

"Yes, it's right out of *The Importance of Being Earnest*," said Dennis Savage.

Our hosts appeared impassive.

"Eh?" added the grandmother.

"What do you put in them?" asked Virgil. "Besides the cucumbers."

"Cream cheese," Simon replied.

"I'm going to give a tea with cucumber sandwiches when we get home," said Virgil, "and have a sensation."

"I expect you must be eager to get back into the swim of your own pond," said Gillian.

"Oh, I could stay here forever," Virgil told her. "And I know where all the buses go already."

"Fancy."

"Yes, they are. Our buses are so dumb-looking."

He plopped down on the couch next to the grandmother. "I wish I were English."

That one she heard. "He's a very nice lad," she
said. "Got his tie on and all."

"I'm growing up now," said Virgil. "I don't need
anyone to show me how to do things. I even got my
passport all by myself, and when it came in the mail,
I was very excited. It's a nice picture, too. You know
what? I'm going to visit here again next year. Could
I come back to another tea with you?"

Startled by this very American informality, this
very un-English confidence, our hosts paused before
uttering firmly polite responses. And immediately,
the entire room froze upon us. Only the most exquisite calibrations could have measured the change
in atmosphere, but we had unmistakably crossed a
line, been forward, mugged the protocol. This was
not merely a faux pas, but a menace of who could
say what further enormities? A man who would invite himself into your home is capable of anything.

Dennis Savage, lost in thought, missed it all; and
Virgil had no idea he had committed an outrage. So
I led off in making our farewells, and we went back
to the hotel to pack and laze around till bedtime.
No, I beg your pardon: Virgil wanted to do some
last-chance exploring, so Dennis Savage and I went
up to his room to split the end of my scotch.

"Interesting party, what?" I said.

"Oh, yes. Yes. Handsome people, aren't they?
The women are so beautifully featured. They all look
like musical comedy heroines. Yet one sort of has
the feeling that they're finding you wanting in some
way."

He seemed distracted, as so often on this trip, dealing out the aperçus as if they were cards for a hand he had no desire to play.

"Have you noticed," he asked, with a fearsome smile, "how young everyone is? Gillian, and Roderick, and Egbert, and Athelstane, and the kids ganging up in the street, and the businessmen with the furled umbrellas in those wonderful striped suits. The last bus Virgil forced me into, I looked around and lo, I was the oldest thing on it, I swear. Young is what it is. *Everyone* is young *everywhere* you go. I can remember what it was like to be twenty-two, and walk into a bar, and believe I could get just about anyone there if I hit the right approach. Remember twenty-two? Remember how that felt? Everyone moved about you, everyone after something they maybe couldn't get; and you're so still, right in the center of it all. Twenty-two, that was. And now . . . well . . . I'm the one doing the moving and the looking and the needing. I'm the one after something."

"I shouldn't have taken you to *Follies*. All this jeering at yourself for not having borne the years well, or made a righter choice . . ."

"Okay, pal." He held out his empty glass. "Fill 'er up. Right in the center of it."

"Easy, boy."

"'How about a country house?'" he asked, quoting *Follies*.

"Unaccustomed as you are to private drinking."

"Sure. Easy." He took a huge swig of liquor. "Simon was very nice-looking, wasn't he? Tall, probably very slim under the sweater. Smooth, I bet. It's supposed to be impossible to tell who's hairy and who isn't. I can always tell. I'm never . . . But you don't care about that, do you? Simon. Aren't they cute, with those names? Did you notice that deftly sculpted mouth? Do you think Little Virgil noticed?''

"Not likely. He treated them all as an audience, not—"

"Simon and Graeme. You could hold a twenty-two contest and it'd be a draw, wouldn't it? Everyone's being young together nowadays. You know—and this may surprise you, in light of the extremely inelegant performance I've been giving of late—I intend to be utterly accepting when Little Kiwi takes off. Yes, I . . . refuse to yell at him, or keep him tied up in some evil place, a slave of love . . . or what? *Blackmail* him with medical juju? It's vicious, but it works. I could tell him I've got plague and if he'd only see me through it, I'll make him my heir. I could play that one for an extra year, couldn't I? It's a really mean stunt, true, but . . . in fact . . . I'm going, when the time comes, to accept it, and bless him, and shake his hand . . .''

"Enough of this.''

"Everyone hates self-pity except the people who need it.''

"You don't need it.''

"Oh, you don't know . . .'' Shuddering, he began to weep, as he did on The Night of Cosgrove out at The Pines. "You don't know what I need.''

I took the glass from him and placed it on the table and sat next to him on the bed and put my arms around him and he held on to me for a bit and then he said, "Oh, this is such a concessive cliché,'' and tried to free himself, but I held on to him. So he stayed put till we heard Virgil's key nudging the lock, whereupon we sprang apart like adulterers in a Whitehall sex farce.

Virgil, getting out of his coat, sensed trouble. First he checked his souvenir counter. Then he went up to Dennis Savage.

"What do you want?" Dennis Savage asked him. "What can I give you? A rent-boy in a leather jacket and bright red corduroy pants? How about a steward with a Scots accent and veined forearms?" Tenderly, he brushed Virgil's hair back. "A piece of candy? A suit? You want a suit?"

"What have you been doing to him?" Virgil asked me.

"What do you want?" Dennis Savage repeated.

"I want to go to *Maurice*. I came back to get you two."

"It's playing in New York."

"I want to see it here."

"Anything. Anything at all."

So we went to *Maurice*; we had nothing better to do, anyway. We got there a little late, but English movie shows always start with commercials; the film itself began just as we had settled down in the top of the balcony, and all three of us connected with it immediately. It is a "beautiful" work, in the classic sense: visually sensitive, enacted with elegance, a radiant presentation. More important, it is agelessly relevant, though set in an older England of murderously homophobic prohibitions. In brief, two friends, both homosexual, choose different paths. One, in terror of prison, swears off his feelings and plays the straight man; the other, after wrestling vastly with his devils, blissfully abandons himself to his real nature in the arms of what the British call "a bit of rough," the gamekeeper on his friend's estate.

Antique stuff, you say? Yet men face this same choice today, take either of the two paths. All gays are born actors, selecting the role they feel most secure in. Your first sixteen years or so comprise the audition, as you juggle your self-enlightenment with what the world will tolerate. You are too young to make sound judgments; but you have learned to act, to judge each scene as you enter it, to finesse the cast and work the house. Sometime later—for a few, as early as in high school or college; for many, one marriage or so after that—you take on your life's role, portraying what the world expects of you or defying the world. Of course, even free-choice gays can choose to maintain a portrayal, to favor certain personae in our dress and speech, to join or boycott the elect covens, to dwell in the ghetto or balance the gay life with the larger culture. But these *are* free choices, whereas deciding whether to be what you are or what They are is fraught with terrible pressures and penalties—and never, before *Maurice*, did a work of art present this so clearly. Never have I felt so truly the sheer tedium of dishonesty, the rapture of the truth.

The movie ends suddenly, and I was still absorbing its lesson as the credits rolled along. But Virgil was so stunned by what he had seen that he refused to move, even to speak. Dennis Savage kept looking from him to me and back. I was standing in the aisle; the houselights were coming on. The theatre was going to close for the day.

And Virgil shook his head.

"What's the matter?" Dennis Savage asked him.

I hadn't seen him like this in years, with the absolutely crushed expression of the orphan who is once again passed over on Adoption Day.

"I thought you were all grown-up now," I said, coming over to reason with him from the row ahead. "Grown-ups don't get blown away by movies. They go out for coffee and discuss them. So come on and we'll try that."

But Virgil wouldn't budge.

"If we do this much longer," Dennis Savage put in, "we'll miss our plane."

"We were so glad about you," I told Virgil, "the way you took charge and led the expedition." Dennis Savage shot me a look. "Some of us, anyway."

"Can't you tell me what's wrong?" Dennis Savage asked, sitting down next to him.

No, Virgil didn't reply.

The theatre had completely emptied. It was just the three of us up in our corner, and I began to worry that we might get locked up in the building all night. Or surely some employee had to make certain that everyone was out. Indeed, the man who had taken our tickets now appeared before us. "Sorry, gentlemen," he announced, "but we're shutting the house."

"See?" Dennis Savage told Virgil. "You're interfering with this man's job. It's late, and he can't leave till we do. You don't want to keep him from his family, do you? So late on a Sunday night?"

"What if he calls the police?" I added. "The reckless English press will drag our names through the muck."

"What's the trouble, then, eh?" said the usher, coming up the aisle to us.

"My friend was so deeply affected by *Maurice*," Dennis Savage explained, "that he can't seem to . . . carry on with . . ."

The usher looked at Virgil for a bit. "'Ere, that's no way," he said. "Goin' on about it like that. It's just a movie, in't it?"

Interesting to note, as soon as the usher went beyond the set idioms of his job, he slipped into his more natural and less polished sounds. In England, speech is class, and class is strictly observed. I imagine the guy couldn't have got hired without this diplomatic effacement of his inflection. Not that anyone handing him a ticket to tear really cares what he is when he's at home. It's all a matter of style, of acknowledging the received values.

"I've seen plenty o' people come chargin' out of a movie," the usher told us. "Mad as hornets they'd be, too, some of 'em. But I never seen a one stop movin'."

"He's mortified by the theme of the movie," I ventured. "What does *Maurice* tell us, after all? It says that presentation is everything, that people—*all* people—get through life by portraying some ideal of themselves."

"No and no." Dennis Savage shook his head. "And thrice no. This film warns us that, however deliriously beautiful sex may be, friendship is more valuable. This is why we pity the closeted man in the movie—not because he's missing out on a night at Boybar, but because he's cut himself off from being able to enjoy the affection and support of his best friend."

"That's all very well, gentlemen," said the usher. "But, if you'll pardon me, the significance of this film is to the gay men in the 'ouse. It says to them, When you're with the main part of the world, you will always be alone. Isolated, like. But when you're with your gay mates, you'll be safe. Now, that may be right and that may be wrong. I don't know. But that's what it says, clear as I can make out."

"I think so, too," said Virgil. "But I want to know one thing. Did Maurice and the gamekeeper stay together, despite the demands of intolerant society? I mean, did one of them ever leave later on?"

"I'm very certain," said the usher, "that they lived 'appily ever after."

And so, trying to smile through his worries, Virgil let the usher lead us to the exit, and not many hours later we were aboard British Airways Flight 177 from Heathrow to Kennedy. It was an autumnal flight, as this is an autumnal story, reflecting on the past and trying to ascertain what point one has reached on what course of action.

In other words: What have I accomplished? There comes a day when one must ask.

There are hard stories and soft stories. The hard ones I define as strongly plotted, based on actions; the soft ones are largely interior, based on feelings. Perhaps I owe my readers an apology for closing this book with a soft story—but this is the third and, I am very nearly positive, final volume of tales on my

New York adventures, and a certain amount of intellection must be allowed.

Certainly that was the atmosphere among my intrepid cohort on the trip homeward. All three of us were quiet, considering the possibilities of stabilization or meltdown, holding on or packing up. There are no permanent solutions, no absolute states. We were confounded.

Virgil had laid in so many trinkets that I had to take some of them in my valise. He wanted to set them up in the living room all at once, in another of those incomprehensible rituals he's forever instituting, so when we reached Fifty-third Street I went to their place first.

Carlo was there, watching television with Cosgrove, and they gave us, respectively, broad and tremulous smiles of welcome. Strange: I had almost forgotten them for the last week.

"Virgil," said Cosgrove, "did you bring me something from the United Kingdom?"

"Did you go to all the play shows, Bud?" said Carlo, switching off the television.

"I took very good care of your house," Cosgrove told Dennis Savage. "Mr. Smith and I made dinner every night and we always cleaned up after."

"He's going to be the top houseboy of the East Fifties," said Carlo.

"I'm a good boy now," Cosgrove agreed.

We travelers didn't say much. We were running on London time, five hours later than New York, and thus had reached the end of our waking hours while our fellow citizens were enjoying the middle of their evening. I gave Virgil his souvenirs and was about to drag myself downstairs when Carlo said, "Now we all have to go and help Cosgrove start his new job."

Cosgrove, standing apart from us all, put his hands in his pockets and looked down at the floor. I remembered his Story. Dennis Savage, his eyes flickering with fatigue, managed a grin. Virgil was brisk and Carlo fleet, gathering up Cosgrove, my bags, and me in a sneaky whirl, and the whole pack of us trooped downstairs to my apartment.

Inside me, voices protested that my right of free choice was being overwhelmed by an officious do-gooder faction. The sanctity of the one-person household was under attack. I was so upset that I couldn't hold my key straight when we reached my door.

"Look," I began; but Carlo calmly took my key and let us all in. Plenty of sex and a happy ending, you know.

"Oh, you'll have a lot of tidying to do here, Cosgrove," says Virgil as the lights go on.

"Don't break anything," I beg. "You can't do it with just anyone. I don't want to be a woggle."

"He's going to be a good boy," Carlo promises me.

"Four against one," I cry. "No fair."

"Just throw his bags anywhere," Dennis Savage tells Cosgrove.

Could I be dreaming this? I've had such dreams before. Sometimes I'm atop a falling building, sometimes I'm going under in an avalanche, and sometimes I'm being assigned a live-in houseboy.

"That little Cosgrove's going to take care of you,"

says Carlo, having a wonderful time, putting a hold on me.

"His veal marengo!" Dennis Savage raves. "His cassoulet!"

"I fix an afternoon tray," Cosgrove tells me, "of cheese and potato chips."

"Kiss today hello," says Dennis Savage. That's what the choice is.

He always goes for the good things; this is my turn, now. The theme demands it. Mission accomplished. I am the bearer, the actor. I say, "The Cambridge Theatre is in Seven Dials, not Cambridge Circus."

"He's babbling," observes Dennis Savage. "The horrid zany. Somebody slap him."

I sink into my desk chair. All this reality. "How can you do this to me?"

"With a certain giddy pleasure, actually," Dennis Savage replies. "Because this ties up everyone's problem, and you can live happily ever after."

"This doesn't tie anything up. Nothing is resolved!"

"Well," he shrugs. "Such is life."

"Oh, suddenly you're in a good mood?"

"I've got all the future to be morose in, haven't I? And some recent moviegoing to think about. Maybe we're not all as grown-up as we think we are."

"Cosgrove," says Virgil, "you're going to be happy ever after."

"Am I?" Cosgrove goes up to Virgil like a felon suing the governor for a pardon. "How do you know that?"

"Because all your friends are here now. Everybody *loves* you, Cosgrove."

"But I don't know if that's true!"

Virgil takes Cosgrove by the shoulders. "I know it's true, Cosgrove. I was always planning to watch out for you."

Pulling Cosgrove to him, Virgil slips his arms around him, and Cosgrove holds on to Virgil.

"Look at those two kids playing Lover Man," says Carlo. "With those little waists and their smooth boyskin."

Cosgrove's eyes are wet when the two break apart, and he whispers, "Everybody loves me."

The phone rang.

As I reached for it, Dennis Savage stopped me and beckoned to Cosgrove. "Let the houseboy do his job," he ordered.

"I'll get it!" shouted Cosgrove, rushing over. As he picked up, he said, "This is Mr. Bud's residence."

"Oh, for heaven's sake!"

"Why, this is Cosgrove . . . the houseboy . . . Yes . . . No, because . . . because I have a smooth boywaist."

I grabbed for the phone, but Carlo held me down in the chair. "Let him do it."

"It might be somebody important!"

"Cosgrove will handle it," said Virgil.

"Well," Cosgrove was saying, "you know he was in London, England, and then he came back . . . I know, but I always have to find out who it is first. I want to do a good job, so nothing bad happens anymore. I don't want to be street grunge . . . Yes, for a while, but there were certain things I wouldn't do even when they threatened to beat me up. I was like a secret to them. But I knew who my friends were. The Elf King left me with a terrible family, but I escaped and came here. I don't have to be a secret anymore. And Miriam said if I don't behave that the Elf King will . . . he will . . ."

Cosgrove is turned away from us, but Virgil knows all about his little comrade and whispers, "You mustn't cry on the job, Cosgrove."

"I'm not crying," says Cosgrove, crying, as he extends the receiver to me. I take it in one hand and gently pull Cosgrove closer with the other. I am thinking of Cliff just now.

"Yes?" into the phone.

"What on earth is going on over there?"

"Hello, Mother."

"What was that young man talking about?"

"He was trying to tell you that . . . that everybody loves him."

Cosgrove burst into sobs at this, and I put my arms around him, and Dennis Savage had to get on the phone and keep Mother busy with the first thing that came into his head, a recollection of the time he and I subverted an all-Jamboree Capture the Flag and were thrown out of the Boy Scouts, woggles and all. Virgil and Carlo pressed close for family support as I realized, startled, furious and full of joy, that I am back where I started, as the middle boy of five brothers: except Carlo and Dennis Savage are kinder to me than Ned and Jim were and I promise not to bully Virgil and Cosgrove the way I did Andrew and Tony. One other difference from the old-style family: no parents. No authority figures saying no. Now the parents are overthrown; we are our own authority.

On the strength of this new union, I told Cosgrove that we would all take care of him, that he was home and free. He held on to me, but his head was shaking, because he has vast doubts that anyone will take care of him for long. True, he has been disheartened by past dealings with incorrect company, by a shortage of Cliffs. But I am determined that my family find a place for the elf child, because I have not forgotten how lonely it felt to be one myself, when I was very young and didn't know the way to Stonewall City.

I've a feeling I'm not in Pennsylvania anymore. And as for what now transpires, I leave you to reckon, boys and girls, for this is the utmost of my report.